ALEXANDER McCALL SMITH

A TIME OF LOVE AND TARTAN

A 44 Scotland Street novel

ABACUS

First published in Great Britain in 2017 by Polygon
This paperback edition published in 2018 by Abacus

1 3 5 7 9 10 8 6 4 2

A CIP catalogue record for this book
is available from the British Library.

ISBN 978-1-4087-1099-9

Printed and bound in Great Britain by
Clays Ltd, St Ives plc

Papers used by Abacus are from well-managed forests
and other responsible sources.

Abacus
An imprint of
Little, Brown Book Group
Carmelite House
50 Victoria Embankment
London EC4Y 0DZ

An Hachette UK Company
www.hachette.co.uk

www.littlebrown.co.uk

This is for Caroline Hahn and
Richard Neville Towle

44

A TIME OF LOVE AND TARTAN

1. *An Invitation to the Elephant House*

When Pat Macgregor received an invitation from Bruce Anderson to meet him for coffee at the Elephant House on George IV Bridge, her first reaction was to delete it. That is one of the great advantages of electronic communications – one can simply delete them. And one can do the same to people – in their electronic incarnation, of course; at the press of a button, or the equivalent, one can send them off into some vast soup of disassembled digital data, reducing them to floating ones and zeros, consigned to a Dantean world of echoes, a shadowy underworld of fading impulses.

And that, thought Pat, was the fate that Bruce so richly deserved. A few years earlier he had played with her affections, as he had toyed with those of so many other young women, believing that to pay attention to this rather shy young student of art history was to confer on her a benison for which, if she knew anything about the world, she should be profoundly grateful. The expression *God's gift to women* came into all this – somewhere. It was usually uttered sarcastically, as in *He thinks he's God's gift to women*, but in Bruce's case this was exactly what he did think of himself. In his view he was one of those people who existed to give pleasure to others – not through anything he actually did – although that, of course, entered into it – but simply by being.

Auden said that the blessed had no reason to care from what angle they were regarded, having nothing to hide. This was true of Bruce: whether you looked at him from the front, the back, or from either side, the inescapable conclusion was that he was egregiously good-looking. As he pointed out to Catriona, a young woman with whom he once visited Florence, 'There's a statue of my double in this city, you know.'

She had looked puzzled. 'Your double, Bruce? Here in Florence?'

Bruce smirked. 'Yes, right here. Would you like to see it?'

She nodded. This was some sort of game, she suspected; but then Bruce was so playful. That was one of the things that attracted her to him – his playfulness. That and, of course, the way he made a girl feel special; now that was a very considerable talent. And then there was his hair gel, that strange, clove-scented potion that tickled her nose when she smelled it, and added, in such a curious way, an erotic charge to the most mundane of situations.

Bruce and Catriona had already visited the Uffizi and had stood for some minutes before Botticelli's *Birth of Venus* before Bruce said, 'That's Venus, you know. That's her standing in the shell.'

Catriona nodded. 'She's very beautiful, isn't she?'

Bruce thought about this for a few moments before he replied. 'Her neck's a bit long, but, yes, she's beautiful all right.' Then, after a short pause, he had observed, 'Beauty's an interesting thing, isn't it? You either have it, or you don't. And that's all there is to it.'

Catriona looked at Bruce. He returned her gaze with all the confidence of one who knew that he stood on the right side of the divide he had just described.

That was in the Uffizi; now they found themselves in the Galleria dell'Accademia, looking up at Michelangelo's great masterpiece, the towering statue of David.

'There,' said Bruce. 'Feast your eyes on that.'

The contemplation of Michelangelo's David is not easy for everybody, but Catriona looked.

'Lookalike?' whispered Bruce.

She stared at the line of David's nose and brow: it was undoubtedly Bruce. Her eye followed the sweep of his arms and the musculature of his torso. And she had to admit it: Bruce could have been Michelangelo's young model.

'I don't tell everybody about this,' confided Bruce. 'But I remember when I first saw a photograph of David, I thought: "Jeez, that's me." I was about sixteen at the time. In Crieff. I was at Morrison's, you know, and one of the girls in the class stuck a picture of David up in a corridor and wrote underneath it *Bruce Anderson*. It was so immature, but somehow . . .'

Pat, of course, had soon detected Bruce's narcissism. But in her state of infatuation – for that, she acknowledged, was what it was – she had persuaded herself that his self-obsession was a harmless quirk, a hangover from adolescence, a passing phase. After all, there were plenty of young females who were just as fascinated by their appearance, spending hours in front of the mirror. It was more unusual amongst males, perhaps, but what was sauce for the goose should surely be sauce for the gander. If women were to indulge themselves in the contemplation of their own beauty, then why should men not do the same?

For a few months, she had circled Bruce, caught in his gravitational field as a moon might be in that of a planet, until at last she managed to extricate herself. When that happened, her father's relief at her escape had been palpable. 'Men like that are very dangerous,' he said to her. 'The only thing to do is to tear yourself away. Believe me – I've seen it in so many of my patients.'

Pat's father, Dr Macgregor, a self-deprecating and scholarly man, was a psychiatrist, and was particularly close to his daughter. He and Pat's mother had divorced after she had gone off to restore a walled garden in Perthshire and had never returned. He had done nothing to deserve the desertion, but had been generous in his response. 'Your mother has found herself elsewhere,' he explained to Pat. '*Il faut cultiver notre jardin*, as Candide (I think) pointed out. The important thing is her self-fulfilment – that's all that counts.'

But there was something else that counted for him, and that was Pat's own happiness. He doted on his daughter and when he realised that she had taken up with Bruce, he had been tipped into depression. At the end of Pat's affair with Bruce – an end that he, at least, had realised was inevitable – he had tried to explain to her that however low she might feel after the break-up, it was as nothing when compared with the risk she would take in staying with him.

And that was why, when she received this invitation to meet Bruce in the Elephant House, Pat said nothing about it to her father. And it was also why she almost deleted it from her e-mail in-box without a reply. Almost, but not quite: she moved the cursor to hover over the delete symbol, hesitated, and then moved it to *Reply*.

'See you there,' she wrote. She added no emoticon – for what emoticon is there to express anticipation of the sort she was feeling?

2. *On George IV Bridge*

Pat arrived at the Elephant House before Bruce. She had not planned it that way: he had suggested ten-thirty in the morning, and she had lingered slightly in Forrest Road so as to be at the café at a quarter to eleven. This was a stratagem to show him that she was not at his beck and call, and that even if she had agreed to meet him, she was not that eager to do so. It failed, however, as Bruce did not get there until shortly after eleven.

When she found that he was yet to arrive, she briefly toyed with the idea of leaving. To do so would at least be to heed the advice – even if rather tardily – of her friend, Janice, with whom she had discussed Bruce's invitation.

Janice's views were very clear. 'Don't,' she counselled. 'Just don't.'

'I'm only going to meet him for coffee . . . '

Pat was not allowed to finish. 'Coffee? You know what coffee leads to?' Her friend uttered the word *coffee* as one might utter *cocaine*, as if a whole hinterland of warning, of decline, of Hogarthian dissipation lay behind the word.

'You see,' Janice continued, 'you should never – *never* – take up with an ex. Everybody knows that. Everybody. *Everybody.*' Janice had a way of repeating words, or verbally italicising them, that added a certain melodramatic force to what she said.

'Do they?'

'Of course they do. The reason why an ex tries to get in touch is always – *always* – to get something from you. Never – never – to *give.* So the only thing to say to an ex is: you're *history*! You're the *distant past*!'

Pat had wondered whether there might not be cases where an ex merely wanted to meet as . . . dare she say it? . . . a friend.

No. Janice was adamant on that. 'As a *friend*? Pat, get real. Men don't do *friendship.*'

'Oh, come on. There are plenty of men who do friendship.'

Janice shook her head. 'But not exes. *Exes* do dependence. They do recrimination. They do insincere attempts to get you back temporarily because they need a partner for a ball or something like that. Or to ask for *money.* That's what exes do, Pat, and if you go to meet this guy, this *Bruce*, at the Elephant House then you're toast. You're on a plate. *Bruschetta*.'

Pat had wavered, and had almost taken Janice's advice, but had eventually decided to meet Bruce in spite of it. The whole point of seeking advice, at least for some, is to get somebody to confirm what you have already decided to do, and Pat had decided that she would meet Bruce. It would just be for coffee, and it would be a single meeting. If he asked her out, she would come up with some reason for saying no. She could even use that time-honoured pretext of having to wash her hair. That was an excuse that was still occasionally used as a signal to a man that he had no chance, and was, in a way, the ultimate put-down. Even Bruce, she felt, would understand that. And yet . . . and yet . . . did she really want to wash her hair?

She found a table at the back of the café, near the window. From there, looking out over Candlemaker Row, she saw the roofs of the Grassmarket and, against the skyline, the Castle. The café itself was busy; it attracted a young crowd, a mixture of locals, students and others, with a chattering presence of foreign teenagers. Pat was at an age where she was unaccustomed to feeling older than those around her, but here she did. She was now twenty-five, the point at which eighteen- and nineteen-year-olds suddenly start to look straight through one. Invisibility to the young, of course, is a quality that grows slowly: by thirty, one is beginning to get fainter; by forty, one is starting to disappear; and by fifty the metaphorical hill has been crossed and one is simply no longer there.

This manifested itself in the conversation that was taking place at a neighbouring table between a boy and a girl of eighteen or nineteen. They seemed oblivious of Pat's presence only a few feet away and well within earshot, and were discussing the slovenly habits of the boy's absent flat-mate.

'His room stinks,' he said.

'He stinks,' she agreed.

'I can't stand it when people stink. You know, we owe it to other people not to stink. It's a sort of . . . '

'Civic duty?'

'Yup. Don't stink. You'd think people would get it, wouldn't you? After all, which part of *don't stink* doesn't he understand?'

Pat stared out of the window, trying to insulate herself from this unwelcome exchange. Why had Bruce contacted her? Did he want to ignite old fires? She would not allow that. She simply would not. She knew that he was not good for her and anyway, she was no longer interested in the sort of short-term relationship that Bruce went in for. But what if he had changed? What if he had matured and was now prepared for longer-term commitment? What then? Could she see herself with him again, giving him a second chance? People did change; they grew up, they stopped being selfish, they thought more of other people's feelings. Sometimes in the case of males this change happened quite late – at twenty-eight, and even beyond; or so she had read. In fact, she had seen something in a magazine recently that suggested that some men did not mature – fully mature – until they were well into their thirties. Bruce could be one of those, perhaps. He was now twenty-eight or thereabouts, or was he even thirty?

Her train of thought was again disturbed by the conversation at the neighbouring table.

'You know what? He hardly ever changes his socks. No, I'm not making this up, but I think he wears them for four or five days and then he leaves them lying on the floor. He has these ghastly trainers – you should see them, you'd want to throw up, I swear you would.'

'He's disgusting. How can you bear to live with him? Why don't the rest of you throw him out?'

'He owns the flat.'

'Oh. Well, I suppose that makes it different.'

'Yes, it does.'

Pat smiled. The world was a difficult place. One had to hold one's nose; metaphorically, of course, but sometimes otherwise too.

3. Bruce Irritates Pat, But Only to an Extent

'Patikins!'

She looked up to see Bruce standing at the end of the table, smiling at her. Her irritation at being addressed by the childish soubriquet was intense, but did not last for more than a few seconds. One had to forgive Bruce – it was impossible to be angry with somebody like him, with his clove-scented hair gel, his narcissism, his incorrigibility, his breezy self-confidence, his propensity to infantilise the names of others . . .

He bent forward and kissed her on the cheek. There was a strong scent of cloves.

'I know I'm late,' he said, as he sat down opposite her at the table. 'But I knew you'd wait.'

Pat frowned. How did Bruce know that she would wait? Was she the sort of person who could be expected to wait because she had nothing better to do – or, because even if she would not normally wait, she would always wait for Bruce? To paraphrase Charles de Gaulle, who said – to those who urged him to take action against the inflammatory rhetoric of Jean-Paul Sartre – that one did not imprison Voltaire; one does not stand up Bruce, no matter how late he may be.

But she simply could not let him imagine that she had nothing better to do than sit in the Elephant House and wait for him.

'I was about to go,' she said. She wanted to sound firm, but the words came out almost apologetically.

'Where?' he asked casually. 'Are you working today?' Pat helped Matthew in his gallery in Dundas Street, but only on three days a week.

'No.' Again it was not the answer she had intended, but Pat was truthful and whatever the stakes for her self-esteem, she could not tell a bare-faced lie.

'Then that's all right,' said Bruce.

It is *not* all right, she thought. It is *not*. But she said instead, 'It's good to see you.'

Bruce inclined his head, as if to acknowledge an act of homage. Of course it was good to see him; he had been good to see for as long as he could remember. Even as a small boy, he had attracted admiration for his looks; the cherub had become an angel, had become a youth from a Giotto painting, had become a matinée idol . . .

'So,' he said. 'How's Patsy?'

This was a complex offence. Bruce had an irritating habit of referring to people – in their presence – in the third person. That was count one. Then there was the diminution of Pat's name. That was count two. And finally there was the question of a possible play on the word *patsy*, as used in the argot of fraud. The patsy was the victim; was that what Bruce was implying? She decided it was not; if Bruce employed word play, it was not that sophisticated.

'I'm all right,' she said.

He reached across the table and patted her hand gently. 'Good,' he said. 'And you were about to ask how I was, weren't you?'

'Was I?'

He winked. 'I think you were. Well, there's nothing wrong with me. *Rien*. But I could do with a cup of coffee.' He paused. 'Are you going to go and get something for yourself?'

Pat seethed. 'What do you want?' she asked. This was intended to be a question about the point of their meeting: Bruce clearly wanted something.

'Thanks,' said Bruce. 'I need to make a phone call. I'll do

that while you're fetching. Hope you don't mind. I'll have a *latte* – semi-skimmed, if poss. I'll keep the table.'

Pat caught her breath. She wanted to storm out; she wanted to tell this outrageous man that his charms would no longer work on her; that she saw through everything; through the hair gel, through the banter, through every arrogant assumption about female psychology; through the whole, outrageous act – she saw right through it. But instead she asked him whether he took sugar.

'*Nyet*,' Bruce replied. 'No sugar, thanks.' Then he added, 'I thought you'd remember that – you know, from the old days.'

As she stood at the counter waiting to be served, Pat reflected on what Bruce had just said. It was typical of his solipsism that he should imagine that she would remember every little detail of his preferences. Who would possibly remember, after some years, whether or not somebody else took sugar? If the other person was immensely important, of course, one might remember a little detail like that – if one went to tea with the Pope, for example, one might say, years after the event, *He doesn't take sugar in his coffee, you know*. Or he might make some small remark about something very insignificant, and one would remember that, with all the clarity with which important events can be incised into memory. Such as, *The Pope said that his watch wasn't keeping very good time*. Something like that. To which, of course, the reply might be that the watch of such a personage is calibrated in centuries rather than minutes and hours . . .

She waited her turn. Two young Japanese women were

ahead of her, talking to one another in hushed tones. One of them glanced at Pat and smiled; it was a tiny feeler of empathy, and she felt it touch her briefly, a flicker of warmth. They were strangers to her, far, she thought, from everything that was familiar to them, visiting this café for its literary associations. They were pilgrims, in a sense, not all that different in their quest from those who went to a religious shrine, to a grotto where some manifestation was said to have occurred a long time ago, or to a river bank where the water was in some way holy and capable of washing away all the pains and cares and grubbiness of our ordinary lives.

She took the tray with two coffees back to the table. Bruce had finished his call, and was tucking his phone back into his pocket.

His tone, when he spoke, was business-like. 'Right,' he said. 'You'll be wondering why I wanted to see you. Here's the inf. I'm going to be setting myself up in business.' He smiled at her and told her what he had planned. Then came the proposition. 'And I want you, Pat, to work with me. How about it?'

She stared at him. 'Are you serious?' she asked. 'I mean, as in *serious*?'

4. Those Things for which We're Grateful

While Pat and Bruce had their conversation in the Elephant House, Bertie Pollock (7) sat in his classroom at the Steiner School, looking out of its west-facing window. He knew it faced west, as he had recently acquired a compass from his friend, Ranald Braveheart Macpherson. In turn, Ranald had been given it as a present by his godfather, who had forgotten that he had given exactly the same present the year before, and even the year before that.

'You have this one, Bertie,' said Ranald. 'It's jolly important to have a compass. If you get lost, you'll always know which direction you should go.'

Bertie thanked him effusively. 'You're really kind, Ranald,' he said. 'I wish I could give you something in return, but I don't really have much stuff.'

'I'd noticed that,' said Ranald. 'But don't worry, Bertie, when you get older you might have more stuff and then you can give me some of it. I'll keep a note of what I give you so that you'll know how much stuff you have to give me.'

That struck Bertie as perfectly fair, and it made it easier for him to accept the compass that Ranald had passed on. There was a small instruction booklet that came with it, and this explained the points of direction, and gave a short note on magnetic deviation. For Bertie, though, the real point of having a compass was to know which way was west, as west was important to him in more ways than one. Directly west of the Steiner School, only one block away, was George Watson's College, where Ranald Braveheart Macpherson was a pupil and where Bertie had spent a brief time – not quite a whole day – in a plum-coloured school blazer to which he was not entitled. That day had ended ignominiously when he had been pushed to the ground and roundly kicked on the rugby field – an experience that had prompted him to run back to the Steiner School, where rugby was blessedly unknown.

Beyond Watson's, over Craiglea ridge and a touch more to the south than to the west, lay the Pentland Hills, where Bertie had once gone fishing with his father and where, after they had been lost in a suddenly-descending haar, they had ended up seeking directions at a farmhouse. Had Bertie had his compass, he felt, they would not have been lost in the first place, but that would have meant that he would never have met the farmer's son, Andy, with whom he had established immediate and deep rapport. So a compass, he decided, like so many things in this life, brought both advantages and disadvantages.

Yet the west still called, and called strongly, because in that direction lay what to Bertie was the promised land – Glasgow. No matter how constrained he might feel in Edinburgh; no matter how trapped in the programme of yoga and psychotherapy planned for him by his mother, there was always Glasgow, an irresistible presence – rather like a great lighthouse in the darkness sending out its pulsating message. *This is Glasgow calling* ... And surely readier than all others to answer the call of Glasgow was Bertie. Glasgow was freedom; Glasgow was excitement; Glasgow was a yoga- and psychotherapy-free zone.

But in Edinburgh that morning the members of Bertie's class had been given the task of writing a list.

'Lists are very important,' said the teacher, Miss Campbell. 'We use them for all sorts of purposes. Can anybody think of the sort of lists people make?'

She surveyed the class. There were a few thoughtful expressions, but no hands went up.

Then Olive put up her hand. 'Mummies make lists of things for daddies to do,' she volunteered.

Miss Campbell hesitated. The staff tried as far as possible to avoid role stereotypes, but sometimes these seemed so accurately to reflect what happened in real life.

'Well, that's true,' she said. 'But daddies may also make lists of things for mummies to do, don't you think?'

Olive shook her head. 'Not in my experience, Miss Campbell. Mummies don't need these lists because they're the ones who decide what needs to be done. So those things are already in their heads, you see.'

Miss Campbell gritted her teeth. She was all for equality in relations between the sexes, but she found it very hard to agree with Olive on anything. She had no desire to encourage her, and agreement might simply urge her on.

A further thought had occurred to Olive. 'Of course, I suppose you might not know about that sort of thing, Miss Campbell, since you don't have a husband, do you?'

Miss Campbell closed her eyes and mentally counted to ten – in Gaelic. She had heard about the reason for the dismissal of Elspeth Harmony, who had pinched Olive's ear in full view of the rest of the class. At the time she had been shocked by what seemed a completely unacceptable lapse in professional standards, but now she was not so sure. It must have been immensely satisfying to pinch Olive, and as she thought of this she felt the thumb and index finger of her right hand move slightly apart, as if in readiness for just such an attack. But she could never do that, of course, whatever the provocation, whatever the temptation. And so she finished counting up to ten in Gaelic and then opened her eyes again.

Pansy now joined in. 'Of course, somebody might ask her to marry him, Olive.' And then to Miss Campbell she said, 'Has anybody ever asked you to marry him, Miss Campbell? And if not, do you think anybody might?'

Bertie turned to Pansy. 'You shouldn't ask that sort of thing, Pansy,' he said. 'And I bet nobody's ever going to ask you or Olive.'

This brought a cheer from Tofu. 'You bet they won't,' he called out. 'Unless they're mad, of course. They might get somebody from the loony bin.'

Olive drew in her breath. 'Did you hear that, Miss Campbell? Did you hear what Tofu just said? He called the Royal Edinburgh Hospital the loony bin.'

'You shouldn't say that, Tofu,' said Miss Campbell reproachfully.

'Make him stand in the corner,' said Pansy. 'For two hours, Miss Campbell.'

'Shall I hit him for you?' asked Larch.

'I think we need to return to lists,' said Miss Campbell. 'Let me suggest a list we could all make – and shall do so right now. A list of all the things we're grateful for.'

The members of the class exchanged glances, but jotters were taken from desks and pencils readied.

Number one, wrote Bertie. *Mummy and Daddy*. Then he paused. He so wanted to cross out Mummy, but he could not; he just could not.

5. *Glencoe Again*

Miss Campbell's eye alighted on Bertie. Of all the children in the class, she imagined that Bertie would be the one who would best understand gratitude, and it was for this reason that she picked him to read out his list.

'We shall start with Bertie,' she announced. 'We're all interested to hear your list of the things you're grateful for, Bertie. I wonder what they'll be?' She paused. 'We shall soon see, shall we not? Please read us your list, Bertie.'

Bertie's heart sank. 'Couldn't we hear Tofu's list first, Miss Campbell?' he asked.

'Hah!' said Tofu. 'You can't, because my list has got nothing in it!'

'Stupid!' crowed Olive. 'You hear that, Miss Campbell? Tofu's not grateful for anything. That's because everybody hates him. If everybody hates you, there's nothing to be grateful for.'

Miss Campbell looked disapprovingly at Olive. 'Hush, Olive dear. That's not a very nice thing to say.'

'But it's true,' persisted Olive. 'Some of the girls have already got a list, Miss Campbell. It's a list of horrid boys, and Tofu's at the top of it because everybody hates him.'

'I don't care,' said Tofu. 'They hate you, Olive, more than they hate me. I've seen lists with your name at the top and Pansy's second. There are bags of lists like that.'

This brought a squeal of protest from Pansy. 'They don't hate me, Miss Campbell. People don't hate me.'

'Of course they don't, Pansy,' said Miss Campbell reassuringly. Turning to Tofu, she administered a stern warning. 'Tofu, you are not to say things like that. I won't have any talk in this classroom of people hating one another; is that quite clear?'

That brought a sullen nod of assent.

'Right,' said Miss Campbell. 'Now let's think more positively. Bertie is going to read us his list of things that he's grateful for in his life and I, for one, am very eager to hear it.'

An air of expectation filled the classroom as Bertie unfolded his piece of paper.

'Things I'm grateful for, by Bertie Pollock,' he said.

'A very good start,' said Miss Campbell. 'Please carry on, Bertie.'

'Number one,' said Bertie. 'My mummy and daddy.'

Miss Campbell clapped her hands together. 'Well, isn't that a lovely beginning, boys and girls! I think it is. Because we all know that without our mummy and daddy none of us would be here. So it's quite right to be grateful for Mummy and Daddy.'

'Or a donor,' muttered Tofu.

Miss Campbell's eyes widened. 'Did you say something, Tofu?'

Tofu shook his head. 'Nothing, Miss Campbell.'

Miss Campbell hesitated. There was some territory best left unexplored, and this was an example of that. She turned again to Bertie. 'Please carry on, Bertie. What's next on your list?'

Bertie looked at the paper. 'Number two,' he continued. 'I'm grateful I live in Scotland.'

Miss Campbell smiled. 'Now isn't that nice, boys and girls? Bertie is grateful that he lives in Scotland. It's very important to be proud of your country, boys and girls – not proud in a silly, boastful sense, but grateful for all that your country gives you.'

Olive looked doubtful. Her hand went up. Miss Campbell tried to ignore her, but she was insistent.

'Yes, Olive?'

Olive looked accusingly at Bertie as she voiced her objection. 'But what about England?' she said. 'Not everybody comes from Scotland.'

'That's true, Olive,' said Miss Campbell. 'But Bertie wasn't talking about England. Bertie happens to be a Scottish boy and so he was talking, quite understandably, about Scotland.'

Olive was not to be easily put off. 'Yes, but there are some people from England in this class. Hiawatha, for instance, he's English. He was born in England, you see.'

Hiawatha frowned. 'I can't help that, Olive. Nobody asked me where I wanted to be born.'

Olive looked at Hiawatha tolerantly. 'I know you can't help that, Hiawatha. I was only thinking of how you must have felt when Bertie went on about being Scottish. You must have felt really small – sort of unwanted.'

Hiawatha did not reply. Pansy, however, always standing by in her role as Olive's principal lieutenant, voiced her agreement. 'Yes, poor Hiawatha,' she said. 'Sitting there being English . . . '

Bertie felt that he needed to explain. 'I didn't mean to say anything about being English,' he protested. 'I like English people. I wouldn't want to say anything nasty.'

'Did not *mean*,' said Olive, with heavy sarcasm. 'Lots of people say things they don't mean to say, but still say them.'

Miss Campbell felt it was time to return to the subject. 'That's enough, Olive. I think we should get back to Bertie.'

'I was only trying to protect others from being hurt,' said Olive. 'I was only thinking of Hiawatha's feelings.' She paused. 'But there's something else, Miss Campbell.'

The teacher sighed. 'What is it, Olive?'

'My dad says that we shouldn't be too pleased with ourselves. He said that we should always remember the bad things that have happened in Scottish history.'

Miss Campbell nodded. 'I think that's quite right, Olive. I think we should always take a balanced view.'

Olive was now in her stride. 'Such as the Massacre of Glencoe. My dad thinks we shouldn't forget that.'

'No, we shouldn't,' echoed Pansy, trying hard to remember what the Massacre of Glencoe was all about.

Larch, who had been largely silent, now joined in. 'Yes,' he said, 'we should remember what the English did at Glencoe.' He stared at Hiawatha as he spoke; Larch was violent, and a historical *casus belli* was as good as anything else.

'The English!' exploded Olive. 'It wasn't the English, Larch. You obviously know nothing about Scottish history. It was the . . . ' She paused. There was complete silence in the classroom. 'It was the Campbells.'

All eyes turned to Miss Campbell, who laughed nervously.

'There may be some truth in that,' she said. 'But we must remember, boys and girls, that it was a long time ago that the Campbells fell upon the MacDonalds.'

'In their own house,' contributed Olive. 'After the MacDonalds had given them their tea.'

'It was a very long time ago,' repeated Miss Campbell.

There was a further silence, eventually broken by Olive. 'Was your grandfather there, Miss Campbell?' she asked.

6. *Unsettling Thoughts*

Domenica Macdonald, anthropologist and resident of Scotland Street, was now Domenica Lordie . . . or was she? Domenica may have married Angus Lordie, portrait painter and stalwart of the Scottish Arts Club, but that did not mean that she had ceased to be who she was – which was Domenica, daughter of the late Patrick Auchterlonie Macdonald and Euphemia Constance Macdonald or Scrimgeour. Identity was a complex matter, but one thing was clear: in Scotland you did not automatically change your name to that of your husband, and there was certainly no legal requirement to that effect.

Domenica had been happy enough to be married, but did not feel that it was the defining feature of her life. Angus was her second husband. Her first, whom she had met and married in South India, had been a mild and rather unmemorable man, a member of a family who owned what they referred to as an electricity factory outside Cochin. This business, a small coal-fired generating station, had been her husband's pride and joy, but it had also been the cause of his death – by electrocution. Widowhood had saved her from a restrictive marriage. She had loved her first husband – vaguely – but she had not been *in* love with him. There was a distinction, she felt, between the state of loving another and being in love. The latter involved a surrender to a state of incompleteness: the object of your love was necessary for your continued existence – or so you thought. Loving another was wanting to *own* that person – to have him or her as completely as possible. You appended the other to your life – you incorporated him within your immediate, personal world.

As an anthropologist, she had spent her entire professional life trying to understand people, how they behaved, and why they did what they did. The scientific study of human society answered some of those questions, but said nothing at all about why we liked the things we did. So an anthropologist might work out how people organised their private lives, might throw light on patterns of courtship and marriage – which were matters of love, after all – but might have nothing to say about the thing that was at the core of all that – about the mystery of love. Nor did psychology throw much light on what made people experience love for another. The psychologist might understand the place of love in the pantheon of emotions, but may say nothing about what it actually was. It was the same with consciousness: we understood how consciousness might come into existence – neuroscience claimed even to have pinpointed the region of the brain that appeared to weld mental activity into an awareness of self – but an understanding of the fundamental notion of consciousness continued to evade philosophers. Love was like that: it happened, and it made a big difference, but what it actually was, what its wellsprings were, was a question that philosophers had yet to answer.

Domenica was not sure if she loved Angus. She was fond of him, of course, but fondness was not the same thing as love. Fondness never set the pulse racing; fondness never made you ache inside, hopelessly, sometimes deliriously, as love so effortlessly did. Yet if anybody were to ask her 'Do you love your husband?' she would have replied, without hesitation, 'Of course I do.' And that, more or less, was what she had publicly professed on that rather fraught day when she had stood with Angus in St Mary's Episcopal Cathedral and exchanged vows. She had promised to love him, because the wording of the 1929 marriage service had been explicit on that point. But how could one promise to love somebody? You might promise to treat him lovingly, which is something that anybody should be capable of, but you could not promise that the bird of love, that shy, elusive creature, would alight on your particular bough.

And so far, she felt that she had kept her promise, and she thought he had too. They had treated one another with kindness and consideration. They had exchanged few angry words, and when they had, they had immediately regretted them. They made one another breakfast turn and turn about; they ironed each other's clothes; they bought small presents that they presented to one another at odd times. She was contented, but could she say that she *loved* him? Possibly – as long as love was defined broadly enough, to include the comfortable friendship that comes with being in another's company over time.

She looked across the kitchen in Scotland Street. Angus was sitting on a rickety chair – one that had belonged to Domenica's grandmother and had been taken from that distant croft on North Uist when she had died. In Domenica's eyes, the chair was a link with that old Scottish past that seemed to be vanishing so quickly; an object that should have been in a museum somewhere but was, instead, here in her house.

How unnoticed, and how speedily, might a whole culture slip away from a people ... The Gaelic voices of Domenica's youth had largely disappeared, those liquid vowels, that soft and entrancing language that could sound like the falling of rain; that had become almost rare, and been replaced by the very different tones of incomers, the flattened vowels of Yorkshire, the chirpy, half-swallowed patois of London. And with the withering of language had gone the stories and the attitudes, the unspoken understandings, the subtle references that had made up the distinctive life of Scotland.

That might go slowly, its passage almost unnoticed, until suddenly you were reminded that the person to whom you were talking did not know what you meant.

She smiled; she was remembering what had happened a few days ago when she had wanted to go to a concert at the Canongate Kirk and had telephoned to book a taxi to collect her. 'I'd like to go to the Canongate Kirk,' she had said. The voice at the end of the line had hesitated, and then said, 'Is that a restaurant?'

Domenica had laughed – but it was a laugh that concealed a sudden twinge of despair. A voice on the telephone – a local voice – did not know the word *kirk* (*anglice* church) which was one of the very commonest Scots words.

She looked at Angus. An important part of love was the

sharing of some valued possession – a tune (*Listen, they're playing our tune!*); children, perhaps; a fund of stories; a country . . . They had all of that, she thought, but still . . . and now it came to her, that awful unsettling question. Did she want to stay with Angus for the rest of her life? If she did, then she knew that this would preclude any passionate involvement. Angus represented friendship and companionship, but was that all that she wanted?

She gasped with shock at her own disloyalty. Angus looked up. He thought she had sneezed. 'Bless you,' he muttered.

She looked away, ashamed and perturbed in equal measure.

7. *Grateful For You*

For Angus, if there was an emotional key to his marriage it was gratitude. He had been a bachelor for longer than most – he and Domenica had married when they were both in their late forties – and he had felt the relief and gratitude that often accompanies a marriage at that time of life. The relief came from the assuaging of that niggling doubt that one of life's milestones was yet to be passed – others, of course, being the driving test, the first session of root-canal treatment, the payment of the last instalment of the mortgage, the first colonoscopy, the marriage of one's firstborn child, and the last examination that one will ever be obliged to take. With marriage came the feeling that one had answered an expectation that others had of one – even if that expectation was tactfully never articulated. One was expected to settle down, to forswear freedom, to assume a commitment to somebody else. All of this may have been watered down to an extent by the recognition of less formal arrangements, but it was still there.

Angus fully understood that people wanted other people to find another person with whom to settle down. Why should they want this? One explanation was that those who were free of commitments of this sort were an affront to those who were encumbered: if people were going to have to knuckle under to the bringing up of children, with all it entails in terms of personal sacrifice, then why should some avoid this and continue to be free? Another, more generous, explanation lay in the desire that people have for others to be happy. It was assumed that everybody without somebody would be happier if the situation were to be changed. This was a notion of completeness: that a moiety requires, by its very nature, to be united with its missing part.

Angus had had his involvements, of course. As a young man there had been a succession of girlfriends, but they had drifted away when they sensed that he was just too preoccupied with his painting to give much thought to committing to any of them. He had treated them well, but it had been as if he were not entirely *there* in the relationship.

And then, as the years went past, he became progressively more covered in paint, as if he were somehow stepping into one of his paintings. He took less trouble with his clothes, all of which were flecked with oil paint of various, sometimes non-matching, hues. It was not very romantic to be embraced by somebody who would leave patches of paint on one's blouse, or who, when running his fingers appreciatively through one's hair, would leave paint there as well.

'My friends think I've been highlighting,' complained one girlfriend. 'But it's you, Angus – you leave paint on everything you touch, including my hair. A Midas of the pigments . . . '

'I have to paint,' said Angus. 'It's what I do.'

Nor did women, by and large, find the smell of turpentine all that attractive, and when Angus adopted Cyril, who was by general repute one of the more malodorous dogs in Edinburgh, the flow of women callers to his studio dried to a trickle and then became a drought.

He did not mind too much. He had a social circle that consisted of painters and sculptors. He was a regular at the Scottish Arts Club, which had passed a special bylaw to allow Cyril to enter the premises as an associate member; he had been elected a member of the Royal Scottish Academy; and he was on the committee of the Scottish Artists' Benevolent Association, the body that distributed largesse (*smallesse*, as Angus called it, in view of the limited nature of the fund) to struggling artists. He had his routine, which included visits to Big Lou's café during the day and to the Cumberland Bar in the early evening, where Cyril would be given a complimentary bowl of stout to drink under one of the tables. He could have continued with this life had it not been for his meeting Domenica and his appreciation of her conversation, of her wit, and of the sheer pleasure that he took in being in her company. When she agreed to marry him, he felt a gratitude more profound than any he had felt before. It took his breath away. (*Me? She has consented to share her life with* me*?*) It was a feeling that all modest people have when it suddenly dawns on them that somebody likes them.

His happiness brought changes in his life. The paint-bespattered outfits were disposed of and an entire new wardrobe of clothes obtained from Stewart Christie & Co in Queen Street: four pairs of moleskin trousers; two waistcoats, one olive green and another mustard; three jackets of Harris tweed in a cut far nattier than anything he had worn before; a new pair of tartan trews in Macpherson tartan; a pair of Dubarry boots into which the legs of the moleskin trousers could be tucked to particularly dashing effect. Even Cyril benefited from this make-over, being fitted with a new collar and put on a course of charcoal pills to tackle his social issues. The transformation was complete and, in a strange way, liberating: familiar routines, old clothes, habits of the years can be like chains; cast them off and one's step is lighter, nimbler, less restricted to the *piste* created by the past.

'You're a new man, Angus,' observed Matthew in the Cumberland Bar one evening. 'Marriage obviously agrees with you.'

'Oh, it does,' said Angus. 'I'm happy, you see, Matthew.'

Matthew nodded. He wondered how many people ever said to themselves *I'm happy*. And did it help to contemplate one's own happiness?

'Do you think,' he asked Angus, 'that happiness is something you can create within yourself just by saying *I'm happy*?'

Angus looked about the bar, at the familiar faces of the other patrons.

'Do you like Hopper?' he asked Matthew. He was thinking of the picture of the people lined up at a counter.

'Of course,' answered Matthew. 'His paintings . . .'

Angus interrupted him. '*Nighthawks*?'

Matthew nodded. 'The people in the diner? The chef in the white hat?'

'The most powerful portrayal of loneliness in art,' said Angus.

'Yes,' said Matthew. 'But the thing about Hopper's paintings is that they provide us with the view that God must have of the scene. If he exists, of course.'

'We can still talk about God even if he doesn't exist,' said Angus. 'God, as an idea, makes perfect sense. We can paint things, you know, that don't exist. The wind, for example.'

He looked at Matthew, as if to challenge him to deny that one might depict the invisible through the effect that it has on the visible.

8. *Head-hunting*

Domenica put the disloyal thoughts out of her mind, at least for the moment: in due course they would return, and return more troublingly. For the present, though, she was more concerned with a letter she had received from the Department of Social Anthropology at the university. Domenica was not on the department's staff, but organised occasional seminars for their postgraduate students or would lecture the undergraduate students if one of the full-time staff was on leave. Her lectures were popular, particularly one she would from time to time deliver on the subject of head-hunting in Papua New Guinea. Like so many anthropologists, Domenica had at an earlier stage of her career undertaken field work amongst remote tribes of the New Guinea Highlands. These people, who were so accustomed to anthropologists that they had a separate guest house in the village reserved for visiting professors, were generally hostile to their neighbours, against whom they had in the past conducted regular head-hunting raids. In a rough-hewn cabinet in the main meeting house, a low, dark building thatched with local reeds, there was a collection of small, shrunken objects, wizened with age. It was explained to the visiting anthropologists that these were human heads, and that each one represented a successful raid on a neighbouring tribe with whom there were ancient disputes, going back, the headman assured visitors, to the time before the earth had entirely cooled and the land taken its current shape.

This tribal cosmology had greatly impressed visitors, particularly a succession of American anthropologists who came from the University of Louisiana in Baton Rouge, and their German counterparts from the *Institut für Sozialanthropologie und Empirische Kulturwissenschaft* in Zürich. For her part, Domenica was sceptical and, in the six months she spent living with the group in question, had set out to examine in a more critical way the claims that were made in relation to head-hunting. Her suspicions were aroused by the difficulty she encountered in finding any member of the group who had actually engaged in a head-hunting raid. There were plenty of uncles – now safely deceased – who were said to have been accomplished head-hunters, and various cousins – since relocated to Port Moresby – who had a reputation for major hauls of heads. Death and distance prevented either of these categories from attesting to their exploits, but this had somehow been overlooked by previous anthropologists. Domenica thought that this might be because to have been exposed to head-hunting had a certain cachet that research in the libraries of North America or Germany simply did not confer.

After being shown the preserved heads in the meeting house, Domenica had managed to pick the primitive lock that prevented access to the home-made display case in which they were stored. She did this privately, when nobody was around, and when her hosts imagined that she would be safely in bed. Shielding the beam of her torch with a cupped hand, she gingerly extracted the first of the heads, a tiny, shrivelled object the size of a large grapefruit or pineapple. A tuft of hair protruded from the top and it was by this that she held the head while she examined it more closely.

There were two sockets where the eyes must have been and a short protuberance that would have been the victim's nose. The ears were flattened against the side of the head; sad, dejected flaps of skin that must once have heard bird-song, the singing of children, the sound of waterfalls . . .

She looked more closely. There was something odd about this head, and as she ran a hand down the back of it, she encountered unexpected ridges and something sharp that pricked at her finger. She almost dropped it, imagining the dormant viruses that might live on a shrunken head like this until a careless anthropologist came and picked it up. That was what had happened to those Egyptologists – was it not? – those unapologetic tomb raiders who had, with the blessing of Western scholarly academies, broken into dusty pyramid chambers and disturbed the rest of ancient pharaohs. They had all died in mysterious circumstances, some from unexplained diseases which could well have been triggered by microbes for which a millennium or two of seclusion was but nothing. These heads could similarly be host to such organisms . . . except . . . except that the ridges and the prickles gave it away. These were, in fact, shrunken pineapples, cleverly made up to appear like shrunken heads.

This conclusion was borne out by examination of the other heads in the collection. Three were pineapples, one was a melon, and another a coconut. She waited until the right moment came to raise the subject with one of her informants in the village, the sister of the headman, who had been delegated to act as hostess to Domenica.

She communicated with this woman in Pidgin, the *lingua franca* of the region.

'This head,' she said, pointing to the painted coconut. 'This head bilong coconut tree, not bilong man.'

The woman looked shocked. 'No,' she said. 'This head bilong bad man bilong people bilong next door. Owner head bilong spirit world now bilong no-head people.'

'No,' said Domenica. 'Me bilong University of Edinburgh bilong Scotland bilong Scottish Enlightenment. Me too much clever; know coconut when I see one.'

The woman stared at her for a moment. 'All right, all right,' she said at last, switching to Australian-accented English. 'There hasn't been head-hunting for ages. But you know how men are – they love to boast about physical exploits.'

'Oh, I know all about that,' said Domenica, also abandoning Pidgin. 'We have rugby back in Scotland. It's much the same thing.'

'We should send one of our people over to do some fieldwork,' joked the woman.

Domenica had laughed, but now, sitting in her kitchen with a letter in her hand, she remembered this conversation from all those years ago and experienced a certain sense of *déjà vu*.

'Angus,' she said, 'I really must tell you about a letter I've received from somebody up at the university.'

Angus looked interested. 'How nice that somebody still writes actual letters. What does it say?'

Domenica unfolded it. 'Apparently they're getting visitors from Rwanda.'

'Ah yes,' said Angus. He was good at maps, and he could picture Rwanda tucked away under Uganda, with, beneath it . . . What exactly was beneath Rwanda?

'Well,' continued Domenica. 'Apparently Creative Scotland has given a grant to somebody to bring some Forest People over to Scotland for a visit.'

'Forest People?' said Angus. 'Who exactly would they be?'

'They used to be called pygmies,' said Domenica. 'These days they're often called Forest People, but they themselves don't object to the term *pygmy*, as long as it's used with respect.'

'I see,' said Angus. 'And what has this got to do with us?'

'They – that is, Creative Scotland – would like us to help to entertain them. I suppose it's because they know I'm an anthropologist.'

'How does one entertain Forest People?' asked Angus.

Domenica frowned. 'I'm sure they require little entertainment. Everything I've ever read about them suggests that they are charming, gentle people, who will make ideal guests.'

'Oh, well,' said Angus. 'They won't take up much room, will they?'

Domenica smiled. '*Guid gear in sma' buik*,' she said.

9. Cavafy's Poem

As Angus and Domenica contemplated the impending visit to Scotland of the Rwandan Forest People, or pygmies, at Nine Mile Burn, just outside Edinburgh, Matthew and Elspeth were busy putting their triplets, Tobermory, Rognvald and Fergus, to bed. Matthew sensed his wife's exhaustion, and had it been possible for him to deal with bedtime single-handed, he would have offered to do so. But it was physically impossible for one person, however adept at handling small children, to cope with the three young boys, now just past their second birthday, and endowed with apparently boundless energy, inordinate appetites, and incorrigible boisterousness.

'I've had it,' said Elspeth, as they manoeuvred the boys into the bath. 'I'm absolutely whacked. Finished.'

Matthew reached out to put a sympathetic arm on his wife's shoulder. 'I know how you feel,' he said.

She glanced at him. She was not sure that Matthew did know: he spent most of the day at work while she looked after the boys, and so it was easy for him to tackle bedtime when he arrived home. He would have the boys for no more than an hour, while she . . . She did a quick mental calculation: she had been on duty for exactly twelve hours, ever since Tobermory, who always woke up first, had called out from his room that there was a lion under his bed.

'You go,' Elspeth had muttered as she emerged into consciousness.

Matthew grunted.

'It's Tobermory,' said Elspeth, louder now. 'Could you go and deal with the lion . . . ?'

Matthew grunted again. 'Where do all these lions come from? He was going on about lions last night. Have you been reading them stories about lions?'

'No,' said Elspeth. 'I haven't. But Birgitte and her friend . . .'

Matthew snorted as he hauled himself out of bed. 'It's their fault – I should have known.'

The girls in question were the two Danish au pairs, Birgitte and Anna, who had stayed with Matthew and Elspeth for some time before their contrariness, manifested in disagreements about virtually everything, coupled with a sullen, resentful sensitivity to even the slightest criticism, had led to the ending of their contracts.

'They had some ghastly Danish children's book that they'd found somewhere or other,' Elspeth continued. 'They used to translate it for the boys. It was all about a lion that ate his way through an entire village, polishing everybody off one by one.'

'Scandinavian *noir* for children,' said Matthew. 'It's completely unsuitable.'

'Well that's where these particular lions come from,' said Elspeth. 'Those girls . . .'

Matthew made his way down the corridor to the triplets' room. Opening the door, he saw that Tobermory was standing up in his cot, rattling the bars, while his brothers continued to sleep.

'There's a lion,' said the child. 'Right under the bed.'

Matthew yawned. 'There are no lions in Scotland,' he said patiently. 'But Daddy will look, just to be sure.'

He bent down and peered under the bed. A stuffed toy lion lay there on its side, its button eyes glaring at Matthew with all the intensity of a real lion on the African savannah. For a moment, they looked at one another. *Don't run away from a lion – instinct will drive them to pursue you.* So what does one do? Matthew asked himself.

'Oh,' said Matthew. 'There's a lion.'

'That's what I said,' crowed Tobermory.

Matthew retrieved the toy and handed it to his son. 'There,' he said. 'Nice lion.'

Tobermory took the creature. '*Løve*,' he said, hugging it to him.

Matthew reached down to pick him up. 'What did you say, darling?'

'*Løve*,' said Tobermory.

'What's *Løve*?'

'*Løve*,' repeated the little boy, flourishing the lion.

That was twelve hours ago – twelve hours that had been filled with domestic crises of one sort or another – a fight between two of the boys, the breaking of a cafetière that covered the kitchen floor with slivers of glass; the regurgitation, by Rognvald, of his breakfast over a newly upholstered chair; the loss, somewhere in the garden, of one of Tobermory's shoes; a difficult telephone call from a somewhat clingy friend; all of which were fairly typical incidents in Elspeth's day. She wondered how many more such days lay ahead of her. The boys would go to school at about five years of age, which meant that she had just under three years to endure, which made about a thousand days.

The thought defeated her, and she made the decision to tackle Matthew that night. She would have to have help. After the experience of the two young Danes they had decided they would try to manage by themselves, but now she realised that this was simply impossible. She would contact Mother's Angels, the agency she had used to find the Danes, and throw herself upon their mercy.

The boys having been bathed, clad in their tartan pyjamas, and read to by Matthew – a short and repetitive book that was chosen as the antithesis of juvenile Scandinavian *noir* – Elspeth retreated to the kitchen. There she poured herself a gin and tonic and informed Matthew of her decision.

'We can't cope,' she said. 'Or, rather, I can't.'

Matthew did not argue. 'We have to get somebody.'

'I'm not going to get another girl,' said Elspeth. 'I want an au pair boy.'

Matthew was surprised, but said nothing.

'A Spanish boy,' said Elspeth, taking a generous sip of her gin.

'Why Spanish?'

Elspeth explained. Her cousin in Dundee had employed a young Spaniard, who had been popular with her children.

'He played football with them,' Elspeth said. 'They loved him.'

Matthew looked thoughtful. 'But will you be able to find one?'

'There are any number of them. Unemployment in Spain is so high. One in five young Spanish males has no job.'

Matthew winced. 'How did that happen?'

Elspeth sighed. 'Something to do with . . . ' She shrugged and mentioned the reason for the economic woes of the Spaniards, the Italians, the Greeks . . .

Matthew smiled. 'How useful to have a scapegoat to blame for all one's problems.'

'But what if it really is the scapegoat's fault?'

'Ah,' said Matthew. And then 'Ah' again. He thought of something. 'Have you ever read Cavafy?' he asked. 'That Greek poet. He lived in Alexandria and he wrote a wonderful poem called 'Waiting for the Barbarians'. The Barbarians don't arrive and the people think about how they were a really convenient solution to their problems – the waiting, that is.' He paused. 'The thing you fear may sometimes be the solution.'

'Are we waiting?' she asked. 'I mean, are we, here, in Scotland, waiting for something?'

Matthew looked out of the window. It was hard to tell. He thought they were waiting – possibly – but then he was not quite sure what they were waiting for.

10. O Tempora! O Mores!

In the Scottish Office of Statistics in Leith, a meeting was being attended by Stuart Pollock, senior statistician, father of Bertie and Ulysses, and of course husband of Irene, although she herself never used the patriarchal term *husband*, preferring *ally*, which expressed, she felt, the conditional, egalitarian goals of the relationship more widely known as marriage. Not everybody, of course, understood the term *ally* in this context. The plumber, for instance, had looked blank when Irene had mentioned that she would need to consult her ally about the installation of a new shower head. 'Stuart,' she explained when she noticed his incomprehension. 'I must talk to Stuart.'

'Ah,' said the plumber. 'Your man.'

Irene had bristled. 'I don't *own* him,' she said.

'No, of course not. But he is your man, isn't he?'

'We are in an alliance,' said Irene coldly.

The plumber had not pressed the point, but had bitten his lip. *You certainly encounter them*, he said to his wife that evening. *Especially in Edinburgh.*

The alliance between Irene and Stuart had lasted for ten years. Irene did not think much of anniversaries, which she regarded as sentimental celebrations largely encouraged by the makers of greetings cards.

'The fact of the matter,' she said, 'is that for many women so-called marriage is a sentence. Would you send a card to somebody when they've served fifteen years, or whatever, of a sentence? I think not.'

Stuart did not argue, confining himself to the mild observation that for some people, at least, an anniversary might be a reminder of happiness and its duration.

'False consciousness,' muttered Irene. 'People don't necessarily know what their true condition is.'

He thought he might say that people who *thought* they were happy probably *were* happy, but he did not. There was no winning an argument with Irene and he merely sighed, but not audibly, of course. Release for him came in the office, whither he could escape on weekdays from eight in the morning until five-thirty, when he returned to Scotland Street to put Bertie and Ulysses to bed. That gave him nine and a half hours of freedom, during which nobody accused him of anything, nobody corrected him, and nobody made him feel that he should be thinking – and saying – something he did not agree with.

He enjoyed his work, which was largely concerned with presenting facts and figures in a way that was positive rather than negative. In particular, he was responsible for making economic prospects look good even if the figures suggested otherwise. So if there were, for example, a fifteen-billion pound deficit in public spending, this could be presented as a marked improvement on the sixteen-billion pound deficit forecast by some others.

'We have such fun,' Stuart observed to one of his colleagues in another department. 'It's creative work, you know – in fact, you'd think Creative Scotland would give us a grant for what we do.'

Stuart was not overly ambitious. He had been an academic high-flier as a young man, graduating with one of the best first-class honours degrees awarded at a Scottish university that year, and this had been followed by two years of work on a PhD. Financial pressures put an end to that, as he had already met Irene and they had decided to buy the flat in Scotland Street. Stuart needed a job, and the Scottish Government post offered a reasonable salary and access to a preferential mortgage.

Over the years he got the promotions that one would expect, moving slowly up the grades, but had now reached the point where, if he were to be promoted further, he would need to go before a special board. This board was informally called the Perspex Ceiling, and it made recommendations for head-of-department appointments and above. The people who occupied these positions were known as *mandarins*, and were, *ex officio*, eligible for membership of both Muirfield Golf Club (subject to certain conditions) and the New Club, should they so desire.

Irene had no time for mandarins, but, rather in the manner of Lady Macbeth, was ambitious for her husband/ally. Apart from anything else, money was tight and the additional salary would be more than welcome; so when Stuart was told at work one day that he was to be invited before the Perspex Ceiling he realised that, whatever his own feelings about occupying a much more senior post, Irene would require him to apply.

The information about his selection came from his closest friend in the office, Morrison Purves. Morrison was only a few years away from retirement and so had no interest in further promotion, but was keen for Stuart to be successful.

'I shouldn't be telling you this,' he said. 'But . . .'

It was the usual preface to an important piece of information.

'Of course you don't have to tell me if you don't want to,' Stuart assured him.

That, too, was the standard reply to such an overture, and it meant the opposite of what it said.

'No, I'll tell you because I know how discreet you are,' continued Morrison.

That again was very much in the script, and once it had been said, the information could be revealed.

'Three of you are going up for interview,' said Morrison, his voice lowered. 'Would you like to know who the other two are?'

For a few moments, Stuart attempted to look indifferent, but then he nodded conspiratorially. 'If you insist,' he said.

'All right,' said Morrison, his voice lowered even further. 'That eighty-four horsepower *sook*, Elaine.'

'Oh no,' said Stuart. 'Not her.'

'And that snivelling toady, Faith.'

Stuart cast his eyes up to the ceiling. 'What a field!'

'You've got to get it, Stuart,' went on Morrison. 'If either of them gets chosen, I'm bringing forward my retirement. Guaranteed. Elaine can't even do long division, let alone statistics.'

Stuart smiled. 'And Faith . . .'

'Have you seen her with the politicians?' asked Morrison. 'She sends them birthday cards. Can you believe it? She gets their birthdays from *Who's Who in Scotland* and she sends a card. They love it.'

'*O tempora, o mores*,' muttered Stuart.

'Come again?' asked Morrison.

'It's Latin for *Jeez*,' explained Stuart.

11. Tolerance and Intolerance

Morrison said to Stuart, 'How about going to the Old Chain Pier? We can talk more freely there.'

The Old Chain Pier was a well-known bar, perched on the shore at Newhaven, once festooned with old fishing floats and maritime paraphernalia.

They were sitting in the staff canteen at the time, and it was there, over a standard civil service lunch (healthy option) that Morrison had given the news to Stuart that he was on the shortlist for promotion.

'Why? Can't we talk here?' Stuart said.

'No,' replied Morrison. 'I don't mean that we can't talk, it's just that . . . well, I detect a certain change in the atmosphere in this place recently. I don't think we can speak quite as freely as we used to.'

Stuart raised an eyebrow. 'You mean there's less freedom of opinion?'

Morrison looked over his shoulder. 'To an extent.' He hesitated. 'And not just here. Everywhere.'

'You aren't over-reacting, are you?'

Morrison shook his head. 'Liberty can drain away very slowly. So slowly, in fact, that you may not even notice it. We lost freedom of speech some time ago. You can't say what you think these days, can you? About some things – yes, but not everything. Far from it.'

Stuart considered this. 'In some areas, perhaps. You certainly can't insult others. You can't whip up hostility against them.' He paused. 'And don't you think that's a good thing? Don't you think it was about time people stopped demeaning others?'

Morrison stared at Stuart, as if weighing him up; as if uncertain whether to trust him. When he answered, he spoke cautiously. 'I'm not suggesting it's a good thing to demean people. What I'm worried about is the creation of a climate of fear – so that people feel they can't say anything that might offend some group.'

'Give me an example,' said Stuart.

Morrison looked about him again. 'All right,' he said, his voice lowered. 'Let's say you take the view that you shouldn't be able to change the sex you're born into. Let's say you believe that people who have sex change operations are still men or women because that's what they are chromosomally. Can you express that view?'

Stuart shrugged. 'Yes, if that's what you think. As far as I'm concerned, though, I see nothing wrong with sex change. People in that position feel very strongly about what they are. Why prevent them from living their lives as they want to?'

'That's not the point,' said Morrison. 'I happen to agree with you on that, but there are some who don't. The point I'm making is this: should those who take a different view be allowed to express it?'

Stuart shrugged again. 'Who's stopping them? It's not illegal to express an opinion on that.'

'Not yet,' said Morrison. 'But you could lose your job if you did.'

'Oh, come on . . . '

'Or be crucified on the social media,' Morrison continued. 'Or de-platformed, like Germaine Greer.'

'Well, I don't condone that,' conceded Stuart. 'But think what's at stake here. In the past we've been so casual about hurting people, about allowing people to be disparaged because they're different in some way. If you disparage people for what they *are*, then you're saying something about their nature, about who they are. You're saying *You don't count as much as others because of what you are.*' He paused. 'And that's pretty devastating, isn't it?'

Morrison looked down at the floor. It seemed to Stuart that his friend looked rather ashamed of himself, and so he added, 'Not that I think you're saying any of that. It's all a question of kindness, isn't it? And you're fundamentally kind.'

He sensed that something unexpectedly raw and difficult had opened up between them; a difference of opinion that went rather deep.

Morrison looked up. 'Look, I don't have any difficulty with people being whatever they happen to be. It's not that at all. It's just that I don't like being told that I can't express a view – or can't even hold a view. And what about religion: what are we allowed to say about that?'

Stuart shrugged. 'You can express a view if you want to. You can say that religious belief is a delusion – if that's what you think. Nobody's stopping you from saying that.'

'But I can't sing certain songs?'

Stuart hesitated. 'You mean "The Sash my Father Wore?"'

Morrison nodded.

'You shouldn't sing that at a football match. No, you shouldn't.'

Morrison sighed. 'Well, there you are. We've now become a society that stops people singing the wrong songs.'

Stuart was reluctant to let that pass. 'That's not about religion, anyway. That's all about group antagonisms. And why would you sing it? You'd sing it to taunt others. You'd sing it to encourage a bit of a rammy between Protestants and Catholics. You'd sing it to promote division and hatred.'

Morrison hesitated. 'I wouldn't sing it. And I don't know the words anyway.'

Stuart began to hum the opening bar; then the words: 'It's old but it is beautiful . . . '

Morrison turned pale. 'Sshh!'

'Don't worry,' said Stuart, smiling. 'I won't sing it. But

there are plenty of people who would. And they'd sing it to stir up trouble. They'd sing it to start a fight – and surely we're entitled to say that we don't want people fighting with one another.'

Morrison was silent. Then he said, 'I wouldn't want you to think I'm reactionary,' he said.

Stuart smiled. 'Anything but that.'

'It's just that I get the feeling,' Morrison continued, 'that there's an imposed consensus. That there are people who want us all to think in the same way and are using pressure of various sorts – social disapproval as well as real sanctions – to ensure that people toe an ideological line.'

Stuart thought of Irene. He almost said, 'I'm married to one,' but loyalty prevented him.

'I've got nothing against much of this,' Morrison continued. 'I've got nothing against correcting the injustices of the past – including all the injustices that women have had to bear. It's just that I still believe that an old injustice doesn't justify a new injustice.'

'Ah,' said Stuart.

Morrison fixed Stuart with an intense gaze. He leaned forward as he spoke. 'And there's a line in the sand right here in this building,' he whispered. 'And if either of those two – Elaine or Faith – gets the job, then it's the end of tolerance and it's hello witch-hunts. I'm warning you, Stuart, this is deadly serious.'

Stuart sat back in his chair. 'Don't you think you're overstating it a bit?'

Morrison shook his head. 'I'm not, Stuart. I'm telling it as it is. Those two have an anti-male agenda. They're every bit as bad as men who have an anti-female agenda. There's no difference. Or there is, perhaps, in that they've got the *zeitgeist* on their side. They've got the rhetoric, Stuart.'

'I think you're being unreasonable, Morrison,' Stuart said evenly. 'The world has changed. Old privileges and old attitudes are out. Accept it.'

Morrison rose from chair. 'All right, but don't say I didn't warn you.'

12. *The View from Dunfermline*

Stuart felt unsettled by the conversation with Morrison. He was fond of his colleague and it saddened him to think that he should feel alienated from the world he worked in. But that, he supposed, was not surprising: Morrison was approaching retirement and at that age people commonly felt at odds with social progress. Every generation made that discovery, Stuart thought; the world changed – of course it did – and not everyone found it easy to accommodate these changes. Yet many of these changes were not bad ones: far from it, they were introduced to help people feel better about themselves, to lead happier lives, to be treated fairly and not discriminated against by those who had an advantage over them. No, he could sign up to all that – and not just because he was married to Irene and had experienced an extreme version of that agenda at full blast, but because he actually believed in the central values that such reforms embodied.

What worried him, though, was that Morrison had been made so anxious – indeed frightened – by the prospect of one of the other candidates for promotion getting the post. Stuart did not like Elaine or Faith. He did not like their only-too-obvious ambition and the fact that they were always calculating the effect that anything they did would have on their superiors. There had been several instances where he had seen the advice they gave to ministers and had realised that what they said was the exact opposite of what he knew they believed; they gave this advice, though, because they knew that this was what the minister would want to hear. Everybody likes those who express their personal prejudices, and government ministers are no exception to that rule. Both Elaine and Faith knew that, and were prepared to act against their own better judgment if that meant a smile or a pat on the head from those in authority. It was sickening, thought Stuart. What's the point of having an independent civil service, he asked himself, if that same civil service is not going to give independent advice?

He felt a strong dislike for those two, but he did not really know either of them at all well. Elaine was the older; she was a tall, rather irritating woman in her mid-forties, who came from Fife – a fact that she never tired of mentioning. Remarks on a wide range of subjects would be prefaced with, 'Well, I'm from Fife, you see, and we . . . ' There then followed some general local prejudice, set out in great detail and presented as if it were an example of deep wisdom only available to those who had the good fortune to be born and brought up in Fife.

Another of her expressions was, 'We don't look at things that way in Dunfermline.' That could be inserted into any discussion at any point, and was very effective in derailing the debate. For the most part, people were unsure what to make of it. Was there something about Dunfermline – some quality of higher rationality – that made it futile to question the Dunfermline view of things? Or was there an implicit suggestion that if any position were espoused that differed from the Dunfermline view, then there would be endless trouble in Fife and, perhaps, in many other places that were somehow in Fife's sphere of influence?

He knew little of Elaine's personal circumstances. He had been told that she was married, but he knew nothing of her husband, whom she mentioned from time to time, invariably adding, 'He's originally from Kirkcaldy, you know,' as if in explanation of all that he stood for. Stuart had heard that he was called Sammy, and that he ran a tree nursery near Auchtermuchty. He felt vaguely sorry for this Sammy, with his tedious wife and his tree nursery, and all the worries and burdens that went with both of these.

Elaine was very friendly with Faith, who was a strongly built woman with broad shoulders and a square chin. She had a master's degree from McGill University in Montreal, and insisted on listing this degree behind her name on any letter or circular she signed. It was also rumoured – although the accusation remained unproven – that the Christmas cards she sent to politicians were signed *Faith McDougall, MSc (McGill).*

Faith very rarely spoke to Stuart, whom she seemed to ignore most of the time. If Stuart asked her a question at a meeting, Faith would answer it, but would not look at him as she spoke, addressing her answer to Elaine, who would nod encouragingly as she spoke.

'She doesn't acknowledge my existence,' said Stuart to another colleague. 'She doesn't see me.'

The colleague laughed. 'She doesn't see me either,' he said.

'I wonder why?' asked Stuart.

The colleague laughed again. 'We're the enemy,' he said.

This explanation depressed Stuart. He felt it was quite unfair to be branded with the misdeeds of other men – men who treated women unfairly and could be thought to deserve this angry *froideur* in return. He was not like that, and yet she refused to hear him out, to see that he was not like the men against whom she was waging her campaign.

'I've never personally been . . . ' Stuart began, only to be cut short by his colleague.

'That's not the point,' the colleague said. 'This is *status* guilt. The moment you were born you became part of the structures of oppression – because you're male. It's nothing to do with choice, Stuart – nothing to do with what you yourself think or feel.'

Stuart sighed. It was the mark of Cain – a burden much the same as that borne by the offspring of enemies of the people in revolutionary Russia. It was inherited guilt, and no protestations of innocence, no rejection or disavowal of the iniquities of the past could remove the stain.

He wondered how long this would last. Would it be there until the memory of the past faded completely, or would it last until men themselves had become the new oppressed class? And if that were so, then how long would the period of revenge last?

He was thinking of this when the summons came for a meeting with the Supreme Head of Personnel. All three candidates were to attend, the note specified, to have explained to them the selection procedures that were to be followed to ensure a process that was transparent, equitable, and designed to achieve the best possible outcome. But what, Stuart wondered, was that? That the best candidate would be appointed? And best for what? That was the real question – that was where the demons lurked.

13. No Boys' Club Here

'Now,' said the Supreme Head of Personnel, 'as you know, there are very carefully set-out procedures.'

Elaine nodded. 'Procedures. Yes, procedures. Unlike the bad old days when . . . '

She glanced at Stuart, who smarted under the implicit

accusation that he had somehow been involved in the procedures of that benighted era.

The Supreme Head of Personnel was reassuring. 'Oh, I can assure you: we're not going back to any of that.'

Stuart struggled. 'Of what?'

Elaine glared at him. 'The boys' club approach.'

'Precisely,' said the Supreme Head of Personnel. 'We now have procedures that meet all the requirements of public appointments. There will be an outside assessor. Then the position will be advertised.'

'Where?' asked Stuart.

'On the noticeboard,' said the Supreme Head of Personnel.

Stuart raised an eyebrow. 'What about people from outside . . . ?'

'Not eligible,' said the Supreme Head of Personnel abruptly. 'This is a category A position. Category A positions are not advertised outside the civil service, as per the relevant agreement.'

'With whom?' asked Stuart.

All three women stared at him.

'With the relevant union,' answered the Supreme Head of Personnel.

Stuart sat back in his chair. 'I see. And the outside assessor? How is he chosen?'

'She,' said the Supreme Head of Personnel.

Stuart corrected himself. 'How's she chosen?'

'I've made an appointment,' said the Supreme Head of Personnel. 'Under the terms of the relevant regulation.'

'Are we allowed to ask who it is?' asked Stuart.

'No,' said the Supreme Head of Personnel. 'Now, on to the procedures themselves. There will be an initial declaration for you all to sign. This will ask certain questions, including one as to where you heard about the vacancy.'

Stuart thought of his conversation with Morrison. Would he have to disclose that? 'I heard about it on the grapevine,' he said.

The Supreme Head of Personnel bristled. 'That's not what we're after, Mr Pollock. In fact, that's exactly the sort of thing we're trying to get beyond – the cosy passing on of information about these opportunities.'

'Well said,' said Elaine. 'We need to expose that sort of thing.'

Stuart turned to face her. 'Where did you hear of it then?'

Elaine was momentarily taken aback, and Stuart pressed his advantage. 'From a friend?'

Elaine exchanged a glance with the Supreme Head of Personnel. Unknown to Stuart, she had heard from the Supreme Head of Personnel herself, who had telephoned her at home to pass on the news.

'You don't have to answer that,' said the Supreme Head of Personnel. 'And I'll regard the question as not having been asked.'

'But it was,' said Stuart. 'I asked it.'

The Supreme Head of Personnel ignored this. 'Now, there's another aspect of the process,' she said. 'The resumé. As you know, we'll be following the new form. We don't want personal details of a sort that would enable favouritism to be exercised. So we don't want any names on the resumé itself – just a number. And we want no details of schools or universities attended.'

Stuart sighed. 'So no reference to qualifications?'

The Supreme Head of Personnel shook her head. 'None. We are seeking to avoid networking.'

Stuart sighed again. 'Surely it will be rather hard for the Board to make a decision if they don't know anything about any of the candidates, such as their educational qualifications, their experience, their gender . . .'

'Oh, that must be revealed,' said the Supreme Head of Personnel.

Stuart nodded. 'Of course.'

'And there's an interesting new requirement,' continued the Supreme Head of Personnel. 'Every candidate must write a short paper – not more than two thousand words – on their vision for the job.'

Stuart frowned. 'Our vision for the job?'

'How you see the job as an opportunity to carry forward departmental objectives,' explained the Supreme Head of Personnel. 'It's not novel. And it's useful for us to know in advance what the successful candidate thinks she will do with the job.'

Stuart raised a finger.

'Yes, Mr Pollock?'

'What *she* will do with the job?' he said quietly.

The Supreme Head of Personnel looked puzzled. 'Yes, that's what I said.'

Stuart closed his eyes. 'I see,' he said. 'You haven't already decided who's going to get this?' he asked, and then added, quickly and apologetically, 'Just wondering.'

'Of course not,' said the Supreme Head of Personnel. 'And, frankly, I'm surprised that you would ask such a question.'

The meeting came to an end. As he returned to his office, Stuart was aware that someone was pursuing him down the corridor. He turned round and saw that it was Elaine.

'I want you to know,' she said as she caught up with him. 'I want you to know that even if this whole process is stacked against us, neither Faith nor I will hold anything against you.'

Stuart caught his breath. 'Stacked against you?'

'Yes,' said Elaine. 'We know what men are capable of.'

Stuart could barely believe what he was hearing. 'But there aren't any men involved in the whole thing,' he stuttered. 'It's all women, as far as I can see.'

Elaine smiled. 'On the surface,' she said. 'But the underlying patriarchy's still there.'

Stuart stared at her. Within him, deep within him, something snapped.

'I think you are seriously deluded,' he said. 'I think you're paranoid.'

Elaine stopped in her tracks. 'You've seriously compromised my personal space,' she said, her voice filled with venom. 'If I chose to make an issue of this you'd be suspended, you know.'

'Oh, do shut your face,' said Stuart.

Elaine screamed. Stuart stared at her. He felt a curious sense of detachment – of freedom.

'Do you realise how ghastly you are?' he said.

Elaine gasped. 'You hateful . . . ' She struggled to find the right words. 'You hateful, hateful . . . '

Stuart tried to help her. 'Hateful man? Yes, I'm a man. I can't help it. I was born that way and that's what I am. I know I'm inferior. I know I'm no longer needed, but that's what I am, for better or worse, a man.'

Elaine shook her head. Approaching him, she whispered her warning. 'Start the count-down, Stuart. Start the count-down to your early retirement – very early retirement.'

14. Silk Sheets

Big Lou's day had begun at six. It had been that way, summer and winter, for as long as she could remember. At Snell Mains, the mixed arable and stock farm on which she had been born and spent her childhood, the idea of staying in bed once you had awoken was anathema. Lying in bed was what lazy people did – people who lived in towns and cities, who had no cows to milk, no chickens to feed, no sheepdogs to let out of their kennels. Such people could lie in bed until unheard-of hours – eight o'clock, in extreme cases – listening to the radio or even drinking tea, leaving other people to do all the work that honest people from places like Angus and Aberdeenshire were up and about doing.

At the age of eight, Big Lou had been taken to Dundee by a favourite aunt. After they had finished their shopping, they had gone into a cinema where she had sat through a parental-guidance-rated film. She had been thrilled at the maturity implicit in being allowed to see such a film, even if the aunt had whispered to her at one or two points that she should avert her eyes. Big Lou had complied, to an extent, clasping her hands firmly over her eyes but discreetly peeking through her fingers at what was happening on the screen. It was nothing exciting, as far as she could make out, but it did show a woman – a well-known actress of whom her aunt had often talked, slightly disapprovingly – lying in a bed with silken sheets. Lou had concluded that this was the part of the film that was viewed as unsuitable for children – the main offence being that the woman in question was lying in bed after six o'clock.

On the way back to Arbroath, Lou said, 'Auntie, that woman in the film . . .'

'That well-kent one? That Madame Bovary? Aye, what of her?'

'She was a bad woman, wasn't she?'

The aunt had considered her response. 'Definitely bad, Lou dearie. And she got what was coming to her.'

'She had that bed with silk sheets . . . Are there fowk who really have silk sheets?'

The aunt did not hesitate. 'Aye, there are fowk like that, Lou. Not here in Arbroath, though, thank the Lord.'

'Where, Auntie? Where do they have these silk sheets? Edinburgh?'

The aunt nodded. 'Edinburgh's one such place. There's a gae lot of that doon there, I think.'

'And they don't get up til . . . '

'Til all hours of the forenoon,' supplied the aunt. 'Some of them stay in bed until the efternoon, would you believe it?'

'Til the efternoon!'

'Aye,' said the aunt. 'But they get what's coming to them, sure enough.'

'Which is?'

'The Lord punishes them. He has a list, you see, of fowk like that. He sorts them out soon enough, don't you worry.'

That attitude to sluggardly behaviour set Lou in good stead during the time she spent working at the Granite Nursing Home in Aberdeen. In all her years there, she was never late for work – not on a single occasion – and never objected to the early shift. Her loyalty to the home was to be spectacularly rewarded when one of the inmates, a man of considerable means, had left Lou his entire estate 'in gratitude', as his will put it, 'for all she has done for me and other unfortunates, for the heart of gold that beats within her'.

Lou did not immediately leave her job as a nurse's assistant, as many might do on benefiting from such a generous legacy, but continued for a good six months before handing in her resignation.

'Ah, Lou,' said the Matron, 'I was hoping against hope that you'd stay, but you've deserved this – every penny of it. Now what?'

‘Back to the farm for a while, Matron,’ said Lou. ‘There’s work to be done.’

Matron smiled. ‘Yes, there’s always work to be done, isn’t there, Lou? And you’ll always do it, won’t you – nae complaint, nae bither.’

‘And then I thought maybe I’d try Edinburgh for a while.’

The Matron’s eyes lit up. ‘Edinburgh! You know, I lived in Edinburgh once – for a year or two. I stayed in the Nurses’ Home at the Royal Infirmary. Oh, we had a grand time, so we did. You had to work hard enough and you had to be signed back in to the home by ten o’clock, but you were allowed to go to the dances in the University Union. They called them the Union Palais and you could meet some awfie nice young men there – medical students often enough. We had a wonderful time back then.’ She paused. ‘I could write to somebody, Lou. I know a man down there who has a nursing home in a good part of town. He’s always looking for reliable staff. I could write to him, if you liked. He’s called Jimmy Watson and I think his mother was from somewhere down your way, from Arbroath, or maybe it was Montrose. There were plenty of Watsons in Montrose, but they weren’t all related, you know ... One of them had a haulage business that he’d advertise each week in the P and J. It was called Watson’s Trucks, I mind. You saw them on the road all the time – muckle trucks that took cattle off to the sales and so on.’

Lou listened. Although disinclined to complain, this was exactly what she wanted to get away from – this sense of being trapped in a world where everyone was somehow connected, where people knew where others came from and who their parents and grandparents had been. Lou wanted to see the world and to achieve something. She had spent her entire life thus far in doing things for others – now she wanted to create something that would be hers.

'I think I'll start a café,' she said to Matron. 'I'll use the money to buy a café in Edinburgh.'

The idea had just occurred to her then and there, but it seemed to be the right thing to do.

'Oh, you'll have the time of your life in Edinburgh,' said Matron. 'Start a café. You might meet a young man from Arbroath – they go down there, you know.'

'I'll see,' said Lou. 'You never know.'

'You could try the Union Palais,' said Matron. But then, on second thoughts, added, 'Well, maybe not.'

15. You Are the Sun

When Big Lou arrived in Edinburgh she used almost the entire legacy to buy a two-bedroomed flat in Canonmills, overlooking a bend in the Water of Leith, and a former bookshop in Dundas Street. The bookshop, known for its associations with figures of the twentieth century Scottish Literary Renaissance, had been frequented by poets such as Norman MacCaig, C. M. Grieve, and Sydney Goodsir

Smith. The proprietor's executors sold the shop with all its stock, which meant that Big Lou became the owner of a library of several thousand books on just about every subject. Big Lou moved the books lock, stock and barrel to the flat in Canonmills, where the motley collection became her private library, to be worked through, title by title, over the years that followed.

Big Lou had left school at sixteen – a decision that was made for her by her parents without her views being sought. They felt that by that age she would be vested with sufficient skills to enter the workplace for a few years before, in due course, she married the son of a local farmer. What would count thereafter would not be skill in mathematics, a knowledge of geography, or even an ability to understand basic French, but familiarity with the cleaning of a milking parlour, the ability to help ewes to lamb, and an understanding of the running of a farmhouse kitchen.

At first her lack of formal education did not trouble Big Lou too much, but as the years passed she became increasingly aware that there was a great deal she simply did not know. She started to read while she was working in Aberdeen, taking up authors who had something to say about the world she knew. *Sunset Song* struck her as being utterly and completely true – she *knew* those people – and *The House with the Green Shutters* shocked her with its accurate portrayal of meanness and greed in a rural setting.

The acquisition of so large a library might have daunted many, but not Big Lou. She decided she would at least start every one of the titles in her new library even if she would not persist with those that she found uninteresting or out-of-date. She started with philosophy and the Scottish Enlightenment – she read Smith, Hume and Hutcheson, along with commentaries on the works of all three of these. She moved on to George Davie's *The Democratic Intellect*, and to Iris Murdoch's *The Sovereignty of Good*, which she appreciated greatly. Next was *The Myth of Sisyphus* by Albert Camus and Martin Buber's *I and Thou*, first courses for a prolonged meal of continental philosophy that included the words of Spinoza, whom Big Lou rather liked, and Schopenhauer, whom she liked rather less.

These studious pursuits, along with the hard work involved in setting up and running her coffee bar, might have been expected to leave little time for socialising, but Big Lou was determined to take advantage of what Edinburgh offered. She met and became involved with a series of men, including a chef, a Jacobite plasterer and an obsessive Elvis impersonator; none of the men she met was anything but a disappointment to her, with the result that she gradually came to accept that she was unlikely to meet the sort of man she would so dearly love to find: a man who would be intelligent, empathetic, and witty company – somebody like Angus (without the dog and the tendency to wear clothes spotted with paint) or Matthew (without his cardigan in distressed oatmeal or his trousers of mitigated beige), but not at all like the narcissistic Bruce Anderson, with his hair gel and constant gazing at himself in any nearby polished surface (Big Lou had caught him admiring his reflection on the front of her Gaggia coffee maker, 'preening himself', she said).

Now she was reconciled to remaining single, or at least to accepting the possibility that she would not find a suitable partner. She would have been content enough with that – men, she had decided, were, on balance, somewhat overrated – and anyway somebody had come into her life who was already transforming it in ways she would never have thought possible. This was the young boy, Finlay, who had been allocated to her by the Social Welfare Department after Big Lou had offered to act as a foster parent. Finlay, who was seven – the same age as Bertie Pollock – had had a difficult start in life. At first, the traumas of his earlier years had made him suspicious and silent, but as he settled in, these defences were gradually lowered. Big Lou was a woman of infinite patience; she knew what it was to nurse an orphaned or rejected lamb back to health – she had done just that so many times in the lambing season, coaxing a tiny confused creature, unsteady on its spindly legs, to take the teat of the milk bottle, encouraging strength and vitality drop by drop. Now she did the equivalent of that with this strange, freckled little boy who had come into her life, bringing him round to an acceptance of the love she offered him. He responded willingly, taking her hand in his when they walked down the street, clutching it to him as if frightened that the world of warmth and security she had created for him might suddenly be snatched away.

He thrived at school, no longer the shy and withdrawn child his teachers had earlier observed, but now the life and soul of the classroom, popular with the other children and appreciated for his winning smile.

He drew a picture that was passed on to Big Lou by his

class teacher. 'I thought you might like to see this,' said the teacher. 'Finlay has drawn a picture.'

She gave Big Lou a typical child's drawing – a house, some trees, a sky in which a sun, human-featured and smiling, beamed down on a woman and a dog, stick-figures both. The woman was wearing a dress on which a large letter L had been drawn.

'That's you,' said the teacher, smiling. 'Finlay explained it all to me.'

But what made the drawing unusual was that the woman in the foreground – clearly Big Lou – was surrounded by exactly the same radiant beams that emanated from the sun above her.

Big Lou caught her breath. 'Me?'

'Yes,' said the teacher. 'And if I were you, I'd be very touched by that. He thinks of you as the sun.'

Big Lou felt the tears well up in her eyes. 'Pair wee bairn,' she whispered.

16. As Much Said as was Unsaid

Each morning Big Lou accompanied Finlay to Stockbridge Primary School before walking back along Raeburn Place, across the bridge over the Water of Leith, and up the gentle slope towards the gardens of Royal Circus Place. She followed the same route each day, as people so often do, crossing streets at precisely the same point each time, finding satisfaction in the routine. And it was not just familiar places that she saw – the same shop-fronts, the same street furniture, the same cracks in the pavement – she also encountered the same people, all following their familiar routine, treading a path that they would follow month after month, year after year, until they no longer had to go to an office, or a workshop, or wherever it was that they earned their living. Sometimes it seemed to Lou that the world was something of a treadmill – a giant treadmill on which we all tramped for our allotted span, covering much the same ground, with much the same view.

She found herself wondering about the people she encountered on this daily trip. There was that man, for instance, who emerged from St Stephen Street and paused before crossing the road opposite the Floatarium. He always stood there for a few minutes before making his way to the other side, as if uncertain as to what to do. She saw him look at his watch, then check it again before he crossed the road, reluctant to cross until exactly the right moment – whatever that was – had arrived; Immanuel Kant, thought Big Lou – Immanuel Kant. She had just read a biography of Kant, extracted from her shelf of old bookshop stock, in which Kant's famous regularity had been explored at length. And if the citizens of Königsberg could set their watches according to the appearance of the philosopher on his daily walk, then Big Lou could do much the same thing with this man.

Further up the hill, she sometimes found herself walking towards a man strolling down the road towards her – a man she thought of as the poet Hugh MacDiarmid because he was on the short side, somewhat bowdy-leggit, and sometimes in a kilt. Big Lou liked the kilt, but had views on those who should wear it and those who should seek some other means of making that particular cultural statement. In general, she felt that the kilt was for taller men, who could carry it off with the dignity that the garment required. Those who were of average height could wear it too, but had to be careful about their swagger. Those who were portly, or vertically challenged needed to exercise discretion, and those who were bandy – or bowdy-leggit, as Big Lou put it – had to think long and hard about wearing it at all if they wished to avoid looking too much like Harry Lauder. There is much to be said for the late Harry Lauder and his couthy songs, but whether he would recommend himself as a style icon was another matter.

Over a period of months, this particular man had progressed from stranger to acquaintance. It had started with eye contact, and this, after a suitable interval, had led to a slight nodding of the head. A few weeks later, this had been supplemented with a smile, and finally words had converted the relationship into a speaking one.

'Aye, aye,' the man had muttered one morning as they passed one another on the pavement.

'Aye,' responded Lou.

That had sufficed for a further week. Although few words were used, such exchanges can be emotionally expressive. The adding of a sigh to the *aye*, for instance, can say so much about the world and its problems; the addition of two sighs can express utter despair at the state of human affairs; just as prefacing the first *aye* with an *oh* can express nuanced emotions ranging from slight doubt to sophisticated cynicism, as in this exchange, where the translations are parenthesised:

Aye, aye (*Good morning.*)

Aye (*Good morning.*)

Aye? (*Is everything all right? Any news?*)

Aye (the tone descending slightly at the end) (*I give up; I really do.*)

Aye? (the tone rising at the end) (*What's wrong? The usual issues?*)

AYE (emphatic) (*Yes, the same old stuff.*)

Oh, aye (resigned) (*Here we go again. It's someone else's fault – as per usual. You'd think that people would . . .*)

Then on to Great King Street, where she saw the same lawyer, an advocate, emerging from his door with its professional brass plate and then beginning to walk up to Parliament House, his formal clothes contrasting with the everyday working dress of most others on their way to work. She came across this lawyer's photograph in *The Scotsman* one day, and read that he had been given a public appointment. Thereafter, when she saw him, she noticed how stooped he looked, his shoulders bent under the increased burdens of office and the cares that came with it.

Big Lou wondered whether it was much different from life in Arbroath or in any of the other small towns up and down Scotland. There were more people in the cities, of course, but within the urban centres, for all their crowds and complexities, the same small units of human activity – the villages – persisted. Out of the throngs they saw about them, people created small communities of one or two hundred, ignoring the rest. In a sense, all the others were extras, as in a film: they were there, crossing the scene, going about their business, but what really mattered was the people you actually saw, the people whose faces were familiar, whose background you understood, the people who knew the people you knew.

She thought about this as she crossed Dundas Street to her coffee bar. She thought about it further as she unlocked the door and turned on the lights. As she switched on the coffee machine and gave the counter its first rub-down of the day, she wondered whether she had ever really left Arbroath and Snell Mains, or whether she carried them still within her, and made a new Arbroath and Snell Mains right here in Edinburgh, amidst these tenements and cobbled streets, amidst all this finance and business and decision-making.

Her first customer of the day came in. It was a young man who worked, she recalled, for the Royal Bank of Scotland. He was training for a marathon and had told her all about it, and the exercise, he said, justified the bacon roll she made him every morning.

She prepared a roll; the bacon sizzled in the frying pan. He sniffed at the air appreciatively. The roll was one of her special *butteries*, of the sort her aunts had been so good at making. This was what Scotland was all about, thought Lou. It was about butteries and people who liked butteries. It was about conversations where as much was said as was unsaid. It was about special ways of breaking the heart.

17. *At Big Lou's*

When Matthew went over to Big Lou's for his morning coffee, he either left Pat in charge of the gallery – if it was one of her days to be there – or he locked the door behind him, putting up a note that said *Back in fifteen minutes – or thereabouts, depending.*

This wording had always amused Pat. 'It's a bit odd to say *depending*,' she remarked. 'People will think you're indecisive. Not that you are, of course – you aren't, if you see what I mean.'

'But it's true,' replied Matthew. 'What it says is true. What we *think* will happen always depends on all sorts of things. And we can't be sure whether those things will happen – or not happen, if you see what I mean.'

Pat thought about this. Yes, human affairs were uncertain. Yes, matters did not always work out as we hoped they would work out, but surely we could not go through life qualifying everything like this. 'So should an airline say the flight to wherever will leave at 3pm or whatever *depending*?'

'Yes,' said Matthew. 'Because it does depend. And that, if I may say so, Pat, is a good example: the departure of any plane often *does* depend on all sorts of things. Whether there's a plane, for a start. You know how airlines cancel flights if they don't have a plane available. They do that, you know. It really does depend. They call it operational reasons. No plane – operational reasons. No pilot to fly it – operational reasons.'

'But that's implicit.'

Matthew shook his head. 'No, it's not. People think that 3pm means 3pm. They're funny that way.'

Pat laughed. 'I'd never call you a pedant, Matthew, but . . . '

He looked injured.

'I'm sorry.'

'No need to apologise,' he said. 'It's just that I think people should be . . . well, a bit more honest. We don't like being told half-truths. Or being lied to . . . People can tell, you know. They know when they're being lied to. Politicians find that out – eventually.'

He looked at Pat. Matthew liked to read history; he liked to watch television programmes about the Second World War. He was interested in Churchill, but he was not sure whether Pat would know anything about all that. There were plenty of people who seemed to have only the vaguest idea about the Second World War, and Pat, for all he knew, might be one of them. She knew about Giotto, of course, and Raphael and Bonnard and Vuillard and so on, but did she know much about Churchill?

'Churchill told the truth,' he said. 'He told people what lay ahead. He said that he had nothing to offer them but blood, sweat and tears. He was a politician! Can you think of any politician – any – who would say that to people these days. *I've got bad news for you: you're going to have to work harder, for longer, and have less money to spend.* Who would say that? Name one!'

'Well, they may not actually say it,' said Pat. 'But there are degrees of willingness to come clean. Some are more prepared to say that sort of thing than others.'

'But they won't say it directly,' said Matthew. 'They won't say it outright. Because people won't vote for people who say it's going to be tough. They just won't. They vote for whoever says they're going to get free sandwiches for life. You tell people that and, boy, do they like you!'

That morning, he knew that Pat would probably arrive while he was out at Big Lou's for coffee, but he nonetheless hung the conditional notice – the *honest notice* as he called it – on the door and crossed the road to Big Lou's. Pat had a key to the gallery and could let herself in.

'This place smells of bacon,' said Matthew, sniffing at the air as he entered.

Lou, who was polishing the Gaggia, turned round. 'It may have something to do with the fact that I sell bacon rolls, Matthew.'

Matthew laughed. 'I'm not saying it's a bad smell, Lou. In fact, it's one of the best smells there is, as far as I'm concerned. The smell of the forbidden.'

'Bacon rolls? Who's forbidding you from eating bacon rolls?'

'Elspeth,' said Matthew. 'She says they're bad for you.'

'Och, away with all that,' said Lou. 'What's wrong with bacon? I know plenty of people who ate bacon every day of their lives. My Uncle Willy, for example. He had three large rashers every morning. Two fried eggs and three rashers of bacon. After his porridge, of course.'

'What happened to him?' asked Matthew.

Lou looked surprised. 'What happened to him? Uncle Willy? He's deid.'

Matthew smiled. 'Well, there you are. He's dead.'

'But not from bacon rolls,' said Lou quickly. 'The tractor ran over him.'

Matthew made an effort to look solemn. 'I'm sorry. That had nothing to do with bacon, obviously.' There were all sorts of hazards in living on those north-east farms. Not only tractors, but the cold, for example. People probably froze to death up there. Certainly they did in Aberdeen.

'I'm not saying that you shouldn't listen to these people telling you what to eat,' said Lou. 'All I'm saying is that you shouldn't worry too much. Look at eggs. We were told not to eat eggs, and now they're saying we should. Well, I carried on eating eggs all the way through. Now they're all right again. Eggs are good. Vitamin D or something.'

'In the yolk,' said Matthew. 'Eggs have vitamin D in their yolks. And we don't have enough vitamin D in us in Scotland, Lou. We're all vitamin D deficient, apparently. Just between October and March, I think. There's not enough sun for us to make the vitamin D we need.' He paused. 'I've got an idea for you, Lou. I've got an idea how you could help improve Scotland's health.'

'I'm not taking bacon rolls off the menu.'

'Oh no, it's nothing to do with that.'

'Because there'd be an awfie lot of people who'd feel pretty sair if I did that,' continued Lou.

'You can carry on serving bacon,' said Matthew. 'But how about putting a touch of vitamin D in your coffee? It wouldn't have to be much, apparently. We each need only ten micrograms a person a day. Put it in the coffee you serve, then we'd get it that way. Simple.'

Big Lou looked at him. 'Are you serious?'

Matthew nodded. 'It would help. It could be your contribution.'

Big Lou looked thoughtful. 'I don't like the thought of all those folk being vitamin D deficient.'

'Well, you can do something about it, Lou.'

'Maybe.'

Lou served Matthew his coffee. He looked down at it. Trust, he thought. We take so much on trust. People give us things to eat and drink, and we trust them. We have no idea what may be in the things before us, but we proceed on the basis of trust.

'Is there anything in my coffee, Lou?' he asked.

Big Lou smiled at him. 'Bromide,' she said.

18. Watsonian Ejected

When Matthew returned to the gallery after twenty minutes at Big Lou's, he found Pat reading at her desk.

He glanced at the book. 'Anything interesting?' he asked.

'It's just something I picked up. There was a book sale at Holy Corner. They had all sorts of stuff.'

Matthew tried to look over Pat's shoulder, but she turned the book over, unhelpfully exposing the back cover.

'All sorts of stuff,' he echoed. 'I love those sales. I go to that one in George Street. They get thousands and thousands of books each year, all sold in a good cause. Lots of the books are quite new – I bought Guy Peploe's book on Samuel Peploe there last year.'

'Yes,' said Pat. 'My father gave me a copy of that.'

Matthew decided to be direct. 'So, what's this book you're reading?' He hesitated, as one had to be careful with Pat. 'You seem a bit defensive, if I may say so. You aren't reading that *Fifty Shades* are you?'

Pat gave him a withering look. 'Do you think I'd read something like that?'

Matthew shrugged. 'A lot of people seem to have read it. Nobody I know, of course, but . . . '

Pat looked at him scornfully.

'I was only joking,' said Matthew, smiling. '*Chacun à son goût*,' he said. He was open-minded, but he blushed at the memory of something that had happened to him.

He had seen the controversial book in a bookshop and had taken a furtive look inside. Unfortunately, a woman had come up to reach for another title from the shelf immediately in front of him and Matthew could not replace the book without her seeing it. What would she think of him if she saw him flicking through the pages of *Fifty Shades*? It hardly bore thinking about. She would think he was one of those people who went into bookshops and flicked through the pages of the latest salacious offerings until the staff eventually rumbled what was going on and asked them to leave. The shame of it! The public humiliation! He imagined the headline in the *Evening News* – WATSONIAN EJECTED FROM CITY STORE. They would be sure to mention that he was a Watsonian because they would want to make the most of that. No, that's absurd, he thought: nobody cares any more what other people read. Prudery and disapproval are things of the past, even in Edinburgh . . .

And then, in a moment of heart-stopping awfulness, he recognised the woman standing beside him at the shelf. It was Mrs Patterson Cowie, his old English teacher from Watson's. She it was who had introduced him, as a boy of ten, to Robert Louis Stevenson's *A Child's Garden of Verses* and to *Kidnapped*. From *A Child's Garden of Verses* to books about . . . well, about the sort of things *Fifty Shades* was about, not that Matthew imagined that anybody actually *did* any of the things described in such books. Why would they? Perhaps there were people who had nothing better to do.

For a few moments – an eternity in his mind – Matthew remained immobile. It could hardly be worse, he thought – or it could be, perhaps. It could have been the Moderator of the General Assembly of the Church of Scotland standing next to him. The Moderator would turn to him and say 'I'm so disappointed in you, young man' or, worse still, say nothing but register his disappointment in his look. And Matthew would blush deep red and mumble, 'I'm doing research, you see,' or perhaps, 'I thought this book was about interior decorating. It's very misleading, don't you think, to call a book *Fifty Shades of Grey* when it's not about interior decoration at all.' The Moderator would agree. But then he might say, 'But what *is* it about?' That would be problematic.

He decided he had to act. Mrs Patterson Cowie gave no sign of recognising him; he thought that perhaps she had not actually seen his face. That was a relief; he could now sidle away from her, taking the book with him, and she would be none the wiser.

He took a step backwards. She was still preoccupied with her scrutiny of the shelves and paid no attention to him. He took another step, but found that he could not retreat any further in that particular direction as his way was blocked by a display stand for a new cookery book. Nor could he move to the left, where a door said *Staff Only*. Well, that did not apply to emergencies, of which this was one. He could go through that door, wait until the coast was clear, and then emerge once more to replace the book where he had found it.

He edged sideways towards the door. He kept his face turned away from Mrs Patterson Cowie as he pushed the handle. It gave easily and the door swung open. He did not turn round to see if she had noticed him.

Matthew found himself in a corridor, empty apart from a few tattered pieces of paper on an old noticeboard. At the other end was a second door, towards which he now made his way.

This second door was locked. There was a key-pad

beside it that would open it, but one would need a code. He tried the handle several times and even applied his shoulder to the door itself, but all egress was barred. He felt his heart begin to pound: he would have to go back the way he came. He returned to the door through which he had entered the corridor. It had locked automatically – from the other side.

Matthew took a deep breath. Had he missed something? There must have been a lock that had been triggered once he pushed the door open. Perhaps ... He stopped. There was no point in searching for explanations of his plight. The inescapable fact was that he was trapped in a corridor that was, to all intents and purposes, a cell.

He leaned against the wall. He would have to think very carefully. It seemed to him that this was some sort of emergency exit for staff who, presumably, would have been issued with the code to get out through the second door. He looked about him. The corridor had a dusty and neglected look to it. People probably only used it during fire alarm practices. He could be there for days unless he called for help and somebody heard him. But who *would* hear him? He had been in a corner of the shop, away from everything else. No, he was trapped – with only one book to read.

He suddenly realised then that the walls of his cell were grey – monotonously so.

19. An Absurd Situation

The absurdity of Matthew's situation was not lost on him. To be stuck in a corridor with locked doors at either end was not the sort of thing that happened in reality: such situations were the stuff of urban myths, those hoary, but readily believed tales of headless motorcyclists, vanishing hitchhikers, and axe-wielding little old ladies innocently picked up by motorists in supermarket car parks. These stories, although apocryphal, evoked a feeling of dread in the listener – *And did the driver only notice the blood-stained axe after he had seen his passenger's unusually hairy wrists?* – just as anyone listening to this story would feel anxiety about the outcome for Matthew. *What did you do? Were you really stuck there for two whole days?* Of course, such things did not really happen … Except, thought Matthew, this really *is* happening – and not having heard the outcome of the story, I must decide what to do.

He sat down on the floor, leaning back against the wall, and attempted to clear his mind. First of all, he thought, I have not done anything wrong, and I therefore have nothing with which to reproach myself. I have simply sought to avoid social embarrassment, which is perfectly understandable and, indeed, even laudable. Not only would he have been ashamed had Mrs Patterson Cowie seen him clasping a copy of *Fifty Shades*, but she herself could have felt embarrassed. So, at least in one view, he had acted thoughtfully and might even be congratulated for his sensitivity.

But that threw no light on his options. As far as he could make out, these were: (1) to bang on the door immediately, in the hope of attracting the attention of somebody, who would then unlock the door; that person, however, could be Mrs Patterson Cowie, and that would be extremely awkward; (2) to wait ten minutes, allowing Mrs Patterson Cowie to move to another part of the shop, then to bang loudly for attention; or (3) to do nothing, hoping that in the fullness of time a member of staff would need to use the corridor and would in this way end his awkward durance.

He weighed these three options, eventually deciding upon the first. There was a possibility that his former teacher would be the one to open the door for him, but he had alighted upon a way of obviating any embarrassment that might be caused by the book – he would simply tuck it into the waistband of his trousers. It was marginally too large to fit into his pocket – he had tried that – but it could easily be concealed under the waistband. Then, at an opportune moment, he could slip it back onto its shelf – or indeed onto any shelf; he had read somewhere that the staff of bookshops were accustomed to reshelving salacious books that had been slipped back into an innocent, but incorrect, place on their shelves.

He rose to his feet. With the book tucked out of sight, Matthew returned to the outer door and knocked heavily three times. Then, feeling vaguely foolish about it, he cried out, 'Anybody there?'

He stopped and listened. There was complete silence. He knocked again, more loudly this time, and was on the point of shouting out once more when he heard a voice on the other side.

'I'm here,' said the voice.

Matthew hesitated. Then he said, 'Would you mind unlocking this door?'

There was silence on the other side. Then, at length, the voice said, 'Are you there?'

'Yes,' said Matthew. 'I'm here – are *you* there?'

'I'm here,' came the reply. 'What do you want?'

Matthew felt a surge of irritation. 'I want you to unlock the door.' He struggled to keep his voice even. He had already asked this person – whoever he was – to unlock the door. How many times would he need to make the request?

'What?' asked the voice. 'What do you want me to do?'

'To unlock the door,' said Matthew, his voice now appreciably raised.

'Who are you?' asked the voice.

'That doesn't matter,' said Matthew. 'I just want you to unlock the door.'

'I'm not sure if I should,' said the voice. 'I'm just a customer.'

'Oh, for heaven's sake,' snapped Matthew. 'Don't be so ridiculous.'

'There's no need to be rude,' said the voice.

'I'm not being rude,' said Matthew, seething now. 'You're

the one who's being rude – not helping somebody who's trapped is being extremely rude.'

'Who's trapped?' said the voice.

'Oh, you complete gowk!' expostulated Matthew. 'I'm trapped. I'm trapped behind this door and all you have to do is to open it.'

'Don't you call me a gowk,' the voice retorted. 'You're the gowk.'

'Shut up!' shouted Matthew. 'Just open this . . . ' And here Matthew swore. He was not given to swearing, but he could not contain himself. This was just so ridiculous – and so intensely frustrating.

'Don't you use that language to me,' said the voice. 'I'm trying to be helpful. That's the trouble with this country, it's become so foul-mouthed. People don't even realise that they're swearing.'

'Just open the door,' Matthew pleaded. 'I didn't mean to swear at you – I really didn't.'

'Are you going to apologise?' asked the voice.

Matthew was now desperate. 'Of course, I'll apologise.'

There was the sound of another voice and a muttered conversation that Matthew could not hear properly. And then there was a clicking sound and the door swung open.

There, standing outside, was a man in his mid-thirties, slightly corpulent, wearing a blue sweater and with an annoyed, disapproving look on his face. This was the voice with whom Matthew had conducted such a fraught conversation. Then, at his side, was the assistant manager of the bookshop – identified as such by the badge on his shirt – and finally, behind the two of them and gazing at Matthew with undisguised interest, Mrs Patterson Cowie.

'What's been going on?' asked the assistant manager. 'How did you get in there?'

'I took a wrong turning,' said Matthew.

'It says *Staff Only*,' pointed out the assistant manager.

Matthew felt his cheeks turning red. 'I know. But I just did. I'm sorry.'

'He said he was trapped,' said the man in the blue sweater.

'Well, I was,' said Matthew.

'And he used some pretty strong language,' continued the man.

Mrs Patterson Cowie looked disapproving; Matthew, though, was relieved that she appeared not to recognise him.

'Why did you go in there?' asked the assistant manager. 'You weren't thinking of shop-lifting, were you?'

Matthew drew in his breath sharply.

'That's what I thought,' said the man in the blue sweater. 'That's exactly what I thought.'

'Oh, don't be so ridiculous,' said Matthew.

'Then why have you got a book tucked into your waistband?' asked the assistant manager.

20. Homo Ludens

Pat stared at Matthew.

'You've gone bright red,' she said. 'Matthew, you're blushing.'

Matthew, who had been leaning forward in his attempt to discern the title of Pat's book, straightened up. 'Am I really?' he mumbled.

'Yes, you are. Like a tomato.'

He moved away. Now he faced the window out onto Dundas Street – a favoured stance from which he occasionally attempted to dictate a letter to Pat – an endeavour that never lasted long as Pat kept correcting him as he spoke. *Do you really want to say that?* or *They're not going to like that, you know.* How could one write a letter in the face of such interventions? How would a real businessman react to being corrected in this way by his secretary? But Pat, of course, was not a secretary, and secretaries, anyway, had ceased to exist, as far as he could make out. And not before time, thought Matthew. The whole role had been designed to keep women in a subservient position in the workforce – as handmaidens to those who did more generously rewarded work. Matthew would never subscribe to that: Pat was an *assistant* or even a colleague, doing much the same work as he did (and only occasionally typing letters).

But now she was gazing at him with one of those unsettling looks of hers – as if she was trying to work out what he was thinking. Real businessmen did not have to put up with that, he imagined: you did not find that sort of thing in banks and legal offices.

'I was thinking of something,' Matthew explained.

'And it made you blush?'

He nodded. He was wary. 'Could be. A rather embarrassing situation I was in a little while ago.'

She looked interested. 'Oh yes? What?'

Matthew did not answer immediately. It was none of Pat's business, and she should not have asked him. It was rather like asking somebody who has mentioned going to the doctor what they're suffering from. One did not do it. And it was the same with blushes, really: if somebody blushed, should you ask them what brought on the blush? He thought not.

'I was accused of shop-lifting.' He would tell her that much, he decided. He need not go into further detail.

She gasped. 'No! What a dreadful experience. You know, I've often wondered what I'd do if somebody stopped me as I was leaving a shop and said *Excuse me, madam, what have you got in that bag of yours?* You know, I'd faint – I'm sure I would.'

'Yes,' said Matthew. 'It's not pleasant.'

'And had you?' asked Pat.

'What?'

She immediately corrected herself. 'Oh no, sorry . . . I didn't mean to say that.'

Matthew looked at her reproachfully. 'Do you think I would . . . ?'

It was her turn to blush. 'No, of course not. I don't know why I asked that. It was stupid. Of course you wouldn't.' She paused. 'Where was it?'

'In a bookshop.'

She nodded. 'I've got a friend who works in a bookshop. She says it's a constant problem for them. People come in and steal books. But they also read them, you know. They come in and stand for hours reading books they're never going to buy.'

'It must be galling for the bookshop.'

'Yes, and then,' Pat continued, 'then there are people who come in and head straight for the erotica section.'

Matthew stared fixedly out of the window. 'Erotica?'

'Yes. The steamy stuff. Like that book . . . what's it called? *Fifty* something . . . '

Matthew resisted the temptation to look at her. He felt the back of his neck becoming warm.

'Yes,' said Pat, 'they stand there in their dirty raincoats reading that stuff. Sometimes the staff have to ask them to leave.'

Matthew said nothing.

Pat laughed. 'She was telling me the other day that they caught somebody with that book tucked into his trousers. Red-handed, so to speak. Apparently, he made a run for it. He pushed one of the customers over – into a pile of recipe books. Jamie Oliver's latest. Then he ran out of the shop.'

Matthew was silent. He had not intended to collide with

Mrs Patterson Cowie – it was her fault for getting in the way. And she didn't really fall – it was more of a slow topple.

'But they've got it all on CCTV,' Pat continued. 'They played it back and saw everything. His face – the works. All there.'

Matthew opened his mouth. 'Oh . . . '

'They called the police.'

'Really?' He sounded distant – as if whispering from somewhere afar.

'Yes.'

'And did they . . . did they get him?'

'They're working on it,' said Pat. 'But it's difficult. The police are not all that bothered about the theft side of it – but they don't like the pushing of the customer. They say that he might be dangerous.'

'Dangerous?'

'Yes, as in those police warnings: don't approach this person – he might be dangerous.'

Matthew cleared his throat. 'They'll probably never catch him,' he said.

'Probably not,' said Pat. 'And anyway, she – my friend – thinks that he was just a harmless perv. He was trying to steal that book, you know. *Fifty Shades*. Poor man. Imagine being a perv.'

Matthew frowned, as if trying to imagine it. 'Yes,' he said.

He turned round: it was time to change the subject. 'What's that book you're reading?'

Pat picked it up again. 'You probably know it,' she said. '*The Eclipse of Art*. It's by Julian Spalding. It's all about . . . '

'I know it,' said Matthew. He was relieved that they had moved on to art. 'I agree with him.'

'It's very amusing on conceptual art. About how the whole thing has become a . . . ' She trailed off.

'A blind alley,' said Matthew. 'A banal nothing, manipulated by a handful of wealthy collectors. Found objects . . . Decaying animal heads covered in flies, sharks in formaldehyde. Bits of string. You should hear Angus on the subject – particularly the Turner Prize.'

'He despises it, doesn't he?'

'Yes. And he's trained Cyril to lift his leg whenever he hears the words *Turner Prize*.'

'A bit childish,' said Pat.

Matthew smiled. '*Homo ludens*.'

Pat looked thoughtful. She had been unable to concentrate on her book and had read the same paragraph three times. It was Bruce. That was the problem. She could not get him out of her mind, and even now, talking to Matthew, he came back to her.

She arose from her desk. 'Matthew,' she said. 'I need your help.'

21. *Waiting for Godot*

It was unusual for Stuart and Irene Pollock to go out to dinner. In fact, as Stuart made his way home from work that evening, he tried to remember the last occasion on which they had gone out together – and initially failed. It was only when he was walking the last few hundred yards through Drummond Place that he recalled their dinner together, shortly before the birth of Ulysses. It had not been a success: they had gone to an Italian restaurant that had recently attracted good reviews but where, at an early stage of proceedings, Irene had fallen out with the waiter. This was a result of her correcting his pronunciation of some of the specials on offer that night – an intervention that had not gone down well; and not surprisingly, as the waiter was Italian. Matters had not improved after that: waiters enjoy a very particular form of power, and are capable of revenge in more ways than one. Some of these acts of revenge may be overt – in the form of delaying service, with exquisite judgment as to the precise delay that can be achieved without causing diners to abandon their meal altogether – others may be more indirect: food may be over-salted between kitchen and table; may be put out to cool; orders may be so easily confused or deprived of a vital element. All of this falls short of that ultimate sanction at the waiter's disposal – spitting in the soup. This is a sufficiently distasteful sanction to be vigorously denied by those who speak on behalf of waiters, but they all know that it occurs.

Since that outing, there had been very few occasions in their mutual social calendar. There had been one or two functions at the school, where they had joined other parents at events of one sort or another, but these, too, had not been conspicuous successes. One of the school plays had in fact been chosen – and directed – by Irene: the class two production of *Waiting for Godot* had not been well received, as Stuart had predicted as tactfully as he could. It was all very well for Irene to claim that she had rewritten Beckett's script to make it more approachable for young actors, but Stuart felt there was a fundamental problem in choosing a play in which only two actors dominate the stage.

Irene had sighed. 'But that, Stuart,' she said, 'is the whole point about *Godot*. It's very intense – even to the point of unbearability.'

'Yes,' said Stuart. 'I find it unbearable. The whole second act is unbearable. It goes on and on – even your version, Irene, I'm afraid, seems to go on and on.' Sensing her reaction, he quickly corrected himself. 'I mean, it goes on and on a bit. Not all that much, I suppose, but I just wonder whether this is quite the right play for seven-year-olds. Just a thought, Irene.'

Irene made a dismissive noise. It was one of those dismissive noises the French are so good at. They say *pouf*, or *bof*, or *pah* with such style that one can be under no illusions as to the fact that whatever is being dismissed is beneath contempt and certainly not worthy of explicit refutation.

'When I say it's unbearable,' she explained, 'I mean the *tension* is unbearable. That's what makes it such a powerful piece of drama.'

So, *Godot* had been chosen and casting had begun. That proved to be a minefield – even if it was a minefield through which Irene sailed, blissfully unaware of the dangers lurking below the surface. Miss Campbell, the class teacher, had willingly handed the class over to Irene towards the end of a school day, going off for a much-needed cup of tea in the staff room.

'Bertie's mummy will be talking to you about this term's exciting play,' she announced. 'She will be what is called the director. Now, children, is there anybody who knows what a director does?'

Olive's hand had gone up, and was with reluctance recognised by Miss Campbell. 'Well, Olive, dear, tell us what a director does.'

'Orders people about,' said Olive.

'Hits them,' suggested Larch.

Miss Campbell smiled blithely. 'Not quite. A director helps the actors to do what is required. The director gets the whole show going – like the conductor of an orchestra.'

With that established, she left the classroom, and Irene began to discuss the play.

'*Waiting for Godot* is by a very famous Irish writer called Samuel Beckett,' she said. 'He wrote a lot in French, but we shall be doing the play in English, which is the only language that most of you speak – apart from Bertie, of course. It's all about two men who are waiting to meet somebody called Godot . . . '

Tofu's hand went up. Irene did not like Tofu; she had never approved of him, suspecting him – correctly – of holding exactly those attitudes from which she wished to shield Bertie.

She made an effort to be polite. 'Yes, Tofu, have you something to say about Beckett?'

'I'll play him,' said Tofu. 'I'll be Godot.'

Irene hesitated. It was irresistible. What a delicious thought: Tofu waiting for his role and then discovering that Godot never comes. 'What a good idea, Tofu. Yes, you can be Godot.'

Tofu sat back in his seat, smirking with self-satisfaction.

Olive did not approve. 'That's not fair, Mrs Pollock. Why should Tofu be Godot when there are lots of much better actors in the class? Bertie could be Godot.'

'Shut your face, Olive,' muttered Tofu.

'Did you hear what he said to me?' protested Olive.

'He told her to shut her face, Mrs Pollock,' chimed in Pansy. 'He's always telling people to shut their faces. He doesn't deserve to be Godot.'

Perhaps he does, thought Irene. She pressed ahead regardless. 'And there are two other very big roles: Estragon and Vladimir.'

'Stupid names,' said Larch.

Irene ignored this. 'I think that Bertie should be Estragon.'

Bertie squirmed. He had been afraid that his mother

would choose him; of course, she would. 'Must I?' he said in a pleading tone. 'Must I really?'

'He doesn't want to do it,' crowed Olive. 'Did you hear what he said, Mrs Pollock? Let me be Estragon.'

'That's a boy's name, stupid,' said Tofu. 'Estragon's a boy, isn't he, Mrs Pollock?'

And so the casting had continued – as had the play. Unfortunately, the actual performance had not been a success, as only the parents of the children appearing in the play came, offence having been taken over the choice of a play with only two characters. Irene had at the last minute eliminated the minor characters from her script; this had led to a boycott by the other parents, and an audience consisting only of Stuart and Irene, and Hiawatha's mother – Hiawatha having been cast as Vladimir.

'I thought that went remarkably well,' observed Irene as they made their way home after the performance.

Stuart was silent, as was Bertie.

22. *At the Carl Gustav Jung Drop-in Centre*

Since that testing evening at the school, Stuart and Irene had not gone out together. There was no deliberate decision to remain at home – it just seemed to work out that way. Irene had a busy schedule, what with her Melanie Klein book group, her other book group, her Pilates sessions, her East New Town Community Council outreach evenings, and her commitments as a volunteer counsellor at the Edinburgh Carl Gustav Jung Drop-in Centre. The last of these, which involved her going out every Tuesday and Wednesday evening for three hours, was a commitment that Stuart would dearly have loved her to drop, but she resolutely stuck by it. In Stuart's view, the Carl Gustav Jung Drop-in Centre should have been closed a long time ago on the grounds that even if people dropped in, most of them soon dropped out. This was because the centre, which passers-by imagined dispensed soup and coffee and handouts of various sorts, in fact was there principally to provide Jungian counselling, including advice on the meaning of dreams.

A typical evening at the centre involved two counsellors waiting several hours for a member of the public to drop in. If anybody did, then he or she would be allocated to a counsellor on a strict rotation basis. After a few minutes, it would become apparent whether or not the dropper-in was prepared to accept counselling. Almost always the answer to this was unambiguous, and became evident through the attitude of the potential client.

Misunderstandings were frequent, as in this exchange:

Member of the Great Edinburgh Public: So, I take my coffee white. Two sugars. Make it three.

Counsellor: Hah! Coffee? Well, this is not exactly that sort of drop-in centre.

MGEP: So what do yous do then? Soup? I wouldn't mind a bowl of something hot and nourishing, ken what I mean?

Counsellor: Hah! No, we don't do soup, I'm afraid. What about your dreams?

MGEP: My dreams? You joking, pal?

Counsellor: Carl Gustav Jung was a Swiss psychologist who . . .

MGEP: You think I need a psychologist?

Counsellor: I didn't say that. That's for you to decide. We are here simply to provide support for those who do. I didn't say *you* did. What about your dreams, anyway?

MGEP: Mind your own business. I'll tell you one thing, and I'll tell you for free: I'm out o' here.

That sort of thing happened distressingly frequently, as the drop-in centre was in a run-down building rather close to two popular pubs on the very eastern fringes of the Eastern New Town – and therefore virtually on Leith Walk, which was, to use Jungian terminology, a whole different ball-game.

With all these commitments, Irene found no time to go out with Stuart, even though Stuart's mother, Nicola, was still living just around the corner in Northumberland Street and had declared her willingness to babysit whenever required. Irene thanked her in the icily polite tones she always used with Stuart's mother, and said that she would think about it. 'Possibly some time,' she said, adding, 'Perhaps. We'll see.'

No casting agency, faced with a talentless hopeful, had ever issued so clear a rejection, and quite understandably Nicola had taken offence.

'Most mothers,' she said to Stuart, 'by which I suppose I mean most *normal* mothers, would jump at an offer of babysitting from a grandmother, but I must remind myself that we are not dealing here with a normal mother. No offence meant, Stuart, and I hope none taken, but that is an observation that I feel compelled to make.'

Stuart had mumbled some excuse on Irene's behalf, but even he knew that he sounded less than convincing.

'She has a lot on her plate these days,' he said. 'There are problems at her yoga class ... '

Nicola looked dismissive. 'Problems at a yoga class? Now that's something to think about! I suppose some people might find themselves twisted into a position out of which they can't escape. I suppose some of them might be left there for hours while the instructors endeavour to disentangle them. Oh yes, I can imagine that problems at a yoga class would weigh very heavily on anybody's mind.'

'Mother,' said Stuart. 'Please! Please! There's no need to adopt that tone. You have to understand that ... '

Nicola, who had shown great patience over the years, erupted. 'Oh, I understand, Stuart – I understand very well indeed. I understand that you have married an eighty-four horse-power, six cylinder, fuel-injection, turbo-charged cow.'

'Mother!' protested Stuart.

But Nicola was in full stride. 'No, let me finish. Let me tell you how it breaks my heart – it breaks my heart – to see my son under the thumb of that selfish, opinionated woman with her Melanie Klein nonsense and her relentless denigration of men. Do you think I don't see it? Do you think I don't say to myself every day – every day, Stuart – oh, I wish my son had the mettle to stand up to that ghastly wife of his. And then I find myself thinking: oh, if only my son would just go out and have an affair – not a pathetically insipid attempt like last time – but a full-blooded, passionate affair with all the bells and whistles and with a woman who doesn't diminish him at every step, who doesn't set out to neuter him, who doesn't subject him and my grandsons to a barrage of politically correct claptrap. With a woman who would cherish him, rather than undermine him. Oh, I wish the day would dawn when he would just stand up to her and push her into the Water of Leith or something like that – not a deep part, of course, but just a bit at the edge.'

'Mother! How can you say such things? How can you?'

Nicola was undeterred. 'Very easily, Stuart, and with utter conviction. Because that is exactly what I wish, and what I know, in my heart of hearts, I shall never get. And that heroic little boy, Bertie, is going to have to continue to put up with a mother who to all intents and purposes is a cross between Carl Gustav Jung and a Stasi officer.'

'Oh, Mother, come on! That's a bit extreme, surely?'

'You say "a bit extreme", Stuart. Only a bit. So that means you see at least some truth in what I'm saying. And yet you let this situation continue. You let it go on and on and never, never do anything to stop it.'

She looked at her son. Now she felt sorry for him, and sighed. 'Oh, darling,' she said. 'Can't you see what's going on? I know you're a lovely, nice man and you don't like conflict, but can't you see what's happening?'

23. Stuart Reflects

He reached the top of Scotland Street and paused to look down the sharp fall of the road. Edinburgh was built on hills, on ridges of rock; if the land were the sea, then these ridges were like the spines of whales, or dolphins perhaps, protruding from the surface. George Street was one such spine from which the land fell away to the north, and Scotland Street was part of that decline.

It was a much wider street than many of the neighbouring streets, which gave it the feeling, Stuart had realised, of a courtyard that was not quite a courtyard, yet could so easily be one if the street were closed off at either end. His friend from university days, Neil, who was an architect, had explained to him once that people feel happiest living in a courtyard-type arrangement because they felt secure. 'People like to face other people,' he said. 'It's as simple as that. Put them in a long line and they feel uneasy. Long lines aren't friendly.'

'So houses in a row are ... what? Uncomfortable?'

'Yes,' said Neil. 'Go to any one suburban street where there's a long line of houses and ask people if they know their neighbours. They may know the people on either side of them, but probably not those living three or four houses along.'

Stuart thought of Scotland Street; he knew – or recognised – just about everybody in their part of the street – and that included those on the other side.

Neil was warming to his theme. 'Have you ever been in an American bar?'

Stuart had been to a statistical conference in America when he had been studying for his aborted PhD. That had been in Bloomington, Indiana, but he had spent several days in New York on his way there. He had been in a bar, he seemed to recall, but he did not remember the details.

'Well,' said Neil. 'People sit in a line along the bar, all facing the bartender. It's very difficult to talk to somebody sitting beside you if that person's facing the same way as you are. And three people in that arrangement can't hold a conversation involving all three of them – unless the one in the middle strains to sit back while the other two strain to sit forward.' He paused. 'And the result? Loneliness. Isolation. Anomie.'

'The same with housing?'

'Yes,' said Neil. 'Modernist architecture loved big shapes, but forgot about people. It erected buildings which paid no attention to people's psychological needs. Those great blocks of flats out at Sighthill – the ones they've now blown up. Or the flats they put people into when they took them out of the Gorbals. No shared space, no connection with the people around you, nor with the landscape. Nothing – just enforced loneliness.

'And the loneliness went further,' Neil continued. 'Not only were people made to feel lonely, but the new buildings themselves had an imposed loneliness, so to speak, because they themselves – the buildings – were designed not to talk to their surrounding buildings. In the past . . .' Neil smiled. 'Am I sounding old-fashioned? Am I sounding like one of those people who grumble on about new buildings?'

'Like Prince Charles?'

Neil laughed. 'The thing about Prince Charles is that even if he may not be right about everything, there are things that he really *is* right about. People snipe at him and condescend to him – but if you look at what he actually says about the world about us, he's often right. He's right about climate change. And he's right about the arrogance of some architects – and the people behind them. He's absolutely right when he goes on about architectural brutalism, about buildings that ignore where they are and just want to make some great, ostentatious statement, or don't care about anything – including statements – and just want to be as big and as brutally functional as they like. And that's all about money, isn't it? About making money without any regard to the effect that your actions will have on the lives of others. Look at China.'

'China?'

'Yes. All they're interested in is making money – whatever the cost. So they've hurled themselves into feverish manufacturing. They suck people in from the countryside and put them in vast urban barracks. Then they belt out the goods and all the pollution that goes with that and now what happens? They find they've made their cities virtually uninhabitable because the air's so bad. They can't breathe – they can't go outside because the air's so poisonous.'

Stuart sighed. 'Oh God, Neil, I hate to think about the future.'

'But we have to. That's the problem – people aren't thinking about the future. That's why we're destroying the planet.'

'Oh, I know that. What I meant was that I can't bear to think about what sort of world my wee boys are going to be living in when they're thirty or forty.'

Neil looked surprised. 'I thought you had only one. Bertie, isn't it?'

'You're out of date. We have two. Bertie and Ulysses.'

'Ulysses! That's a bit unusual, isn't it?'

'My wife . . . '

Neil had looked away, embarrassed. He had met Irene. 'It's an interesting name,' he said quickly.

'Homeric.'

'Of course.'

Stuart returned to the state of the world. 'Did we worry about these things when we were at university? I don't think we did.'

Neil shook his head. 'Of course not. You look at things differently when you're twenty. You're pretty much immortal, for a start. And then you're . . . you're . . . ' He struggled to find the right way of describing what it was like to be twenty, but he was distracted by the thought that when you're twenty you don't know that there's a way of looking at things that goes with being twenty; whereas when you reach thirty you begin to understand that there's a way of looking at the world that goes with being thirty, and with being forty, and fifty, and so on.

And what was the view from twenty? It was that people weren't a problem – it was as simple as that.

'You like everybody when you're twenty,' said Neil. 'You trust them. You make friends at the drop of a hat. It's all great.'

Stuart thought about this. Neil was right. 'And then?'

'Cynicism sets in. Or perhaps we should call it realism. Very slowly, but it sets in. You stop being a puppy – you know how puppies lick everybody? You stop that.'

'And you start being a cat? Selfish – self-interested?'

Neil laughed. 'Precisely. Cats are the quintessential psychopaths, you know. Every one of them.'

'And dogs?'

'Enough metaphors,' said Neil.

24. Second Chances

When Stuart reached 44 Scotland Street, he fished in his pocket for the key of the stair door. The old bell-pulls were still there, along with the names of the earlier occupants of the various flats. An Edinburgh doorway could be a palimpsest, with layer upon layer of the building's history displayed in the names accompanying each bell-pull or more modern invention: push buttons from the nineteen-sixties, oblong boxes with automatic opening devices, and in some cases unblinking fish-eye camera lenses allowing scrutiny of those who sought entry. The newer technology tended, like all newer technology, to isolate, and certainly discouraged the public exchanges of the past, when a caller might tug on a bell-pull, a window above might open, and 'Who's there?' might be shouted. To which the proper reply, it seemed, was 'Me'; and then, 'You?', 'Aye', 'Well, I'm no in.'

Stuart glanced at the names. He saw his own, of course, or rather Irene's. She had commissioned a small plastic nameplate inscribed with *Irene Pollock*. There was no mention of Stuart's name, which he would not have wanted, anyway, as the appropriate legend should simply have been *Pollock*. Why then did it say *Irene Pollock*? He had been hesitant to ask her directly, but had once muttered, 'I live here as well, you know.'

This had brought the retort, 'I heard that, Stuart. I know you live here – I never said you didn't. I'm just making the point that there is no such thing as a head of the household. People always say – and they still say this, unbelievably – that the man is the head of the household. Well, not this household.'

'I don't think they say that,' said Stuart. 'They used to, but not any longer.'

Irene made a dismissive gesture. 'You have a touching faith in the capacity of society to change. The reality of the situation is that many men – probably the vast majority – still think of themselves as the head of the household.'

He protested again. 'I don't think they do, you know. Men and women share these things now.'

'Not sufficiently. Some men have adjusted; others haven't.'

'Oh well, I suppose you're right.'

'I am right, Stuart.'

That had been the end of the discussion, and the nameplate had remained in place. Above it was a small brass plate stating *Macdonald and Lordie*. That was newer and was by far the most aesthetically pleasing of the various nameplates, but Angus was, after all, an artist and could be expected to appreciate these touches. Then there were nameplates from the past: *Abbot*, *Michie*, *Donaldson* … These were people who had lived at No. 44 between the nineteen-fifties and the nineteen-eighties. Stuart had heard of Michie, who had been a photographer, he had been told, and who had served with Hamish Henderson in Sicily during the war. He was long gone, as was Donaldson who, according to tradition, had been an amateur racing driver and had for a brief period kept his racing cars in the Scotland Street tunnel.

Immediately above *Irene Pollock*, reflecting the physical layout of the stair, and next to *Macdonald and Lordie*, was a badly tarnished nameplate with *Collie* on it. Stuart rubbed at it with his finger, trying to remember how long ago it was that Antonia Collie had left Scotland Street to join that convent in Italy. He had never had very much to do with Antonia, and he had only heard indirect reports of what had happened in Italy. She had contracted some sort of condition, he seemed to recall; Angus had said she had gone off her rocker, as he put it, and had added that her rocker was probably never very firmly fixed to the ground anyway. Where was she now, he wondered? In a warmer place, no doubt – some Tuscan valley with olive trees and thyme-scented air and . . . well, there were consolations to going off one's rocker in such surroundings.

He entered the stair and began to make his way up to his flat. As he did so, he thought: 'Am I happy to be coming home?' He did not answer his own question immediately, but let his thoughts follow their own course for a while. There were people at the office – most of them, in fact – who positively looked forward to getting home in the evening. They said as much; they referred to the bliss of having a day off.

Did he feel that? The answer came rather quickly. No, he did not. He did not relish the thought of talking to his wife. And this evening they were due to go out to dinner for the first time in ages and he was not looking forward to it. He had tried to persuade himself that he would enjoy it, but he had failed. He did not want to go. He would far prefer to nip round to the Cumberland Bar and meet up with old friends, none of whom Irene showed any interest in seeing, but who were his lifeline.

He reached his doorway, and took out his key. There were voices emanating from within: there was Bertie. And then there was a gurgling sound, which was Ulysses, and this was followed by Irene saying something. He could not work out what it was.

He stood there and listened. Bertie spoke again. He was telling Irene about something that Ranald Braveheart

Macpherson had said to him; it was something to do with rockets and with Mars. Irene said something in reply and Ulysses emitted a strange squeaking sound.

Stuart sighed. He felt strangely disconnected – as if he were listening to a play on the radio, not to the voices of his own family. *I'm an actor*, he thought. *I have my role and my lines, and the play is using up my life …*

He unlocked the door and entered the flat. Irene and the boys were in the kitchen, and so he was alone in the hall. He put down his briefcase. There were no papers in it – just his lunchbox and a copy of *The Scotsman* with its half-finished crossword. He was particularly proud of solving one of the clues that day, 3 across, which had been *A Scotsman followed by another Scotsman – of the Middle East.* It had come to him suddenly, from some strange part of the subconscious mind that does crosswords. *Arabian*. Rab and Ian.

He sighed. How long was this going to last? How long would his unhappiness continue? Some people were unhappy for their whole lives, which was terribly sad, he thought, since we have only one chance. Or did we? Could we not do something about it? Could we not somehow or other find a second chance?

25. Homeric Thoughts

Irene said to Stuart, 'You haven't forgotten, have you?'

Stuart pretended to look blank. 'Forgotten what?'

She drew in her breath. 'So you have. Really, Stuart . . . '

Stuart smiled. 'Only joking. Of course I haven't forgotten. We're going to the cinema.'

There was a further intake of breath, and he quickly brought his joke to an end. 'No, I know: how could I forget? Dinner. We're going out for dinner. You and me . . . '

'I, Stuart, you and I.'

He bore the correction. 'You and I are going out for dinner – as per long-established plan. And my mother will be babysitting.'

Irene looked away. 'Actually, Stuart, I've rearranged things. I thought it better.'

He looked at her enquiringly. 'Thought what better?'

Irene's manner was casual, as if this were a matter of little importance. 'Oh, I cancelled your mother. I thought it more convenient to have that girl from over the road – you know the one who's at St Mary's Music School. Teenagers always like to earn a little bit of money, and I thought I'd give her a chance. She has a babysitting certificate, and Ulysses seems to like her.'

Ulysses seems to like her. That meant that he refrained from being sick when she picked him up, in contrast to his reaction to Irene. But Stuart said nothing of this; he was thinking of the insult to his mother.

'But my mother agreed. She probably had to cancel something to do it. Isn't it a bit rude to call off like that?'

Irene shrugged. 'I don't think she'll mind. She probably has lots to do. You know how old people seem to be so busy these days, doing all sorts of things. The University of the Third Age, for example. She's spoken about that. Bridge, or whatever it is she plays. She's got lots of things to do.'

Stuart bristled. 'My mother isn't old,' he said. 'And I don't think you should condescend to her.'

Irene glanced towards the kitchen. 'Stuart, the boys are in there. Please don't pick a fight within earshot. I've changed our arrangements – it's as simple as that. There's no need to make an unholy fuss over it.'

'She's my mother, and she has her feelings.'

Irene put a finger to her lips. 'Don't make a mountain out of a molehill. Go through to the kitchen and say hello to the boys. They're dying to see you.'

He swallowed hard. He knew that Nicola would be offended by having been cancelled – he was sure of that – but equally he knew that he would not get anywhere in an argument with Irene: he never did. So he made his way into the kitchen where Bertie was sitting at the table with a book open in front of him; Ulysses, perched in his high chair, was toying with a piece of toast and peanut butter.

Ulysses waved his hands about enthusiastically when he

saw his father and uttered an unintelligible babble. Bertie looked up at Stuart and grinned.

'Ulysses isn't talking English yet, Daddy,' he said. 'Do you think he may be talking some other language altogether? Gaelic, maybe?'

Stuart bent down to kiss Ulysses on the top of his head. He caught a faint whiff of vomit; Irene must have picked him up.

'He'll start soon enough, Bertie,' he said. 'Children start to talk in their own time. Some people don't begin until they're quite a bit older than Ulysses is.' He remembered something about Thomas Carlyle – hadn't he said nothing for year after year, until he was seven? And then had said, when a woman inadvertently scalded him with hot water and enquired how he was: 'Thank you, madam, the agony has abated'? Or what about the German child who had been silent for years before, and, when asked why he had not spoken until then, replied, 'Because up until now, everything was satisfactory.'

Bertie was looking up at him. 'Why are you smiling, Daddy?'

'I was thinking of something, Bertie. I was thinking of people who didn't speak until they were much older.'

'Tofu says that he knew the alphabet by his first birthday.'

Stuart looked doubtful. 'Highly unlikely, Bertie. Tofu has a vivid imagination.'

Bertie was looking at Ulysses. 'I was wondering about something, Daddy,' he said. 'I was wondering how we'd look after Ulysses if . . . ' He hesitated. He was fingering the spine of his book, twisting the cover. 'I was wondering how we'd be able to look after Ulysses if Mummy weren't here.'

Stuart frowned. 'But, Bertie, Mummy *is* here.'

'But if she weren't. What then?'

'I don't think we should bother about things that aren't the case, Bertie. Mummy *is* here and she looks after Ulysses very well, and we give her all the help we can. He has everything he needs, doesn't he? And he's a very happy little boy, don't you think?'

They both looked at Ulysses: Stuart inadvertently, Bertie deliberately. Ulysses stared back, his mouth full of toast and peanut butter. There was peanut butter on his chin and a certain amount in his hair.

'Let's talk about something else, Bertie. What's that book you're reading?'

Bertie turned it over so that his father could see the cover. Stuart read the title. *The Odyssey.*

'My goodness, Bertie,' he said. 'That's a very grown-up book.'

'It's all about Odysseus,' said Bertie. 'The Romans called him Ulysses, Daddy. Just like our Ulysses.'

'Well, there you are, Bertie.'

'Yes. He went on a very long journey, you see, and all sorts of things happened to him. You know there's this person called the Cyclops, Daddy, and he was really tall. He only had one eye, you see, and Odysseus had to push a big stake into it to escape from the Cyclops's cave. He hid under a sheep.'

'I believe I've heard of all that,' said Stuart. 'You know it's not true, I take it?'

'Yes,' said Bertie. 'It's just a story. Mr Homer made it all up.'

Stuart tousled his son's hair. 'Yes, Mr Homer did,' he said, smiling. He closed his eyes momentarily; he loved this little boy, with his quaint expressions and his earnest manner. He loved him so much. People talked about loving others with all their heart, and this is what that expression meant. You felt it right there, in your heart, a feeling that was intense and unambiguously physical, as if something within you, roughly where your heart was said to be, was swelling with emotion.

But this situation – this living in a state of lovelessness when it came to his marriage – surely could not continue. He could not bear another day of it – not a single day. But then he thought: don't be ridiculous, you have to, because this is the life that is given to you and you have to accept what is given to you. Half of human unhappiness, if not more, was due to the fact that people did not accept a certain measure of predestined, unavoidable unhappiness. He thought that, and then, for a few moments, wondered whether he really thought it, and whether it was true, or as fictional as *The Odyssey*. Unless *The Odyssey* was, in a sense, true, and we were *all* Odysseus.

26. *Irene Overheard*

Stuart gave Ulysses his bath, dressed him in his candy-striped pyjamas, and put him to bed, while Irene attended to e-mails in her study at the end of the corridor. There had been a recent increase in e-mail traffic to Irene's computer – the sort of thing picked up by intelligence agencies monitoring suspects – but Stuart had no idea about Irene's correspondence and did not dare to ask. He had noticed her expression as she typed many of the messages – it was a sort of grim, determined look, accompanied by pursed lips, as if she were upbraiding the recipient for something, which she probably was. Sometimes there was also a look of satisfaction, suggesting that somebody had been corrected, disproved, or even put in his or her place, the Send button being pressed with an accompanying, even if unspoken, *so there!*

Ulysses, for all his tendency to regurgitation, never took long to fall asleep, and Stuart was free to devote half an hour or so to Bertie before Bertie's own bedtime. This time was often spent reading or sometimes playing a board game. That evening Bertie asked Stuart to read part of his children's version of *The Odyssey*, but became tired after fifteen minutes and was tucked up early.

Stuart sat for a while by his son's bedside, holding Bertie's hand; Bertie was sometimes nervous in the dark, and the presence of his father, and the comfort of his hand, helped him to drift off to sleep.

A small voice spoke in the darkness. 'Do Cyclops really exist, Daddy?'

'No, Bertie. The Cyclops was a complete invention. There are no giants, whether or not with one eye – they just don't exist. Not real, very tall giants.'

'I wouldn't like to meet a Cyclops, Daddy.'

'No, but then it won't happen, Bertie. We shouldn't frighten ourselves too much about things that won't happen.' Stuart remembered their earlier conversation, when Bertie had asked how they would look after Ulysses if Irene were to go. That was typical of the sort of insecurity children could experience – he remembered that when he was a boy, probably about Bertie's age, he had been terrified that his father would die. And he remembered carrying out various superstitious rituals to forfend the possibility: making sure that his shoe-laces did not come untied – that was one of them; getting out of the bath before the last of the water had drained out, that was another. Your father could face mortal peril if you overlooked one of these observances, and as a result you made sure that you did not. Was Bertie worried that Irene would die? That must be it. And how did one tackle that, other than to say to the child that his parents would certainly *not* die, which of course any child could see through? Parents did die.

It was easy to explain death to a child if one believed in an afterlife. 'Granny has gone to heaven' is not too bleak a thing to have to say, and was certainly easier than saying, 'Granny has ceased to exist.' Mind you, that was thinking of the parent's ease – the child might be more capable of taking in the fact of non-existence than that of heaven, which was vague and difficult to define, short of resorting to a thoroughly old-fashioned description of Elysian fields or some cloudy place in the sky. His own father, he remembered, had been evasive on the issue, and questioning by Stuart when he was a boy had simply resulted in the matter being referred to his mother, who had confessed that she was unsure if heaven still existed but it was a nice idea even if it did not.

'Bertie,' he said carefully. 'You aren't worried that something will happen to Mummy, are you?'

Bertie was silent.

'Because,' Stuart continued, 'there's no reason to be worried about Mummy's health. She's very healthy, you know. And she takes lots of exercise.'

'I know she does,' said Bertie. 'She has her Pilates-Tai Chi-Yoga Fusion classes.'

'Exactly,' said Stuart. 'So you shouldn't worry about her. I know that people sometimes worry that something bad will happen to members of their family, but they shouldn't really worry, you know.'

'But bad things can happen,' said Bertie, through the darkness.

'Yes, bad things can happen. But they don't happen all that often.' The only thing to do, he thought, was to allay anxiety by reassurance. 'And I know all about the chances of bad things happening, because that's what I do, after all. I'm a statistician – as you know.' He paused, waiting for the information to be absorbed. 'So if I say that there's not much chance of anything bad happening to Mummy, I know what I'm talking about. That's not just any old person saying that – it's one of the Scottish Government's statisticians.'

'Yes,' said Bertie. 'I understand all that, Daddy, but I was wondering . . . ' He broke off.

'Yes, Bertie? You were wondering?'

'I was wondering why Mummy might go to Aberdeen.'

This brought complete silence: nothing could be heard in the darkened room but the sound of the two of them breathing.

Eventually Stuart spoke. 'Why do you ask that, Bertie? Has Mummy said to you that she might go off to Aberdeen?'

'Not to me, Daddy.'

'To somebody else then?'

Bertie shifted under the bedclothes. 'I heard her talking on the telephone. I was reading in my room, but I heard Mummy talking on the telephone in the kitchen. I had my door open and I could hear.'

'Who was she talking to, Bertie?'

'I think it was Dr Fairbairn. She kept calling him Hugo, and that is Dr Fairbairn's first name, Daddy.' Dr Hugo Fairbairn, now Professor Hugo Fairbairn, had been Bertie's first psychotherapist, and Bertie was convinced that he was mad. It was only a matter of time, thought Bertie, before Dr Fairbairn was taken off to Carstairs, where he would almost certainly have to be put in a padded cell and be watched very closely.

Stuart lowered his voice. 'And what did she say, Bertie?'

'She said: "I can't wait to come to live in Aberdeen." That's what she said, Daddy.'

Stuart closed his eyes. So she was ready to make her move. And it was, as he suspected, connected with Hugo Fairbairn. He might have known.

Bertie had more. 'She said that she had decided what she was going to do for her PhD, Daddy. I think she wants to do a PhD in Aberdeen.' He paused. 'What's a PhD, Daddy?'

Stuart did not answer; his mind was elsewhere.

'It's interesting,' said Bertie, drowsily now, as sleep was overtaking him. 'It's interesting how Ulysses looks so like Dr Fairbairn. It's his ears mainly . . . '

Stuart heard the note of Bertie's breathing changing. He rose to his feet and quietly left the room.

27. *At the VinCaffè*

Irene had chosen the restaurant at which she and Stuart would have dinner that night.

'The VinCaffè,' she announced. 'It's a Contini place and they're the Valvona & Crolla people.' Irene was a customer of Valvona & Crolla, where she took Bertie when she went to purchase sun-dried tomatoes, pasta, and occasionally, as a treat for Bertie, his favourite *panforte di Siena*.

The restaurant was in a small street that ran off St Andrew Square. This street was lined with fashionable shops of which Irene did not particularly approve, and she pointedly refrained from looking in the windows until she reached the restaurant itself. But then, in the warm embrace of Italian hospitality, she seemed to relax, using her Italian sufficiently loudly to attract glances from neighbouring tables.

'*Allora!*' she enthused. '*Insalata Caprese* made with genuine *mozzarella di bufala. Mi piace molto questa*.'

Stuart squirmed, noticing the expression on the face of a woman at a neighbouring table. 'Buffalo mozzarella,' he muttered as quietly as he could. 'Very nice.'

But Irene was just getting into her stride. A waiter had appeared and began to take their order. There followed a prolonged discussion, in Italian, of the merits of various items on the menu. The waiter was patient, and eventually choices were made and duly noted down.

'I rather like this place,' said Stuart. 'Perhaps we should go out for dinner more often.'

'But we're always going out,' said Irene.

Stuart stared at her. She was talking about herself, and her various activities. She went out a great deal, but he very rarely.

'Well, now,' said Irene. 'What news from the office?'

Stuart hesitated. He had not told Irene of the possible promotion, but realised that he would have to do so. 'There's a vacancy coming up,' he said. 'It's a very senior appointment. I'm applying.'

Irene looked interested. 'Well, that's about time, if I may

say so. How long have you been in your current grade? Four years?'

Stuart shook his head. 'Five, coming up for six.'

'Then promotion is well overdue,' said Irene firmly.

'I'm happy enough doing what I'm doing,' said Stuart. 'I've got nice colleagues. We get along well. There's Morrison, for example. I like working with him.'

Irene smiled indulgently. She had met Morrison once or twice when he had called at the house with office papers. 'Oh him,' she said. 'Morrison . . . *Un po' noioso*.'

Stuart was defensive. 'What does that mean?'

'A little bit . . . well, sorry to say it, Stuart – which is why I said it in Italian – a little bit on the boring side.' She paused. 'I imagine he belongs to a golf club.'

Stuart tried to contain his irritation. He liked Morrison, and, yes, Morrison did belong to a golf club – in fact he was on the committee of the Duddingston Golf Club, and often spoke about their meetings . . . but what was boring about that?

'But Morrison's not the point,' Irene continued. 'The real point is your career. You're in a bit of a rut, Stuart. I don't mean that unkindly, but you are, aren't you? You need a new challenge.'

Stuart bit his lip. 'I don't think I am.'

Irene ignored this. 'I take it the salary will be much improved?'

'Yes, it is better paid. It's more senior. It's several notches above where I am at the moment.'

Irene looked satisfied. 'Then you must make sure you get it, Stuart. You *are* going to get it, I take it?'

'There are two other candidates,' said Stuart.

Irene reflected on this. 'Who exactly? Not Morrison?'

'No, not him. Morrison's going to retire quite soon, anyway. He's been in the office for ages.'

Irene enquired further as to the identity of the other candidates.

'A couple of female colleagues,' said Stuart. 'I don't think you've met them. Elaine and Faith.'

Irene sat back in her chair. This required thought. The fact that the other candidates were women changed the picture a bit – one of them should, by rights, get the job on grounds of restorative justice, but Stuart needed the salary increase, especially with her plans being what they were. That trumped it. Any salary increase would benefit her and her work, and therefore weakened the claims – strong though they undoubtedly must be – of the two female candidates.

'You've got to get it, Stuart. Elaine and . . . what's her name?'

'Faith.'

'Yes, Elaine and Faith will obviously be very strong candidates, but think of your experience. No, you have to go for this one, Stuart – really go for it.'

'I'm doing my best,' he said. 'We have to write a sort of mission statement.'

'Leave that to me,' said Irene abruptly. 'I'll do that. I know what they'll be looking for.'

Stuart said nothing. This discussion was all about the future, but what about Irene's own future? What about Aberdeen? He looked at her. His heart was beating hard within him; his mouth was dry. He had to ask her.

'And you?' he said. 'What about Aberdeen?'

She gave a start, sitting bolt upright in her chair. 'Aberdeen?'

'Yes. I gather . . . '

She blushed. 'I was going to tell you this evening. Or discuss it with you, rather.'

'So you haven't made up your mind?'

Her blush deepened. 'I've been thinking of doing a PhD, Stuart. In fact, I've pretty much decided. I'm going to start a PhD in Aberdeen.'

Stuart remained calm. 'I see. And this will be with . . . with Dr Fairbairn?'

She nodded, but he saw that she was avoiding his gaze. 'He's very kindly offered to be my supervisor. And he's actually Professor Fairbairn now. He has a chair.'

Stuart waited for Irene to look at him, but she resolutely did not. 'So you'll need to move up there?'

She looked at him at last, and he saw several things very clearly. She did not love him. She wanted to go to Aberdeen. Her lover was in Aberdeen. And then, finally, he thought: Ulysses isn't mine.

'I've thought about that,' said Irene. 'I'll need to go up there for much of the week. But I'll come back at weekends. Some weekends.'

Stuart held her gaze. 'And the boys?' he asked.

She hesitated, but only briefly. 'There's your mother,' she said. 'I thought . . . '

He took a deep breath. She had rejected his mother as a babysitter, and now here she was proposing her as substitute mother.

He leaned forward. 'You know, Irene, I think this is the most wonderful idea. No, I really do. You've always wanted to do a PhD and you must do, you really must. And as far as my mother is concerned, I'm pretty sure she'll leap at the idea of looking after the boys.'

The waiter appeared with a couple of plates. '*Insalata Caprese*,' he said, with a smile. '*Buon appetito!*'

28. We Stole It

While Stuart and Irene were at dinner at the VinCaffè, out at Nine Mile Burn, on the road to Biggar, Matthew and Elspeth were entertaining their neighbour, the Duke of Johannesburg, the former owner of the house in which they now lived, his own seat being Single Malt House, a converted farmhouse. Although the Duke described his house in those terms, he was not quite sure what it had been converted from or into.

'Lots of people live in a converted something-or-other,' he once observed to Matthew, 'but what exactly the converted doo-dah has been converted into may not be entirely clear – as in my own case right at the moment.'

Matthew tried to be helpful. 'I think it means that the house has stopped being one thing and has become another.

So a converted garage means it used to be a garage and now it's . . . well, whatever it's being used as.'

This reminded the Duke of something. 'My friend, Paddy Auchtermuchty . . . '

Matthew interrupted him. 'The Earl of Auchtermuchty?'

The Duke laughed. 'Well, I suppose he is. I find it very difficult to think of him as that. Personally, I think he's a little bit on the bogus side, rather like myself. But the Lord Lyon appears to recognise him as the real thing, although Lords Lyon, like anybody else, can make mistakes.' He became thoughtful. 'The criterion for membership of that particular slice of Scottish society, as far as I can work out, is that your ancestors bumped off more people than other people's ancestors, or pinched more land than others. Not something to be terribly proud of, I would have thought.'

Matthew hesitated. The Duke was a very relaxed and agreeable man, and he felt that he could speak frankly to him; but he must have been sensitive about *something*. 'Whereas, you're not tainted by any of that?'

The Duke did not take offence. 'Oh, heavens no. You know our story already, I believe – it's pretty much an open secret. My grandfather – or it might have been my father, I'm a bit hazy on these details – promised to do the government of the time some sort of favour. Anyway, those chaps down in government said "Jolly good, roll it on and we'll make you a duke or something like that." They may not actually have said *duke*; it may have been something a bit less impressive – an MBE, perhaps, not that there's anything wrong with an MBE. But, of course, they didn't really mean it because you know how these chaps are – they say whatever comes into their mind as long as they think it will please the voters and then . . . Well, they break their promises. That's what they do with their manifesto promises, you know. So when push came to shove, they denied all knowledge of the bargain.

'The old man was pretty furious and said that he was entitled to the dukedom, or whatever it was that he had been promised, and so we just assumed the title. And without stealing anybody's cattle or land, or slitting anybody's throats! Rather good performance on our part, I'd say.'

The Duke was warming to his theme. 'Of course, Paddy Auchtermuchty's people were a bit run-down – rather on their uppers, truth be told. Angus Auchtermuchty, who was Paddy's father, or possibly grandfather – who knows? – went out to Kenya when it was the sort of thing people did. We Scots like to say that the British Empire was nothing to do with us and that it was all the doing of the English, but my goodness, who do we think we're fooling?' The Duke shook his head in wonderment. 'Ourselves, of course. We tell that to ourselves in the same way as we make these claims about our educational system – which is rapidly declining – and feel all warm inside. *Wha's like us, Matthew?* Anyway, we were completely implicated in the British Empire, and it wasn't just in the engine rooms or the plantations, or whatever, it was actually governing great chunks of it. We were one hundred per cent involved, and then we say, "But oh, we were different . . . " We weren't.

'The Auchtermuchties had a farm in Kenya. Now you

don't get land in Kenya, or anywhere else for that matter, without taking it from somebody, and so let's have none of that nonsense. We stole it. We took vast chunks of land all over the globe. Stuck up a flag and that was it. Have you heard of *terra nullius*, Matthew? Complete nonsense. I'm not exactly sure what it means, of course, but I've got a Latin dictionary somewhere in the house and I'm going to look it up one of these days.

'I sometimes wish I had a bit more Latin than I do – and also a bit of Greek. I never had the chance to learn Greek, you know, Matthew. There was this chap appointed to teach Greek when I was at school, but he didn't last long. A rather portly man with a moustache, as I recall, who looked a bit furtive, as these chaps often do. I think it was only a day or two before they took him away. Some of the boys said that he was put in Carstairs, but one fellow said he had seen him in Glasgow when they went to have dinner at Rogano with his parents. He said he was there, as large as life, tucking into a fish supper and reading the *Dundee Courier*, of all things.

'Anyway, Matthew, back to Kenya and Angus Auchtermuchty. There he was growing coffee but probably not doing it terribly well. Somebody said that he tried to grow decaffeinated coffee – that he had a decaffeinated coffee estate – and that this was the flaw in the business plan. People in those days liked a real jolt when they drank a cup of coffee – it was said to wake them up, and they weren't as interested in decaffeinated coffee as they are today. So he pretty much failed and lost what little money he had. Yet he had a good time, by all accounts, and ran around with that Happy Valley crowd, you know the ones who were always shooting one another. Terrible business. You'd go out for dinner with that bunch and fully expect that one of the guests would get shot during the course of the evening. That happened to poor old Errol, didn't it? Got shot after the pudding was served. Dreadful for everybody, but particularly him. Some of those people, Matthew, were real shockers. Not him, of course, rest his soul, but some of the others. There was that woman, for instance: I forget her name, but you know what they said about her? Apparently, she went out for her honeymoon on the boat to Mombasa or wherever and on the way, on her actual honeymoon, Matthew, she had an affair with some young man she met on the boat. On her honeymoon! That takes some doing, Matthew, to have an affair on your honeymoon. They don't make them like that these days, do they?'

Matthew looked doubtful. 'I wouldn't be so sure,' he said.

29. Who was Homer?

The Duke of Johannesburg continued. 'I mentioned my lack of Greek?'

Matthew nodded. 'I didn't learn it either. We could

choose to do it at the Edinburgh Academy, but I didn't. I did art instead. But there was definitely Greek being taught – there are Greek inscriptions in the stonework.'

The Duke shook his head. 'It's a pity, isn't it? As you go through life you realise what gaps there are in your education. Mine had major gaps, as I suppose just about everybody's did – unless you were very lucky.' He paused. 'Did I tell you about the prep school I went to?'

'No, not that I recall.'

'Well,' said the Duke, 'in those days it was rather more common for really quite young children to be sent off to boarding school. I have no time for that – it's a ridiculous, absurd thing to do – but it happened. Can you imagine it? Seven, or whatever? Being packed off, sent away from home, to some distant place? It's inhuman.'

'I don't like the idea of it,' said Matthew.

'What's the point of having children if you're not going to live with them?' asked the Duke.

'Precisely,' agreed Matthew. 'I've often thought of the psychological damage done to those poor children. The maternal deprivation.'

'The world was very cruel,' said the Duke. 'Positively Dickensian. But be that as it may, it happened to me. I was sent to a place down in Dumfriesshire. It's long since closed. A small place that you could easily miss if you drove past too fast. In fact, people used to say that some boys never actually got to the school – their parents took them down but couldn't actually find it, and so drove back to Edinburgh or Glasgow and put them into schools there. I'm not sure if it's true, but it's a nice story.

‘We found it and I was dumped there and put in a dorm with a lot of other boys, and we all cried our eyes out for days. Then somebody said, “No use crying, may as well get on with it,” and we did. I’ve actually used that as my motto for life, you know: *No use crying, may as well get on with it*.

‘I spent four years at that school you know, Matthew, and I sometimes reflect on what I learned. And you know what? I can’t recall a single thing they taught me – not a single thing, except for one thing. We had this teacher there – he was my form master – who had made a special study of the Boer War. He’d actually written a book on it – probably published it himself – called *The Boer War Reconsidered*. The school was very proud of the fact that one of the staff had written a book – the rest of them having not much more than a DipEd from Jordanhill, if that. So they put it in the brochure and described him as a ground-breaking historian.

‘Well that was all very well, but the fact of the matter is that all he ever taught us was the Boer War. We had the Boer War in the morning, and then again in the afternoon. Every day for four years. That was it. It was very tedious. And then I came to school in Edinburgh and I learned about the French Revolution. Still, there we are, Matthew – none of us knows quite as much as we might like. And so, I can’t read classical Greek, nor modern Greek, for that matter. Not even the alphabet. I can start, of course: Alpha, beta, gamma . . . then it gets a bit hazy.’

Matthew sighed. ‘Me too. I wish I could read Homer in the original.’

The Duke agreed. 'A great regret, that.'

Matthew thought of something. 'You know, I used to think of Homer as a person.'

'Most people do,' said the Duke. 'Wasn't he?'

Matthew had chanced upon Adam Nicolson's *The Mighty Dead*. 'I used to think he was. I remember seeing a bust of Homer in the Louvre. He had a rather long face, a flowing beard, and some very poetic-looking curls.'

'But how could one tell?' asked the Duke.

'They couldn't. This one was based on a Roman copy of a Greek original. But even that original was made long after the poet died – if he existed, of course. One has to exist first to die.'

'So, nobody knows what he looked like?'

'No, and the point is that *The Iliad* and *The Odyssey* are ancient, traditional stories rather than the work of one hand. There may have been somebody who gathered them, so to speak, and that might have been the person we refer to as Homer, but it's all shrouded in the mists of . . . '

'. . . of antiquity,' supplied the Duke. 'The mists of antiquity are a lovely notion, aren't they? I can just see them rolling in, coming off the Firth of Forth, covering the low plains of East Lothian, and people, seeing them, would say, *Oh, my goodness, here come those mists of antiquity again, it's going to be a cold day!*'

Matthew stared at the Duke, who smiled blandly. 'Like the waters of oblivion,' he said.

'Don't swim,' said the Duke. 'Rip tides there.'

'Hah!' said Matthew. 'And the grapes of wrath?'

'I looked for them in the supermarket,' said the Duke,

laughing. 'Nowhere to be seen. *On order* they said.' He paused. 'Seriously though: Homer – I'm dismayed to find I never knew he didn't exist.'

'Not only that,' said Matthew, 'but there are theories that he was a woman. I came across a book that makes a case for that – the author says that there is a very clear feminine sensitivity at work in the poems. He makes quite a strong case.'

'Interesting,' said the Duke. 'And are there those who say that Jane Austen was a man?'

'If you look hard enough you'll find somebody who says just about anything. Including . . . ' Matthew searched the recesses of his memory. 'Yes, there's an Italian scholar, believe it or not, who argues that *The Iliad* and *The Odyssey* don't belong in Greece at all, but actually come from the Baltic. He's looked at the geography of the whole thing and finds that it fits the Baltic perfectly, whereas it doesn't really square up when applied to Greek geography.'

'*Quot homines, tot sententiae!*' exclaimed the Duke.

'You said you didn't know much Latin,' Matthew pointed out.

'Don't assume that people always know the meaning of what they say,' the Duke confessed.

30. The Evening Sun, Warm and Buttery

Now, from the kitchen window of their house at Nine Mile Burn, Matthew and Elspeth watched the Duke of Johannesburg's car make its way slowly up the drive, disappearing briefly amongst the rhododendrons before emerging on the final stretch of drive. Matthew, who had been polishing a wine glass as he remembered his last conversation with the Duke, put down the glass and left the kitchen to welcome their guest.

The Duke's car was driven by his stockman, Padruig, who climbed out of the driving seat to open the door for his passenger.

'Thank you very much, Padruig,' said the Duke. 'If you'd be good enough to fetch me at eleven.' He looked enquiringly at Matthew. 'I hope that's about right. One should never assume too much.'

'Perfect,' said Matthew. 'Elspeth gets rather tired, you know. What with the triplets and everything.'

The Duke nodded. 'I understand. I'm an early riser myself and I like to get to bed in good time.'

Padruig, the driver-cum-stockman, joined in the conversation. 'Early to bed, late to rise,' he said. 'In Gaelic we say . . . ' He declaimed a rather long Gaelic sentence, which neither Matthew nor the Duke understood.

'There you are,' said the Duke, a note of pride in his voice. 'Padruig speaks a great deal of Gaelic. He understands all our road signs.' He paused. 'Although, without wishing to boast, I understand quite a bit myself. The other day I successfully translated a sign to a place called *Cupar*.'

'Oh yes,' said Matthew. 'And it was?'

'Cupar,' said the Duke.

Matthew turned to Padruig. 'What does that mean? What you've just said?' he asked.

Padruig gave him a penetrating look. 'It cannot be translated,' he replied. 'I'm sorry.'

The Duke tried to explain. 'Padruig tells me that Gaelic is a very subtle language,' he said. 'There's a lot that can't be exactly rendered into English.'

Padruig nodded. '*Eiridh tonn air uisge balbh*,' he said.

Matthew stared at him, wondering whether this was also so subtle that there would be no translation. The Duke intercepted the stare. 'I think you should translate that for Matthew,' he admonished. 'You can't leave him in the dark.'

Padruig looked up at the sky. 'Waves will rise on silent water,' he muttered.

Matthew looked first at the Duke, and then at Padruig, who in turn stared at the Duke.

'I see,' said Matthew at length.

'Oh well,' said the Duke. 'There you have it.'

They waited as the car drove off.

'Such an interesting-looking car,' observed Matthew.

'I must confess I'm rather fond of it,' said the Duke. 'I think I told you before: I bought it from a chap I met at Haymarket Station. I know you shouldn't buy cars from people you meet at Haymarket Station – or at any station, I suppose – but he was very enthusiastic about it and was offering it at a good price.'

'And have you had any trouble with it?' asked Matthew.

The Duke shook his head. 'No, not really. I had to replace the engine – and the wheels – but otherwise it's been a pretty good buy.' He paused. 'There's been a bit of a mystery about it, though. My mechanic said he was totally flummoxed as to what make of car it is. He said that initially he thought it was German, but then there was no sign of any German parts in it. Then he wondered about Italian, but there was no sign of that either. Eventually he concluded that it was Belgian. But I'm not too sure about that: it doesn't *feel* like a Belgian car. Padruig says that it was made in Stornoway, although I can't imagine why he thinks that.'

They made their way inside, where Elspeth greeted the Duke with a kiss on both cheeks. Then they went into the drawing room, which faced due west, and through the windows of which the evening sun, warm and buttery, was streaming. Matthew poured the Duke a dram, while Elspeth dispensed red wine for the two of them. The Duke raised his glass in toast.

'It's Johnnie Walker Blue Label,' said Matthew. 'Somebody gave me a bottle for my birthday.'

The Duke inclined his head appreciatively. 'So very smooth,' he said. He looked at Elspeth. 'I hear you've dispensed with the services of those unusual Danes,' he said.

Birgitte had been gratuitously rude to the Duke and this had not been forgotten.

'They had to go,' said Matthew. 'And they went.'

'But then Clare went as well and that left me a little bit in the lurch,' said Elspeth. 'It's all very well for Matthew – he doesn't have to . . . '

Sensing marital disagreement, the Duke quickly took control of the conversation. 'You must be shattered,' he said. 'I'd have no idea nowadays how to cope with one – let alone three. And tell me, are you going to replace your errant Danes?'

Elspeth nodded. 'That's the plan.'

'And who will you get?' asked the Duke. 'Not more Danes, I take it?'

'We were thinking of somebody Spanish,' said Matthew. 'A young man.'

The Duke looked surprised. 'I thought au pairs were female.'

Matthew smiled. 'You're a bit out of date, Duke. That used to be the case, but now there are bags of male au pairs. We're thinking of a Spaniard because we know somebody who employed a young man from Spain and he was terrific.'

For a few moments the Duke seemed to mull over this. Then he said, 'Couldn't you get somebody local?'

Matthew glanced at Elspeth, who looked embarrassed. 'I'm not sure we could find anybody,' he said.

There was an awkward silence. Then Elspeth spoke. 'Perhaps they're too busy. That's why we import people all the time.'

‘So, what are our local young people doing?’ asked the Duke.

There was another silence, more awkward than the last. This was not the sort of question one asked.

‘I have no idea,’ said Matthew. He had read the figures somewhere for youth unemployment. ‘I think, though, that roughly ten per cent of them are unemployed.’

Elspeth sighed. ‘I’d take on a local boy if I could find one,’ she said. ‘But . . . but . . . ’ She shrugged in a gesture of hopelessness. ‘Can you name one, just one, who would be prepared to do this job?’

‘My nephew,’ said the Duke. ‘He’s a fine boy, and he’s coming up for a gap year.’

‘But they all go to India and Thailand,’ said Matthew. ‘Or at least the privileged middle-class ones do. They don’t work as au pairs.’

‘Not this one,’ said the Duke. ‘He’s not privileged and he wants to work. He’s just finished his Advanced Highers at James Gillespie’s and he’ll do anything.’

Matthew gave Elspeth a glance.

‘Speak to him,’ said the Duke. ‘Give him a chance. He’s a lovely boy. A keen cook . . . ’

Elspeth brightened. ‘Keen on cooking?’

‘And flower arranging,’ added the Duke.

‘We’ll give him an interview,’ said Elspeth.

‘And rugby,’ the Duke added.

31. A Conversation Under the Night Sky

Elspeth said goodnight to the Duke at the end of dinner, leaving Matthew to see their guest to his car. Padruig had already arrived and was parked under the oak tree at the front of the house. Emerging from the car as they approached, he opened the rear passenger door for his employer.

'You and Elspeth are very good to me,' said the Duke as he shook Matthew's hand. 'It's not easy, you know.'

Matthew was not sure how to respond. He was not quite sure what was not easy, and so he simply made a noncommittal noise – something that could have been agreement or simply an acknowledgment of having heard.

But if elucidation was necessary, it was provided by what the Duke said next. 'We live in difficult times, Matthew – very difficult times.'

Matthew felt he could agree with that; and yet, he reflected, people had always thought they lived in difficult times. He thought of his father's generation, and his grandfather's before that. His paternal grandfather had lived through the Depression as a boy, at a time when the family had had very little money. Matthew had never known him, as he had died before he was born, but he had heard how hard it had been. Then there had been the war, in which his grandfather had served with the Cameronians. His entire life, it seemed to Matthew, had been overshadowed by crisis and the moral disaster of war – difficult times by any standards. And his father? He had been born in the post-war period when, for a brief time, it looked as if the sunny uplands might have been reached, but then there had been the Cold War and the threat of nuclear annihilation. His father had been twelve at the time of the Cuban Missile Crisis and even at that age had understood that at any moment the country might have been reduced to ashes – difficult times again.

'Haven't we always lived in times of crisis?' he said to the Duke.

The Duke, about to climb into the car, pushed the door shut, indicating that he wanted to finish their conversation before he left.

'That's all right, Padruig,' he said. 'I'll just be a few minutes.'

He turned to Matthew. 'You're right, of course – every generation thinks its situation is uniquely worrying – but the world has always been on the brink of disaster. Yes, that's right, but that doesn't detract from the particular difficulty of specific times.' He paused, appearing to think through the next stage of his argument. 'All that I'm saying, I suppose, is that there appear to be some periods where the dilemmas seem greater than those experienced a few years previously, or where there is marked decline in something we value. That's what I was thinking about.'

Matthew waited for the Duke to continue.

'It's the destruction of civility,' said the Duke. 'Twenty years ago, people may have had their differences of opinion – of course they did – but they did not abuse one another for it. They respected those with whom they disagreed. They spoke courteously.'

Matthew was silent.

'Oh, I know that we shouldn't romanticise the past,' the Duke continued, 'and I don't, you know. But there are times when it seems that the social glue that holds people together is weakened and . . . well, brother is turned on brother, so to speak. My American friends report something very similar in their society. Friendships have been broken, families sundered because of the polarisation that has taken place. Who can be happy about that? I can't.'

'Nor I,' said Matthew. The Duke was right – he was talking about something that was there, that had been noticed. And Matthew felt sad even to think about it.

'And now,' said the Duke, 'there's something very unpleasant on the loose. We may pretend that it isn't; we may deny it, but we know that there are more and more people who hate those whom they used not to hate. And there are even some who encourage this hate, who harbour that hate within themselves and are happy to see it flourish in the breasts of others.'

Matthew felt his heart beating hard within him. This was true; it was the uncomfortable truth that nobody wanted to acknowledge, to look at squarely in the face.

'I sometimes wonder,' said the Duke, 'whether this isn't because we started to dismantle nations. Nations gave people a sense of common identity and encouraged concern for others – because of the community implicit in the idea of nation. We started to chip away at that in the name of a wider, transcendent identity but . . . but perhaps that hasn't worked and as a result we've been cast adrift, our previous links and bonds dissolved or discredited, suspicious of one another, ready to distrust our neighbours.

'Hate is very easy to unleash,' the Duke continued. 'All you need is the Other. And then people will take over from you and do all the hating that needs to be done, all the belittling, all the insulting and bullying.'

Again, Matthew waited for the Duke to continue, but it seemed that he had said all that he wished to say on the subject. For his part, all that Matthew could say was, 'I know what you mean.' It was not much of a response, but it was accurate. He knew exactly what the Duke meant.

The Duke reached to open the door of the car. Padruig brushed his hand away, though, and took the handle.

The Duke looked at Matthew in the moonlight. 'Matthew,' he said, 'have you read what Hamish Henderson had to say in one of his poems? He says, somewhere or other, *let us not disfigure ourselves with hatred*. Let us not disfigure ourselves . . . how apt, how resoundingly true. We should not disfigure ourselves with hatred, Matthew, and yet we do, and dear Hamish Henderson, that softly-spoken, good man, who believed that we should treat one another with gentleness and love, understood the dangers of that and will be birling in his grave, Matthew, *birling*, to hear some of the things that people say to one another these days.'

Matthew had not read the poem, but he had heard Henderson's great hymn to fellowship and sympathy, 'Freedom Come All Ye', and knew the sentiments.

The Duke eased himself into the car. He wound down the window and addressed Matthew from within. 'A final point, Matthew. We unleash these forces at our peril: a virus behaves in exactly the same way wherever you release it. Nobody is above it, and we are just as vulnerable as anybody else. That's why I'm sad, Matthew; that's why I'm sick at heart.'

32. Scouting for Boys, etc.

Friendships between children often result in friendships between sets of parents. Conversations between waiting parents at the school gate do more than provide information on what is happening in the world of the school – and the latest gossip, of course – they may lead to exchanges of e-mail addresses, invitations to dinner, games of bridge, and the negotiation of numerous playdates for the children themselves. Or they may encourage animosities and feuds.

It was not at the school gate that Irene had come to know the mother of Bertie's friend Ranald Braveheart

Macpherson. Bertie and Ranald were at different schools – Ranald at Watson's and Bertie at the Steiner School, but they were both in the Morningside Cub Scout pack that met at Holy Corner in Bruntsfield. It was while they were waiting to collect their sons after the cub scout meeting that Ishbel Constance Macpherson first met Irene. The meeting was not a success by any standards, and both women conceived a perfect dislike for one another – a dislike that subsequent acquaintance merely served to intensify.

'I met an extremely ghastly woman this evening,' Ishbel told her husband. 'You should have heard her.'

'Loud?'

'No, it wasn't the volume, it was the whole attitude. It's difficult to describe, but she was the sort of person one just couldn't help disagreeing with – whatever she said. You just wanted to disagree.'

'Oh dear. Difficult.'

'And her son, little Bertie . . . '

'Oh, he's marvellous,' said Ranald's father. 'I've met him. Very earnest. Very polite.'

'That's him,' said Ishbel. 'He has to put up with this train crash of a mother. He deserves a medal.'

These cold relations had not been improved by a famous telephone call between the two mothers, in which salvos had been fired from Scotland Street across the rooftops of the Old Town to Church Hill, and then returned with interest. But although they were barely speaking to one another, both were compelled by their sons' friendship to negotiate times to drop off and collect their offspring from the other's house on those occasions when the two boys met.

So, when Ishbel came that day to drop Ranald off for a play session with Bertie, she rang the Pollock doorbell somewhat gingerly, as if prepared to receive from it a reproach, or even a minor electric shock.

Irene knew who it was at the door and was determined to wait as long as possible before she answered.

'I think that might be Ranald Braveheart Macpherson at the door, Mummy,' said Bertie.

'Ah,' said Irene, 'you *think*, Bertie, but do you *know* that it's Ranald at the door? How can you be certain?'

Bertie looked puzzled. 'Because it's three o'clock, Mummy, and that's the time that Ranald said he'd arrive.'

'No, Bertie,' said Irene. 'One should not act on mere surmise – I've often told you that, *n'est-ce pas*?'

Bertie looked down at the floor. 'I can't remember, Mummy. But I . . . '

Irene interrupted him. 'That person at the door, Bertie, might be an unsolicited caller. We wouldn't want to encourage them, would we?' She paused, and then continued, 'Shall we see whether the person rings again? If she does that, then we'll know that it might be a genuine caller – possibly even Ranald What-Not.'

'Ranald Braveheart Macpherson,' Bertie reiterated, just as the doorbell sounded again.

'Well,' said Irene eventually, 'perhaps now we can go and investigate. And who knows . . . ' and here she raised her voice, as they had reached the door '. . . and who knows what manner of surprise awaits us?'

Bertie opened the door to reveal an irritable-looking Ishbel and a beaming Ranald. 'Hello, Ranald,' he said brightly. 'I told Mummy it was you, but she said we were to wait.'

The frown on Ishbel's forehead intensified. A weather forecaster, interpreting it as a meteorological map, might have used the words *thunder*, *gathering storms*, and *ice*.

'I hope we didn't disturb you,' said Ishbel.

'Not in the slightest,' said Irene. 'And here's young Ronald – how nice to see you!'

'Ranald,' muttered Bertie. 'Not Ronald, Mummy.'

'Of course,' said Irene. 'How silly of me. And Isabel, how are you?'

'Ishbel,' whispered Bertie.

Ishbel spoke through gritted teeth. 'Very well, thank you. Just catching my breath, though, after all these steps. I must say I admire you, living in a tenement – it must keep you all so fit! All these funny little stone steps every day. Up and down.'

Irene's eyes narrowed. 'Of course, you don't have that in suburbia, do you? I suppose that's quite comfortable, but I must say give me Georgian proportions any day, steps or not.'

Ishbel smiled sweetly. 'So, here's Ranald all eager for his play session with Bertie. Shall I come back in about two hours?'

'Perfect,' said Irene. 'Bertie has to go to his yoga round about then.'

'Yoga!' exclaimed Ishbel. 'All that stretching and posturing.'

'Positioning,' corrected Irene.

'Of course – positioning.'

Bertie decided to take control. 'Let's go inside, Ranald,' he said. 'I want to show you something in my room.'

'Good idea,' said Ranald Braveheart Macpherson.

The two boys went off, leaving the mothers facing one another for a moment. With an icy smile, Ishbel turned to leave.

'*A bientôt*,' said Irene.

Ishbel turned round. 'What?'

'*A bientôt* . . . French for *see you soon*.'

Ishbel muttered her way down the common stair. 'Common stair,' she whispered to herself, and felt a great deal better for the remark.

Once in his room, Bertie showed Ranald Braveheart Macpherson his contraband copy of Baden-Powell's *Scouting for Boys*. They examined diagrams relating to the positioning of tents and the making of a camp fire.

'I bet Mr Baden-Powell made really good fires,' said Ranald.

'Yes,' said Bertie. 'He never used matches, you know. He just rubbed sticks together over some tinder. Or he sometimes used a magnifying glass to focus the rays of the sun.'

'He was jolly clever,' said Ranald. He looked at Bertie. 'You know something, Bertie? My mummy hates your mummy. Does yours hate mine back, do you think?'

Bertie looked thoughtful. 'It's difficult to tell, Ranald. You know how grown-ups are – it's hard to work out what's going on in their minds.'

Ranald Braveheart Macpherson nodded. 'I asked her once why she hated her, and she just smiled and said that everybody did.'

'Everybody did what?' asked Bertie.

'Hates your mother,' said Ranald. 'I'm really sorry about that, Bertie. It can't be easy having a hate figure for a mother.'

'Let's not talk about it, Ranald,' said Bertie. He looked out of the window. 'You see, you can't change the mummy you get, can you? You have to accept her.'

Ranald looked at his friend with admiration. 'You're very good at that sort of thing, Bertie,' he said.

Bertie looked more cheerful. 'Thanks, Ranald. So, let's go to the Drummond Place Gardens and play Walter Scott.'

33. In Drummond Place Gardens

Given permission by Irene to go out to the Drummond Place Gardens, provided they did not wander off anywhere else, Bertie and Ranald Braveheart Macpherson made their way through the narrow garden gate into the world of luxuriant shrubs and towering trees that made up the handsome green retreat. Like most of Edinburgh's private gardens, this was a quiet, rather staid place, criss-crossed by walkways and dotted here and there with benches from which to contemplate the *rus in urbe*. A small sign saying *Authorised dogs only* dissuaded lesser dogs – or their owners perhaps – from intruding; another sign, saying *No ball games, shouting, or otherwise behaving improperly is permitted under any circumstances*, made it clear that these were gardens in which a certain standard of decorum was expected. Yet this was not enough to deter two small boys, away for the moment from the adult gaze, from starting an exuberant game of Rob Roy, in which they took it in turns to be Rob Roy, a hairy and frightening Highlander, whose main purpose in life was to chase after the other boy, who represented the settled, cattle-owning classes of Scotland. If Rob Roy caught his quarry, he had to be able to hold him for the count of ten, whereupon he gained one point. On reaching three points, that Rob Roy won the round and the whole thing started again – rather like Scottish history, in which some things seem to go on forever and indeed sometimes started all over again.

It was when the game was at a particularly crucial stage that Angus Lordie, exercising his dog, Cyril, turned a corner and was cannoned into by the two breathless boys, one wielding a stick designed to represent a claymore, and the other doing his best to evade capture.

'Whoa!' shouted Angus. 'My goodness, this is a frightening scene I stumble upon. Pirates? Corsairs pursuing an unfortunate Sicilian? The Zulus chasing Redcoats?'

The boys stopped, panting to regain their breath.

'I'm Rob Roy,' said Bertie. 'And Ranald is one of Montrose's men.'

'How very interesting,' said Angus.

'Walter Scott wrote all about it,' said Bertie. 'Have you heard of him, Mr Lordie?'

Angus smiled. 'I believe I have.'

Bertie knew about Walter Scott from a visit to Abbotsford, Scott's Borders home, that he had made with Ranald and his parents a few weeks before. Irene had been reluctant to let him go, being dismissive of Scott and his oeuvre, describing it as both romantic and reactionary. Stuart, however, had taken Bertie's side, and eventually he was allowed to go.

For the two boys, the trip had been one of unadulterated excitement, their imagination being fired by the towers and turrets of the great writer's home. And the interior was every bit as exciting as the exterior, with its displays of the historical relics that so fascinated Scott. The coats of arms of Borders families, displayed around the entrance hall, spoke to Scott's abiding interest in matters heraldic – and were gazed upon with fascination by Bertie and Ranald.

'Macphersons have got that stuff,' said Ranald proudly. 'Our clan has a cat and a glove as its crest. I don't suppose you've got one, Bertie?'

Bertie looked disappointed; he did not know whether he was so entitled, but Ranald's father came to his rescue. 'I'm sure the Pollocks have got their own family crest,' he said. 'And even if they don't, Bertie could make one up.'

'You could have a picture of a sword,' said Ranald. 'And perhaps a lion – because you're jolly brave, Bertie.'

'Thank you,' said Bertie. He was not sure that his mother would allow a sword, or indeed a lion for that matter. He rather feared if she had anything to do with it – and she would certainly want to be in charge – he would end up with heraldic devices rather different from those on display in Abbotsford. A yoga mat, for example, or a picture of Sigmund Freud or Carl Gustav Jung. It would not be a crest one could display with any pride.

After they had finished their tour of the house, Ranald's mother announced that she had packed a picnic in the back of the car and they would be able to have this in the woods to the west of the house.

'I saw a rather attractive spot,' she said. 'And you boys can do a bit of exploring afterwards.'

The picnic basket retrieved from the car, the Macphersons and Bertie made their way up a gently sloping brae towards a cluster of broad-leaf trees. Finding a suitable picnic place, they laid out a tartan picnic rug and on this placed their picnic hamper. Vacuum flasks of hot water were used for tea, while for the boys there was Irn Bru, the sickly orange national drink of Scotland's youth. This was a great treat for Bertie, to whom Irn Bru and all other sugary drinks were normally strictly forbidden. Ishbel knew this, of course, and for this reason said, 'Don't forget to tell your mummy about the Irn Bru, Bertie. I'm sure she'll be really interested.'

It was a delicious thought, and both Ishbel and her husband exchanged amused glances. 'That'll give her something to think about,' whispered Ishbel. 'She's such a food fascist.'

'I don't really approve of Irn Bru,' said Ranald's father. 'The next generation risks turning into a tribe of puddings. I fear that Irn Bru is not the best thing for them to be drinking.'

'Of course it isn't,' said Ishbel. 'I know that. But the point is to get right up her nose.'

Ranald's father understood how tempting that might be. 'Very satisfactory,' he said, savouring the thought. 'But what astonishes me is that Stuart puts up with it. Where's his backbone?'

'All worms eventually turn,' said Ishbel. 'Even the mildest ones.'

While this conversation was taking place, the boys had drifted off and were scrambling around in the undergrowth not far away. And it was from a clump of brambles that a cry came.

'Are you boys all right?' shouted Ranald's father.

Back came the reply, 'Yes, but ... but we've found something.'

Ranald's father rose to his feet. He would go and investigate because it crossed his mind that boys guddling about in the undergrowth could find anything, and it might be something unsavoury – possibly even a body. That, after all, was how Scandinavian noir dramas started: a body was found by a walker or a child, or even a dog. The innocent stumbled across the *corpus delicti* and gave a shout – just as Bertie now had.

34. A Significant Spurtle

It was Bertie who saw it first, sticking up out of the ground, half-hidden by a trailing sprig of bramble. Gingerly, avoiding the thorns, he pulled back the bramble, while Ranald Braveheart Macpherson peered at the half-exposed piece of blackened stump.

'What is it, Ranald?' asked Bertie. 'Do you think it's a bone?'

'Could be,' answered Ranald. 'Maybe it's an arm – or a bit of an arm.' He gestured to his forearm. 'This bit here, see. Maybe the fingers have come off.'

Bertie bent the bramble back upon itself so that they could both get an uninterrupted view. 'I think I should dig it out, Ranald,' he said. 'Then we can find the rest of the body.'

'What about germs?' asked Ranald. 'There could be tons of germs around here, Bertie.'

Bertie considered this. 'I think all the flesh has gone, Ranald,' he said. 'Once all the flesh drops off . . . '

'Or is eaten by worms,' interjected Ranald. 'Most of it gets eaten by worms, Bertie. That's what happens, you know.'

'I know,' said Bertie. 'But I think this is a really old arm,

Ranald. I think this goes way, way back and there'll be no germs or anything left.' He paused. 'But if you like, I'll start pulling it out, and if anything happens to me you can run and get help.'

'You're very brave, Bertie,' said Ranald. 'Tofu says that you're scared of things, but I don't think that's true.'

'Tofu's a well-known liar,' said Bertie.

'You can say that again,' said Ranald. 'His pants will catch fire one day, Bertie. All those lies he's told will catch up with him. And, boy, is God going to punish him when he eventually gets hold of him.'

Bertie had now moved forward and was crouching alongside the strange object. Reaching into his pocket for a handkerchief, he wrapped this around the top of the protrusion and gave it a gentle tug. The earth in which it was buried was dry and loose, and it did not take long for the thing to come free, bringing with it a small clump of attached soil. Bertie brushed this off with his free hand, while holding the top of the object with the handkerchief.

'I think it's wood,' he said. 'I don't think it's bone.' He brushed more soil away. 'No, Ranald, this is a bit of wood – it's not an arm, or anything like that.'

Ranald Braveheart Macpherson looked disappointed. 'It's a pity it's not a body,' he said. 'It would have been really exciting to have found a body, Bertie. We could have taken it to school to show people.'

Bertie did not reply. He did not think it likely that his mother would allow him to keep a body in the flat; there were so many restrictions in his life, and that was just one more of them.

‘It’s a piece of carved wood, Ranald,’ he said. ‘It’s a stick – maybe a baton. Look at this.’

Bertie pointed to a small round bobble at the top of the stick. As he polished it with his handkerchief, the shape became more recognisable. ‘That’s a thistle, Ranald. You see that bit there – that’s the smooth bit at the top of a thistle.’

Ranald had spotted something. ‘And down there, Bertie,’ he said. ‘There’s some writing.’

Bertie looked at the small carved letters pointed out by Ranald. Peering more closely, he read out M R.

‘Mr somebody?’ asked Ranald. ‘Could that be the name of somebody who owned this?’

Bertie looked doubtful. ‘If it was Mr there would another name.’ He examined the stick again. ‘But there isn’t.’

Ranald wondered whether it was a ceremonial wand of some sort. Bertie considered this and was about to answer when Ranald’s father appeared and asked them what they were doing. Proudly, the boys showed them their find. ‘We thought it was a bone,’ said Ranald to his father. ‘But it’s really a sort of . . . sort of . . . ’

‘That looks rather like a spurtle,’ said Ranald’s father. ‘You know what a spurtle is, don’t you?’

Bertie did. ‘It’s something you stir your porridge with, Mr Macpherson.’

‘Precisely, Bertie. And should we go and show that to somebody in the house? Just to see whether they can throw any light on it?’

The two boys followed Ranald’s father back into the house, Ishbel having tidied up the picnic things and taken them back to the car. In response to Ranald's father's request to speak to somebody about a find, one of the custodians said that James Holloway, Chairman of the Trust, was in the house and they could speak to him.

James arrived and examined the spurtle carefully. 'Where did you find it?' he asked.

Bertie explained, and James listened attentively. Then, addressing the two boys, he said, 'This is a very important find. These initials here – M R – stand for Maria Regina, and this, boys, could well be nothing less than the lost spurtle of Mary, Queen of Scots!'

Bertie drew in his breath. 'You mean . . . ?'

'Exactly that, Bertie,' said James. 'The place where you found it is the spot where Sir Walter Scott used to like to have picnics. He possessed Mary's spurtle, but it went missing. He must have used it on a picnic and then dropped it by mistake.

'The spurtle was not heard of after that,' continued James. 'But then, in 1975, there was an article about it by Professor Sandy Fenton, published in the *Scots Magazine*. That raised interest in the subject, but nobody knew of its whereabouts – until, quite possibly, now.'

Ranald's father was visibly pleased. 'This is quite wonderful,' he said. 'You boys have made a great discovery.'

'We shall, of course, evaluate it further,' said James solemnly. 'But in the meantime, a small reward is payable to both of you.'

James reached into his pocket and took out a one-pound coin for each of the boys.

'Thank you very much, Mr Holloway,' said Bertie, pocketing his reward.

Ranald echoed the thanks.

'Who would have thought it?' said Ranald's father. He glanced sideways at James, who smiled. Ranald's father understood. He knew that the world was a place of wonder and excitement for seven-year-old boys – as it was for the rest of us, if we are willing to open our hearts to things beyond the things we see – and if that sense of wonder could be enhanced and made to last just a little bit longer, then why not? The world was a vale of tears – who could doubt that? – but there were moments when the tears might momentarily be wiped away.

35. Mission Statement

While Bertie and Ranald Braveheart Macpherson were explaining the rules of Rob Roy to Angus Lordie in the Drummond Place Gardens, in their flat in 44 Scotland Street Irene and Stuart were discussing their plans. The campaign to which their strategy related was Stuart's application for promotion in the Scottish Government's Department of Statistics. When Stuart had first revealed to his wife that a senior vacancy had opened up and that he, along with two colleagues, was a candidate for the promotion, she had given him her support without hesitation.

Irene was not interested in the activities of the Scottish Civil Service, and had even less interest in statistics. What motivated her, though, was the higher salary that went with the post; the Pollock household may not have been on the breadline, but with only a single income coming in – Irene did not work – their budget was a tight one. The new position, Irene learned, had a salary that was twenty thousand pounds a year higher than Stuart's current point on the pay-scale, and that, in her view, clinched the matter: Stuart needed the job, and she would do whatever she could to help him get it.

Stuart had explained to Irene that there were two other applicants – both of them current colleagues of his in the department, and both, in their individual ways, insufferable. Irene had listened to his description of Elaine and Faith and his account of their shortcomings. She agreed that neither had particularly attractive personal qualities, and that Elaine's inability to do long division would be a serious drawback. But she felt that she had to tell Stuart that notwithstanding these drawbacks, the other two candidates had a major advantage.

'Whatever you may think of them as people,' she warned, 'don't forget that they have one formidable advantage.'

Stuart tried to imagine what this would be. Perhaps what people said about Faith was untrue; perhaps Elaine really could do long division if given enough time.

'Can't you see it?' asked Irene impatiently. 'It's very obvious, you know.'

'I'm sorry,' said Stuart. 'I can't. I'm trying to think positively about them, but, frankly, it's beyond me.'

Irene sighed. 'Really, Stuart, you're being a bit slow on the uptake, if you don't mind my saying so. It's chromosomal, I'm afraid.'

Now it dawned on Stuart what Irene's point was. 'You mean, they are at an advantage because they're women?'

Irene nodded. 'They are both women, and therefore entitled to the job. So you are battling against a major handicap right from the start.'

Stuart frowned. 'But surely the job will be allocated on merit?'

Irene smiled. 'Yes, it will be. Women candidates are more meritorious – it's as simple as that.'

'Why?'

Irene gave him a discouraging look. 'That's just the way it is, Stuart. It's to do with historical injustice. It's to do with hidden male networking. It's to do with the persistence of patriarchy. Take your pick, but in essence it means this: you are not as meritorious as they are because, well, because you're a man.'

'But that's outrageous,' said Stuart. 'Why should I be punished because I happen to be male?'

Irene made a dismissive gesture. 'That's just the way it is, Stuart. We can't reopen that issue all over again. Learn to live with it.'

Stuart bit his lip.

'So,' said Irene, 'let's get down to work. You said that you have to submit an essay in which you set out your stall, so to speak.'

'Yes,' said Stuart. 'It's to be my vision of what I think about the issues facing the department and what are the values I would try to assert if I were to be appointed.'

Irene listened carefully. 'I think I know what to write.'

Stuart stared at her. 'But I'm meant to write it. It's meant to be from me.'

'Oh, Stuart, that's the merest formality. You can have an input, but I know what these people are looking for. You must let me handle this.'

This last injunction was made in a voice that Irene used when she was giving a final and definitive ruling on some domestic matter, and Stuart knew that it was futile to argue. This was Irene speaking *ex cathedra* and with an authority only slightly eclipsed by the authority with which the Pope issues an encyclical on some matter of dogma.

Irene took the form from the folder in which she had filed the application papers. 'Here we are,' she said. 'You had better write it out in your handwriting, Stuart – I'll dictate.'

'I'm ready,' said Stuart.

'Very well,' said Irene. 'Now, note this down – I shall begin. "I believe that I (that is you, Stuart) am the right person to take forward the implementation of the department's goals on transparency, accessibility, inclusiveness, stakeholder involvement and consultation, and rectification of historical imbalances."'

Across the paper scratched Stuart's pen, committing Irene's prose to the official form before him.

'As a department, we must seek to implement in the most cost-effective and productive way the goals of ensuring that vertical job stratification should be conclusively and convincingly neutralised. For this reason, I would support a policy of non-shortlisting of male candidates for any future vacancies. I would further support and seek to implement a policy affording existing male employees the opportunity to leave prematurely, either to pursue alternative careers in the catering/service sector or to take early retirement.'

Irene paused. This was very good stuff, she thought, and it would tick the boxes that she knew would need to be ticked if Stuart were to succeed, in spite of the obvious handicaps of gender, against the weight of opposition against him.

'I think that might be enough,' she said.

Stuart looked doubtful. 'Shouldn't I say something about my educational background?'

Irene shook her head fiercely. 'Certainly not, Stuart – not when you have the background you have.'

'Middle class?'

Irene sniffed. 'Yes,' she said. 'That would be fatal. I suggest you say nothing about that – and nothing about the years you spent working for the PhD. The last thing you want to sound is elitist – and PhDs are elitist by their very nature.'

'But you're going off to Aberdeen to do one,' protested Stuart. 'What's the difference?'

Irene looked at him with ill-concealed pity. 'Oh Stuart, the fact that you need to ask that question in fact precludes my answering it. Only an elitist would ask that, I'm afraid.'

Stuart gritted his teeth. 'Don't they want applicants to be highly qualified?'

Irene looked at him with a cool directness. 'They don't want the typical, highly educated male. They don't want him to come in with all his baggage of assumptions. They don't want that, Stuart – they certainly don't.'

Stuart decided to concede. He had conceded throughout his marriage – right from the very beginning – and he saw no reason why he should try to change now. He was defeated. Irene was right – as always. He should trust in her in exactly the same way that a pilot trusted his instruments in fog. He should trust her absolutely and not try to do things himself. And in the background was the thought that this was not forever. Irene would be going to Aberdeen one day – oh, blessed, blessed day on which our freedom dawns at last.

36. She Wanted a Man So Desperately

Pat Macgregor looked out of the window of her Marchmont flat. By standing in one corner of the room and craning her neck, she had a view of the Meadows, of the trees that lined Jawbone Walk, and of the skyline of the old Royal Infirmary beyond that. Jawbone Walk was rich in associations for her, as in her student days, now a few years behind her, it had been along that path that she made her way into the university each morning – to Professor Thomson's lectures on French art that she so enjoyed, or to the tutorials on Scottish painters of the twentieth century, or to the cups of coffee with fellow students in the cafeteria of the University Library when everything – and nothing – would be talked about with the passion – and certainty – that comes so naturally at that stage in life. Now, of course, she was not so sure. The world and its issues seemed so clear-cut then because almost everyone about you, or at least your coevals, held the same views, and if only those in authority would stop being so mean and grudging and agree to the things that people were asking for, then everybody would be so much happier. Could they not see that? What perversity of spirit stopped them from acceding to such patently reasonable demands?

And then, almost imperceptibly at first, the realisation came that the world was not as simple as one imagined it to be, and that there were choices to be made, and that not everybody was benign. The truth then dawned that there simply was not enough for everybody to have what they wanted or needed; that everything was finite and that what one had taken for granted had actually been paid for by years of work by somebody whom one would never know, who might never have been able to enjoy any of it anyway.

Her university days had been carefree – her generous father had supported her through her course, not only paying her rent but giving her a monthly allowance as well. Other students had to sign up for student loans, large sums that hung about their necks on graduation like albatrosses – the bill for four years of privilege; Pat did not have that, and felt guilty about it. Then, on top of everything, Dr Macgregor had bought her rented flat when the landlord put it on the market, cashing in savings to pay the exorbitant purchase price. Now she lived rent-free, courtesy of her father's kindness, and used the rent paid to her by her two flatmates to cover living expenses. Topped up by the part-time salary Matthew paid her for her work at the gallery, she had enough to live on reasonably comfortably.

She realised, though, that this was not how her life would be forever. In particular, she was beginning to feel vaguely irritated at having to share the flat with two other young women. Her flatmates, Bernice and Andrea, were tidy enough in their habits, and, in objective terms, no trouble at all. They paid their share of joint expenses without demur, they never left washing-up in the sink, they scrupulously avoided eating food Pat left in the fridge. That last matter was the cause of so many rows in shared flats – cheese wars that raged for months over who had encroached on whose lump of cheddar. There had been none of that, thank heavens, and yet, and yet . . .

The problem with Bernice, Pat felt, was a certain lack of . . . And here Pat faltered. What exactly was it that Bernice lacked? Was it engagement? Or intellectual curiosity? Whatever it was, it had begun to annoy Pat, who marvelled that anybody could be as passive as Bernice was, in the face of things that really should have produced some sort of reaction.

Bernice had a boyfriend called Terry. He was an IT man with a finance company, a slightly flabby young man whose nose Pat had never liked. She knew it was wrong to judge a person by his nose, but in this case that is what she did. Terry's nose said everything that needed to be said about his character. It was a dull, directionless nose. It was not the sort of nose, she thought, that could ever point anywhere specific – it would wander about like a weather vane in shifting winds. It was a pointless, dispiriting nose.

When Terry visited Bernice, which he did on most evenings, the two of them would sit in front of the television and watch endless pre-recorded programmes about home improvements. There would be no conversation, although Terry would occasionally make a comment about somebody's choice of kitchen units or paint.

'Can't stand that colour,' he would say. Or, 'I wouldn't choose green, would you, Bernie?'

And Bernice would say, 'No, not green, Terry.'

And then there would be silence until, some time later, Terry would remark again on some point of décor and say, 'They'll regret that, you know.'

Pat could not stop herself from speculating about Bernice and Terry's love life, and once or twice these thoughts came to her unbidden while the two of them were sitting watching their home improvement programmes. Unfortunately, the thought made her want to laugh, and there was an embarrassing moment – for Pat at least – when Bernice turned round and said, 'What's so funny, Pat?'

Andrea was quite different. While Bernice was overweight and rather bovine in her manner, she was petite, and showed a lively interest in the world about her. What annoyed Pat about her, though, was the large social chip she carried on her shoulder. Andrea came from a large Catholic family in Airdrie, and she clearly resented what she saw as Pat's privileged Edinburgh background.

'It's all very well for you,' she once said, 'but you don't really know what it's like.'

'Excuse me,' said Pat. 'I don't know what what is like?'

'Real life,' said Andrea.

'Why?'

Andrea smiled condescendingly. 'You live in Edinburgh. You went to that stuck-up school – no offence, but you did. You don't know what it's like to live in Airdrie.'

Pat defended herself. 'But what's wrong with Airdrie?'

'There you are,' said Andrea. 'You don't know.'

The argument stopped there, but it left Pat angry. Nobody likes to be condescended to, and to be condescended to by Andrea, who had, after all, chosen to leave Airdrie and come to live in Edinburgh, was more than Pat could bear. She decided that she had had enough of this; she simply did not want to share any longer. And that meant that she must get rid of these flatmates and replace them with a man. She wanted a man. She wanted to come home to one person – one male person – and sit together and watch programmes that were not about home improvement. She wanted a man so desperately. I want a man, she thought. I really want a man.

And that man was Bruce, for quite against her better judgment, she was falling for Bruce, again, and she knew that this was a disaster, even if she yearned for him terribly. She was aghast at what she was being drawn into by some weak, irrational part of her; yet she could not stop herself. That sort of attraction, anarchic in its effect, seemed irresistible, overcoming all intellectual reservations, all scruples.

And here she was, standing by the window, waiting for him, because he had said that he would come and see her to discuss his project. Every minute weighed heavy upon her; every minute increased her desire.

37. *A Visit from Bruce*

When the doorbell rang, Pat stayed where she was at the window, counting backwards with painfully slow deliberation. It was something she had done since childhood, using the countdown to prolong the pleasure of anticipation of some treat. Counting down from fifty to one, and then to the zero of fulfilment, increased the pleasure of the reward; but now she did it so as not to appear too eager. She wanted to rush to the door, but would not – for all her eagerness to see Bruce, it would be better to give the impression that there were other things to do before admitting him to the flat.

Now she stood on her side of the door, took a deep breath, brushed hair from her forehead, and then reached for the handle.

'Br . . . ' She stopped herself just before the vowel would have given everything away.

‘I almost gave up,’ said Dr Macgregor. ‘You took so long to answer.’

‘Daddy . . . ’

‘Aren’t you going to invite me in?’

She stepped aside, trying to hide her confusion. ‘Of course.’

He entered the small hall that formed the heart of the flat. ‘I was walking past,’ he said, putting his hat down on a chair on top of a half-opened bill. ‘I thought I might pop in for a quick cup of coffee – if you had the time.’

She looked at her watch. ‘I was planning to go out.’ She did not like lying to her father, and her voice sounded strained.

‘I won’t stay long,’ he said. ‘Ten minutes or so. I wanted to talk to you about your grandmother’s pictures. I’ve been thinking we should do something about them.’

She invited him into the kitchen, where he sat down in the chair that he always chose when he visited her. As with most of the furniture in the flat, it had come from the family house in the Grange, this one from his study. When he had given it to her, he told her that he had thought some of his best thoughts in that chair, and perhaps she would carry on thinking them for him.

She filled the electric kettle with water. ‘Granny’s pictures?’

‘Yes, the ones in the attic. Remember, I showed them to you? Five or six of them. All gathering dust.’

She nodded. ‘Yes. You said that you couldn’t find a place for them on the wall.’

‘Exactly. Unless I put them in that spare bedroom at the back – the one we never use.’

'You could do that.' She glanced surreptitiously at her watch. Her father was the last person she wanted to have in the flat when Bruce called. His dislike of Bruce was intense and she knew that he would be dismayed if he knew that she was seeing him again. She loved her father deeply, and would never wish to hurt him, but her feelings for Bruce were ... well, they were not her fault. That was it: they were not something she had chosen; they were like a bad cold or flu – they had simply happened. You don't choose to have flu, and you don't choose to fall for Bruce Anderson, or a man like him.

Her father watched as she ladled coffee into the cafetière.

'I don't want to tuck them away where they'll never be seen,' he said. 'Your grandmother was very fond of them. She knew him, you see. She knew Adam Bruce Thomson, the man who painted them. I think that some of them were birthday presents from the artist.'

'I see.'

He fiddled with a place-mat on the table before him. There was a small yellow stain of congealed egg yolk on the mat, and Dr Macgregor picked at it idly. That was Bernice, thought Pat; she had been making an omelette for Terry and she had spilled some of the mixture. Terry loved cheese omelettes, which had put Pat off them now.

Dr Macgregor abandoned the place-mat and looked across the room at Pat. 'I've decided that it's wrong to keep things like that in the attic. If you have something that other people might like, I think you have a duty to let them enjoy it.' He paused. 'What do you think, Pat?'

She had been thinking of what she would say if Bruce arrived while her father was still here. Could she express surprise, or would that be insulting to her father, who would see through the pretence? Or should she say to him, right now, Bruce is coming to see me. He has a scheme … She could tell him about Bruce's scheme, but that would probably just make matters worse, as he would worry about her involvement in anything to do with him; after all, he had once said to her, 'That young man is toxic to you, darling – toxic.'

She struggled to answer his question. 'What do I think about … about keeping things in the attic?'

'Yes.'

'I suppose it could be selfish. Yes, I suppose you're right about that. We shouldn't sit on things that other people might enjoy.'

He nodded. 'That's my general view. But then, I've been trying to square that with the whole notion of private property. If you carry that sort of approach to its logical conclusion, then you would end up believing in a fairly radical redistribution of just about everything. I wouldn't be allowed to live in my house in the Grange, for example, because there's just one of me and it could accommodate six people.' The example was as extreme as it was personal; but that, he thought, was where tyranny lay: a tyranny that would not allow people to live in their own houses.

Pat shrugged. 'It's a question of degree, isn't it? Really large discrepancies in what people have are wrong, but there'll always be some. I don't think you need to worry – not yourself. And Granny's paintings, well, you could probably put those in an auction if you were feeling really guilty about them – which I don't think you need to. It's not as if you were a terrifically rich fat cat, Daddy, you're just . . . '

The bell rang.

'Are you expecting somebody?' asked Dr Macgregor.

Pat stood quite still. A way out had occurred to her. She could simply not answer. Bruce would ring again, no doubt, but after a while he would assume that she had forgotten he was coming and had gone out, or he might think he had got the time wrong.

Her father was looking at her. 'Aren't you going to answer?'

She made her decision, and she shook her head. 'Mormons,' she said. 'They came yesterday at about this time and I put them off. I said I couldn't talk to them and they could come back some other time. That's who it'll be – and I just can't face them right now. I can't face saying no to those clean young guys and seeing them look disappointed and trudge off downstairs again. I just can't.'

Dr Macgregor smiled. 'They do tend to be very well-scrubbed, don't they?'

The bell rang again.

'Do Mormons ring twice?' he asked.

'Always,' said Pat. 'It's part of their training.'

There was silence for a moment, followed by a brief hammering on the door.

'Do the Mormons do that?'

Pat's gaze was fixed on the ceiling. 'They can be persistent,' she said.

38. An Invitation to an Encounter

In his studio, a short walk from Scotland Street, Angus Lordie settled behind his easel, his palette on a table beside him, the paint upon it small extrusions of freshly squeezed colour. The smell of stand oil and turpentine hung in the air – a smell as suggestive as that which pervades a bakery or a coffee shop. If smells are redolent of place, then this one transported Angus back to those echoing studios at the Edinburgh College of Art where, as a student, he struggled with the frustration of not being able – yet – to achieve on canvas the effects he yearned for. It had all been so exciting in those days; the world lay before him with all its possibilities. He would use his art college postgraduate scholarship to go to Paris, perhaps to Rome; his work would be fêted, dealers would lay siege to his studio; there would be glamorous women to accompany him to openings, hanging on his every word, basking in his reflected glory.

He smiled at the thought. Every young man must think the same – must believe that something significant will happen to him, before slowly it dawns on him that life, after all, is going to be a routine, undistinguished affair. Not that Angus worried about that any more. He still entertained thoughts of painting the really great picture – the work that would be described as his masterpiece – but this painting steadfastly failed to materialise, and now, in moments of honesty, he knew it never would. If he was to make a statement about the world, then it would not be in the form of a painting, but in a few lines of the poetry that he wrote when the spirit moved him. People told him that his poems made them think – and few people said that about his paintings. Of course, portraits were not really expected to challenge; a portrait was intended to capture something rather than create it.

His mahlstick with its leather-covered tip, an accoutrement as reassuring to a portrait-painter as a baton is to a conductor – or a field marshal – lay on the floor beside him, as yet unremarked upon by the man seated in the chair before him. Sitters were usually curious about the stick and its uses; Angus would demonstrate, although he used it to steady himself only relatively infrequently as he rarely experienced the muscular strain that could come from hours of holding a paintbrush.

He was seated directly in front of the canvas, but in such a position as to make it possible for him to see the sitter without craning his neck. The look of the portrait-painter is a very particular one; he gazes rather than glances – it is an unashamed assessment, a scrutiny, much like the stare of a doctor examining a patient for diagnostic clues.

Angus had discovered that the portraitist's gaze could be disconcerting; a few reacted by looking tense, others adopted a fixed expression – a mask of rectitude that betrayed the existence of guilty secrets. Still others, it seemed, coped by pretending that they were somewhere else altogether.

Then there was the issue of conversation. Angus preferred not to talk too much, as the face of one involved in conversation was too volatile for portraiture. He wondered why few – if any – portraits show people in the act of talking, and had concluded that a portrait that showed the sitter speaking would be oddly unsettling – the viewer would be excluded from the other side of the conversation. This would kill the intimacy of the encounter between viewer and subject; none of us feels comfortable in the company of one whose attention is directed elsewhere.

'A portrait should invite you into an encounter with the subject,' pronounced his tutor at art college. 'Let me repeat that, Mr Lordie, because it may be the best piece of advice you'll ever be given: a portrait is an invitation to an audience.'

But now, with the canvas ready for his attentions, he looked at the man before him, and noticed the small scar on the side of his face. The sitter, a middle-aged man with thick, wavy hair, suddenly fingered his cheek. It was as if he had noticed the attention, and for a moment Angus felt embarrassed.

'It happened a long time ago,' said the man. 'When I was a student.'

Angus dipped his brush into a small circle of paint on the palette. 'You were at Heidelberg? A duelling scar?'

The man laughed. 'Heavens, no. Nothing dramatic, I'm afraid – a bicycle accident in Orkney, when I was a student – more than thirty years ago.'

Angus painted a tentative line on the canvas. 'Strange,' he said. 'I was there as a student too – also about thirty years ago.'

'I was working on an archaeological dig – as a volunteer,' the man said. 'We were digging up a broch. I was staying in Stromness and I used to ride up from there to the dig. Coming back to Stromness – you know, on one of those summer evenings when it never really gets dark – I hit something in the road. It was a rock, I think; it had probably toppled off one of those stone dykes and then rolled down a bank. Not a big rock – something the size of a tennis ball, I think. Anyway, I went flying off the bike and ended up in a barbed wire fence.'

Angus made a sympathetic noise. 'Very painful.'

'Oddly enough, it didn't bother me too much. They took me into Kirkwall and stitched me up. It left my distinguished-looking scar, though.'

'Of course.'

'Which you mustn't ignore.' He paused. 'You don't do improvements, I take it?'

Angus laughed. 'If asked. I'm happy enough to remove double chins. There's a lot you can do with shadows.'

'Not necessary. I'm not vain – or at least, I hope I'm not.' A pause. 'Does anybody actually ask for a portrait for himself – I mean, does anybody actually commission a picture for his own glorification?'

'You'd be surprised,' said Angus.

The sitter reflected on this. Then he said, 'What is it about Orkney?'

Angus hesitated. 'The rain?' he said. 'The wind? The absence of trees?'

'Fishermen with ploughs?'

Angus drew his brush across the canvas; an almost

transparent line of light brown paint. 'The Italian Chapel,' he said suddenly, and remembered, so vividly, so powerfully, that he had to lower his brush.

39. Send Him Hame, Send Him Hame

He had gone there all those years ago with his friend from the hotel, a student from St Andrews, whom he had met on the ferry across from Scrabster. They had discovered they were both destined to spend the summer months working together and with the ease of youth had immediately become friends. For Angus, the job at the anglers' hotel was just something that would help keep the wolf from the door; for David it was a chance to do the thing he liked above all else: catch trout. Even as a ghillie, a paid assistant of the anglers who made the pilgrimage to the lochs of Orkney, the thrill of the pursuit of trout was reward enough.

'You sound as if you know what you're doing,' said Angus, as they sat on the deck of the ferry as it made the short crossing to Stromness. It was a calm day, and the Pentland Firth, so often the wildest stretch of water in the north of Scotland, was touched with the gold of the afternoon sun.

‘Oh, not really,’ said David. ‘I suppose I know a bit, but you could spend your whole life learning about fly-fishing.’ He paused to smile. ‘And you? What’s the thing you love above all else?’

Angus shrugged. ‘I like art, I suppose. I want to be able to paint like … Well, there are a whole lot of painters I’d love to be able to paint like. John Duncan Fergusson’s one. Have you heard of him?’

David looked thoughtful. ‘He’s the one who painted those angular women?’

‘You could say that. And other things, too. And Bonnard. I’d love to be able to paint like Bonnard. Do you know his work?’

David replied that he had difficulty remembering who was who. He was not sure about Bonnard.

‘He did interiors,’ said Angus. ‘He liked painting women in the bath, or sitting reading – things like that.’

‘I envy you,’ said David. ‘I envy you doing the thing you really love doing.’

Angus looked at his new friend. ‘Aren’t you?’

David explained that he was studying history. ‘I like it – to an extent,’ he said. ‘It has its moments.’

‘Only to an extent?’

‘It depends. There’s a lot that I find boring. I don’t really enjoy the European stuff. The Holy Roman Empire. The endless wars. I like Scottish history.’

Angus said that he thought Scottish history was a bloody enough affair. ‘I thought our past was a long story of plots and betrayals and scraps with the English.’

David laughed. ‘I suppose our dealings with them were a bit fraught.’

'Well, they kept invading us, didn't they? There was that small matter with Edward . . . '

'Yes,' said David. 'But then we so enjoyed stealing their cattle.'

'And so it goes,' said Angus. 'But we do like to see ourselves as the victims of the English, don't we? We always have. David and Goliath – and we were always David.'

'Perhaps we were. Stronger powers have always tended to lean on their weaker neighbours. They cast an eye on what they've got. In one view, that's the key to all history – a fight over territory: a struggle for dominance.'

Stromness was in sight, and the conversation had ended there. But that evening, in the hotel, they were able to meet in the bar after they had been given their instructions for the next day.

'I'm going to be hopeless with flies,' said Angus.

'Concentrate on the rowing,' advised David. 'The client will know what flies to use – and if he doesn't, recommend the Butcher. You can't go wrong with a Butcher.'

The hotel bar was busy, and a group of folk singers was expected. They arrived late, but to a rousing cheer from the locals who were drinking in the bar. David bought Angus a pint of Guinness; he blew the froth across the top of his glass. The folk singers struck up as somebody in the bar called out, 'Callum, you're the man! You're the man!'

'*My Love's in Germany*,' announced Callum.

'Germany!' somebody shouted.

The musicians started. My love's in Germany, send him hame, send him hame . . .

Angus listened to the words. This is very sad, he thought.

My love's in Germany, fighting brave for royalty,
He may ne'er his Jeanie see;
He's as brave as brave can be,
Send him hame, send him hame . . .

They finished, the last chord followed by silence. Then there was applause, and shouts of appreciation. David looked at Angus. 'It makes some want to cry, that song,' he said. 'It's about . . . Well, what do you think it's about?'

'About being separated from somebody you love?'

'Yes.'

Angus looked down at his glass. Had it ever happened to him? Had he ever been separated from somebody he loved? No.

'Or not being able to speak about how you feel,' said David.

Angus was not sure what to say. He was nineteen; what time was there to be separated when you were still nineteen? Separation, he thought, would come much later.

'Where does that come from?' asked Angus.

'Here,' said David.

'Here?'

'Yes, the music was written by an Orcadian. He was called Thomas Traill. And the words are from a poem written way back. Seventeen-something, I think.'

Angus was impressed. 'How do you know about that?'

'I just do. I listen to songs. I learn the words. I know who wrote them.' He paused. 'Sometimes I feel that the people who wrote these songs – you know, the people way back . . . I feel that they're talking to me. Personally. I feel I know them, although . . . '

Angus raised an eyebrow. 'Although . . . '

'Although it was a long time ago. I still feel that.'

Angus took a sip of his Guinness. The singers had moved on. 'Love is Teasing'. The words were clearly articulated; they were full of longing.

I wish, I wish, I wish in vain,
I wish I was a young lad again,
But a young lad I will never be,
Till apples grow on an orange tree;
For love is teasing, and love is pleasing;
Love is a pleasure when first it's new . . .

He looked at David. There was a smile playing about the other young man's lips. 'Do you wish you could stop the clock?'

Angus asked him what he meant.

'I mean, keep the feeling of a particular moment alive. Right now, for example. Wouldn't you like to keep hold of this moment? Us sitting here in Orkney, with these people singing these particular songs? Scotland . . . the whole works. Keep it as it is?'

Angus did not reply.

'Because I would,' said David. 'I like where we are, if you see what I mean. I find that just as I get used to something, the future comes and takes it away. So when you're happy being nineteen – that's us – somebody says: *But you're going to be thirty, one of these days, oh yes you will, and then forty.*'

Angus leaned forward. Without knowing why, he put his hand on David's forearm. David looked down, and

Angus withdrew his hand. You did not do that, even in a bar in Orkney, with songs being sung about being away in Germany and friendship, and talk about being nineteen, and loss, and the still evening and the light, the light, reminding you where you were.

40. At the Italian Chapel

Two weeks later the manager of the anglers' hotel gave them both a day off. There was a break in the hotel's bookings, with one set of guests leaving the day before another large party arrived.

'You boys have been doing a good job,' he said. 'Go fishing.'

They both laughed. Even David had had enough.

They caught the post bus to the other end of the island and got off at St Mary's, a small village on the edge of Scapa Flow. 'Now?' said Angus.

David pointed. 'Over there. You can just see it. That low white building.'

'Everything's low here,' said Angus. 'The houses look as if they want to burrow back into the land.'

'The wind!'

'And no trees!'

'The wind!'

They walked slowly along the road that led to an island causeway. On the other side, barely a few hundred yards away, was the island of Lamb Holm, and on it the small building David had pointed out.

'See those barriers?' said David. 'The Churchill Barriers. They built them to keep U-boats out during the war. They managed to sneak in at the beginning and get our ships. The Italians built them – Italian prisoners.'

Angus looked up at the sea. The wind had risen again, and there were waves against one side of the barrier. 'Aren't you glad,' he asked, 'that you weren't around then?'

'Why?'

'Oh, everything,' said Angus. 'Having to join the Navy, for example. Having to be in a ship on that . . . ' He gestured towards the sea. 'Knowing that there was somebody out to sink you, to kill you.'

'And nobody wants to kill us now?'

Angus shook his head. 'Not immediately. They're not actually hunting us down.'

'I suppose you're right,' said David. 'I imagine they didn't think about it too much. You did your duty. You just did it, like everybody else.' He paused. 'How brave would you have been?'

Angus smiled. 'Not at all. I expect I would have been scared stiff.'

'I don't think so,' said David.

'I do.'

They walked the rest of the way in silence – each alone with his thoughts. Angus thought of the sea, and of its colour, a blue that shaded into emerald in the shallows. And then there was the land itself, with its intense Orcadian green and the greys of the stone dykes, stretching across the fields in the gentle curve of the hillsides. And black rock at the edge of the sea; angular black rock. There would be a palette for this place, he thought, that would be different from the palette he used for other parts of Scotland.

Once on Lamb Holm they had only a short distance to walk to reach their destination.

'The Italian Chapel,' said David.

Angus looked at the building before them. It had been built around a curved tin Nissen hut of the sort used in older military camps. The façade, which was only slightly higher than the low-slung hut, would not have been out of place in an Apennine village: a white church front, pillars to each side of the front door, with a small arched recess for a bell. It was very small.

Angus felt awed. 'They built this while they were prisoners? Here . . . in the middle of nowhere?'

David smiled. 'Yes. The prison camp was over there.' He pointed to the field behind the chapel. 'That was full of these huts. They're all gone now. This is all that's left.'

They went inside. The arched roof had been painted with trompe-l'oeil brickwork and stone arches. Behind a screen of elaborate metalwork, an altar had been set against the back wall of the hut; a mural showing the Madonna and Child, along with saints and angels as envisaged by the Italian imagination, formed the backing of the altar.

David went forward to the screen. He crossed himself. Angus caught his breath. It had not occurred to him.

'You're Catholic?'

David nodded. 'Yes. Should I have told you?'

'Not at all.'

David moved forward. 'Look at these lovely paintings.'

Angus winced. It was typical Mediterranean religious art; over-stated, sentimental, naïve.

David noticed. 'You don't like the subject? Does it offend your Presbyterian soul?'

Angus tried to make light of it. 'Some people like this sort of thing.'

David looked serious. 'But these men were so far from home. They were just trying to create something that would remind them of their past – trying to make something beautiful.'

Angus reassured him. 'Oh, I can see that. And, look, I understand what this means.' He paused. 'Do you want me to leave you here for a few minutes?'

David looked amused. 'So that I can pray?'

'If that's what you want.'

David shook his head. 'I haven't been to Mass for over a year. I stopped when I was eighteen – when I left school.'

'I see. So you no longer believe?'

'Not in all this,' said David. He pointed to the saints. 'Yet for me it's still the thing I don't believe in, if you see what I mean. It's where I'm from, I suppose.' He stared at the mural behind the altar. 'I think this place is all about forgiveness.'

Angus frowned. 'Why do you say that?'

David did not answer. 'We should be getting back,' he said. 'We're going to have to hitch back to Kirkwall.' And then he said something that Angus did not at first understand, but came to do so years later. 'The Church doesn't really want me, you know.'

They left, and fifteen minutes later were in the back of a chicken farmer's van, heading for Kirkwall. When they arrived back at the anglers' hotel, they walked down the staff corridor to the rooms they occupied at the back of the building. David stopped. 'Thanks for today, dear friend.'

Dear friend. 'That's all right. I enjoyed myself too.'

'It's going to rain tomorrow.'

Angus made a gesture of acceptance. 'It always does.'

The next day, heavy squalls moved across the loch, whipping the water into white-topped wavelets. A recently arrived angler, impatient to begin fishing, persuaded David to take him out in one of the boats; no trout would take a fly in that wind, but he was determined. In the middle of the loch, a gust of wind tipped the boat and David and his charge fell in. They might have drowned, but David was a strong swimmer and dragged the fisherman to the shore.

He was blamed, and dismissed by the manager. 'I cannot have you risking the lives of our guests,' he was told.

Angus said goodbye to him in the car park behind the hotel. David was on the point of tears, ashamed and embarrassed. Angus put his arms around him. 'Dear friend,' he said.

And now, with this mention of Orkney, so many years later, he thought of all this: of the trip to the Italian Chapel; of forgiveness; of friendship; of the future that takes the present away from us.

41. Irene Prepares Stuart

'Now, just keep calm, Stuart. Keep calm.'

Irene Pollock was addressing her husband, Stuart, in much the same voice she used when telling Bertie what to do. Boys and men were much the same general proposition, she thought: they needed firmness, they needed to be told what to do, and how to do it; they needed to be watched.

'Of course I'll keep calm,' said Stuart. 'I always do.'

'No, you don't, Stuart; you just don't. You have a tendency to speak too quickly when under stress. You're not quite as bad as Glaswegians in that respect, but you do speed up and that's not the way to get your message across.'

Stuart said nothing. He had Glaswegian grandparents and he did not like the way Irene spoke about Glasgow. One could get oneself headbutted for less, if one spoke that way in Glasgow itself. Not that Glasgow really went in for headbutting, of course: the 'Glasgow kiss' was a canard put about by people who did not really understand the city and its warm and affectionate ways. But one could never be too cautious.

'So,' continued Irene, 'when you go into the interview take a deep breath and try to smile a bit – but not too much. Remember: you're there on sufferance, Stuart. You're a man – you're there on sufferance. Then, once the conversation gets going, make sure you get your points across. I've told you what they should be. Transparency. Sensitivity to the needs of stakeholders. Compliance with broader social policy goals.' She paused. 'And most importantly, Stuart, gender-neutral toilets. Make sure you mention those.'

'Yes, I've got all that,' said Stuart somewhat wearily. 'And what about statistics? This is, after all, a senior statistician's post.'

'That's not the issue,' said Irene dismissively.

'Not the issue? But the job is about statistics. Surely my track record . . .'

Irene made an impatient sign. 'No, Stuart, you're just not getting it. You're still thinking in a linear, male way. This job is about how the civil service is responding to needs. In a very real sense it is about toilets. It is not about statistics; it is never just about statistics or whatever. Never. There's a sociopolitical context, Stuart.'

'I see. So should I say nothing about my experience? Should I say nothing about those papers I published?'

Irene sighed. 'We'll take that point by point, Stuart. Firstly, your experience: experience tells us one thing – you have used your inherent advantages to claim contested territory. You have occupied a post that has given you experience that others have not been able to have.'

'But if somebody else had occupied it, then I'd have been denied the experience myself.'

Irene was not impressed. 'Yes, but remember you got where you got through inherent advantage. You didn't deserve it.'

Stuart drew in his breath. 'Really? Didn't deserve to be where I was? How about all my hard work, making up figures for the Scottish Government? How about the first class honours degree? How about the couple of years of postgraduate work? How about those papers I wrote?'

Irene had an answer to this. 'Those were all things that came to you in the context of your privileged position.' She paused; she was clearly getting irritated. 'Really, Stuart, I'm surprised that you can't seem to grasp that things have changed. You seem to believe in some sort of . . . some sort of . . . ' She waved a hand airily. ' . . . in some sort of meritocracy.'

'Yes, I do,' said Stuart.

'Well, you're completely out of date. Belief in meritocracy is naïve.'

'So the best qualified person shouldn't get the job?' He paused. 'Or get to go to the toilet?'

Irene glared at him. 'Not funny, Stuart. Not in the least funny.' She sighed. 'How many times do I have to explain it? Really, Stuart, it's like talking to somebody of Bertie's age. Qualification is a shifting concept. The least well-qualified person in terms of diplomas and degrees and whatever might be the best-qualified in terms of social goals – in terms of how an appointment may progress the objective of a fairer society.'

Stuart gritted his teeth. He hated arguing with Irene . . . but, but . . . It was a shocking moment of realisation. Irene was an unrepentant social engineer. She was post-factual. She was a . . . He searched for the metaphor, and then he found it. She was an archetypical named person! He closed his eyes. Well, it would soon be over. She would be off to Aberdeen where she could talk to her heart's content to Dr Fairbairn, who was her lover, after all, about Kleinian theory and such matters.

He heard her saying something else. He had stopped listening, but her words gradually began to impinge on his consciousness.

'. . . so that's your only hope, you know. Embrace change. Try to persuade them that you subscribe to their objectives even if – as I fear is the case – you don't understand them or support them. Accept the new agenda. Show them that you are ashamed of what you are and that you would much rather be something else.'

He did not reply – what was there to say? And anyway, it was time for him to leave the house if he were not to be late for the Board. So he said goodbye, cursorily, and made his way out into Scotland Street. In an hour's time he would be waiting outside the room where the Board was due to sit, and yet it was not too late to pull out. He could still withdraw his candidacy, and that would mean that he would be saved the indignity of failure. Yet somehow he could not bring himself to do that. There was an awful fascination about what he was about to do; it was like going to the dentist for root-canal treatment without the benefit of anaesthetic; it was like standing in the dock in court and awaiting sentence; it was like an interview with the bank manager when you had knowingly exceeded your overdraft. It was like all of that, and were there a bell, it would be tolling for him, loudly, incessantly, and ominously. And then he thought: Scotland is becoming a tiny bit like North

Korea – just a tiny bit, of course, no more than a smidgen, but enough to notice. Or was he imagining it? Was it just because he was married to Irene that he felt that way?

He suddenly imagined he was in the King's Theatre, at a performance of Barrie's *Peter Pan*, and Tinkerbell's light was fading. He stepped forward and said, 'Clap your hands if you believe in freedom.' From every corner of the theatre there arose a great sound of clapping, and it lasted for a long time, and it rose to the height of the theatre and beyond, and it came from the heart.

42. Male Networking

Stuart's interview was scheduled for ten o'clock. When he arrived at nine-thirty, Faith was in the waiting room.

'I decided to come early,' said Faith. 'Elaine's been in five minutes already.'

'It's always best to be early,' said Stuart, lowering himself into one of the government-issue chairs.

'Oh yes,' said Faith. 'The early bird catches the worm et cetera et cetera.'

Stuart had long been aware of Faith's annoying habit of adding several etceteras to any observation. In his state of anxiety, and with the awareness that nothing he could do now would affect the outcome of the selection procedure, he added his own et cetera out of sheer recklessness. 'I suppose they're going to ask us our view on various things et cetera,' he said.

Faith did not appear to notice the obvious mimicry. 'Yes, they can ask anything at all. Except for things that are not allowed, of course, such as where you went to university and so on. Things that used to carry ridiculous weight.'

'Yes,' said Stuart, and then added, 'McGill in your case, I believe.'

Faith looked at him sideways, unable to decide whether he was being sarcastic or not. 'Anyway,' she said. 'One of the reasons I came early was so that she'd be able to tell me what questions they asked. She can tell me while you're inside for your interview.'

Stuart narrowed his eyes. 'But that's not fair,' he said. 'You'll have an advantage. I won't be able to ask her what to expect.'

Faith thought for a moment. 'Well, you've had other advantages. All we want is a level playing field.'

Stuart mentally counted to ten before he responded. 'All right,' he said. 'Tell me what those advantages are. Just tell me.'

'Male networking, for one.'

Stuart stared at her. 'What networking?' he asked. 'And how? How do I network?'

Faith smiled. 'How do I know?'

'But you've just accused me of something; you've just accused me of networking. Tell me how I network. When? Where? How? With whom? Tell me.'

'You can't expect me to know the details,' said Faith. 'Secret societies probably. I imagine that you belong to a couple of secret societies – most men in Edinburgh do.'

'Name them,' said Stuart.

'How can you expect me to name them?' answered Faith. 'They're secret, aren't they? A secret society that lets people know its name would be a pretty weak secret society.'

'So how do you know they exist?' pressed Stuart.

'Oh, they exist all right,' Faith said. 'They exist to help men get an advantage over women.' She paused. 'Do you have lunch with your friends?'

Stuart shrugged. 'Yes, sometimes.'

'Well, there you are. That's networking. Men who have lunch with one another network. That's how they do it.'

'So, men can't have lunch with one another. Can women have lunch?'

'Of course they can.'

'But men can't?'

'That's different. Women don't network when they have lunch et cetera et cetera.'

Stuart looked incredulous. 'I see.' But then he thought: Yes, it's true men have excluded women from so much in the past; they have been massively unjust. And if women were doing the same things now that men used to do – and still do in many cases – then he had no grounds to be indignant. Men could hardly complain after such a long history of discrimination.

He looked down at the ground. He realised that what he was now feeling – this sense of being excluded, this sense of being treated unfairly – was exactly what women had been obliged to put up with for years. And it was painful, just as it had been painful for them.

They sat in silence for the next twenty minutes. Then the door opened and Elaine emerged. She was smiling, and she winked conspiratorially at Faith. She did not look at Stuart.

Stuart was called in. There was the Board, all three of them, seated on the other side of a large square table, facing the candidate's seat. In the chair was the Supreme Head of Personnel herself, flanked on one side by the Deputy Supreme Head of Personnel, and on the other by a thin woman with grey hair who was introduced as the external assessor. After Stuart was seated, the Supreme Head of Personnel said, 'Well, Mr Pollock, you're applying for this very senior post – may I ask you: what makes you think you're the right person for this job?'

Stuart felt his heart beating hard within him. 'If you want an honest answer, then it's this: I think I'm the best person for this post because the other two candidates are, well, not very impressive.'

The Supreme Head of Personnel drew in her breath sharply. 'Really, Mr Pollock, it's not for you to judge other applicants. That's quite out of line.'

'Is it?' said Stuart. 'Well, is it out of line to point out that one of the other applicants can't do long division? Or that the other is a classic operator? Yes? Is that out of line? I suspect it is. But I don't really care, you see, because I know that you've already decided whom you're going to appoint.' He paused. 'No, don't look so outraged. You have. And I have absolutely no chance at all of appointment because this isn't about merit any more. We've given up on merit and it's all a question of who you are or where you're from. Just like the old days! Isn't that amazing – we spent a long time trying to overcome that sort of thing – appointing people on the basis of where they came from – and now, hey presto, we're back doing exactly that. But with a different set of beneficiaries this time.'

The Supreme Head of Personnel seemed to be struggling for breath. 'You do yourself no favours,' she said at last.

'No, I don't suppose I do,' said Stuart. 'But you know what? I don't care in the slightest. I'm withdrawing from this farce. I'm no longer an applicant.'

The Board sat quite mute. They had lost the ability to appreciate truth, so concerned were they with appearance and the insubstantial.

'So,' said Stuart, rising to his feet. 'I don't need to waste any more of your time. Oh, and by the way, that essay I wrote . . . '

'Actually, we thought it very impressive,' said the Supreme Head of Personnel.

'You would,' said Stuart. 'Because it's utterly meretricious, from start to finish. It embodies every meaningless cliché of our times. It employs every cheap shibboleth by which people like you identify one another. And finally, my wife wrote it.'

He left the room. Outside, Faith and Elaine were in a huddle. They looked up, surprised to see Stuart emerge so quickly.

'That's me out of the running,' said Stuart. And then to Elaine, as if as an afterthought, he said, 'Elaine, can you tell me what 2456 divided by 145 is? I don't need the answer right now, but I'd love to know sometime.'

They stared at him. He left.

43. A Road to Freedom

That day, Stuart left the office at lunchtime. Working flexi-hours, as he did, he was well in credit for that week and could take the afternoon off if he wished. A meeting had been pencilled in for three that afternoon, but since that involved only two others, one of whom was the insufferable Elaine, Stuart felt he could ask for it to be transferred to the following day.

'That's a pity,' said Elaine, when he called her to put her off. 'I was looking forward to going over this morning's ordeal with you.'

Stuart grimaced. It would not have been an ordeal for her, nor indeed for Faith; rather, it would have been what people called a shoo-in for both of them.

'I withdrew my candidacy,' he said tersely.

There was a shocked silence at the other end of the line. 'You? You withdrew?'

'That's what I said. I thought it best. There are good reasons why one should not take that particular job.'

Again there was a silence – this time one of unease. 'Why do you say that, Stuart?'

Stuart took a deep breath. 'Something of a poisoned chalice,' he said quietly. 'But I can't talk about it freely over the phone.'

Now Elaine sounded alarmed. 'What do you mean by that?'

'I mean that I don't fancy being in that seat when ... Look, I really can't talk about it.'

Elaine was quiet for a few moments before continuing, 'By the way, what did you mean when you said something about division? When you left the waiting room this morning, you said something about division and ... '

'Oh, that was nothing,' said Stuart. 'Just a little joke.'

'Well, I didn't think it was terribly funny. You know that we're not meant to make jokes in the office. Jokes can be offensive.'

Stuart felt his anger rise up within him. 'Oh,' he said, 'I'd forgotten. We have to be humourless.'

'I didn't say that. You really twist people's words, you know, Stuart.'

'Well, anyway, I have to go now. Congratulations on getting the job.' He knew that the results would not be known officially for ten days, but he was confident enough of his prediction.

Elaine gasped. 'How did you know that? I was told that nobody would be informed until ... ' She stopped herself. But it was too late, Stuart's suspicions had been confirmed.

'I hear that they told you this morning. On the spot.'

'You're not meant to know that.'

Stuart smiled to himself. It was so predictable. 'Well, I do, but don't worry, I won't tell anybody. I'll let them keep up the façade of open competition.' He looked up at the ceiling, trying to imagine Elaine's expression as she took his call. Smugness would have changed to disquiet and then returned to smugness once more.

He rang off and walked across the floor of his office to the window overlooking the harbour. The thought occurred to him that he could go to sea. People did that in the past – they gave it all up and went to sea. But he could not do that; there was Bertie and little Ulysses and years of wage slavery ahead of him. Wage slavery . . . it was not an expression he would have used of his own position, but now that he came to think of it, it was not all that inappropriate. Everyone – or just about everyone – was a wage slave, in a sense. They went to the office, put in the hours, often working with people they did not like (Elaine and Faith), sometimes with people who could not even do long division (Elaine) or who kept going on about Dunfermline and what people in Dunfermline thought about this, that or the next thing (Faith) or who were fanatical about some issue (that man in the post room who listened in on his portable radio set to ground-to-air transmissions from Edinburgh Airport Control Tower), or who were sycophantic to those in authority over them (Faith, principally, but Elaine too when the opportunity arose).

He watched as a small boat nosed its way out to sea. Boats were a metaphor for freedom. Setting sail meant more than simply slipping away from the quayside; it meant putting the constraints of *terra firma* behind you; it meant turning your back on the security of the land for the uncertainties and risks of the sea. The sea was water ... there's an insight, thought Stuart ... and those who went upon it put themselves, composed largely of water, at the mercy of that medium that would dissolve us all. And the sea did that, as sailors in the past used to recognise; if they went overboard they would simply compose themselves and wait for an end that was ordained to be.

Existential freedom ... As a young man he had flirted briefly with philosophy, and had read, in a directionless and untutored way, various paperback books he had found in an Oxfam shop. He had stumbled across a book on the philosophy of Jean-Paul Sartre and had been taken by the whiff of freedom that emanated from its pages. Authenticity, it seemed, was everything: you had to make choices about your life, you had to live in the fullest way, to be authentic. That was real freedom, the author suggested, and M. Sartre, sitting in his Left Bank café with ... what was her name again? Simone de Beauvoir ... that was echt authenticity. They were no wage slaves, Jean-Paul and Simone; they did not have to clock in to their café at nine in the morning and stay there, being appropriately authentic, until five o'clock.

He moved away from the window. I shall never be authentic, he said to himself, as long as I work in this place, with these people, doing the sort of thing they want me to do. I'm fed up with inventing inauthentic figures; I'm fed up pretending that things are better than they are and expecting the public to believe it all. I've finished with that now. No longer. No more.

He went downstairs to the floor on which the office of the Supreme Head of Personnel was located. He went to her assistant's door and knocked.

'Do you have an appointment to see me?' asked the assistant.

Stuart laughed. 'To see you? Are you seriously suggesting that people need to make an appointment to see you to make an appointment to see her?'

'Yes,' said the assistant. 'I am.'

'In that case,' said Stuart. 'Please note down this message – to yourself, to pass on, in due course, to her. Pollock, S, Department of Creative Statistics: resignation, with immediate effect, coupled with a request to be allowed not to work one month's notice, as per contract, and to take the notice period as accumulated leave in lieu.' He paused. 'Did you get that?'

'Yes,' said the assistant. 'I did.'

'Good,' said Stuart, and he left by the door that, although unmarked, was in his mind labelled Freedom; the door we all long to find, and sometimes never locate, but sometimes do.

44. Stuart Has Lunch

Leaving the office, Stuart was light-headed, almost to the point of feeling intoxicated. The full enormity of what he had done was yet to come home to him, but he knew that his life had changed – and changed irrevocably. Handing in his resignation to the Supreme Head of Personnel had been a simple enough affair: a few minutes with her assistant, the dictation of a resignation note in the language that bureaucrats so loved, and then . . . into the street – not metaphorically, he thought wryly.

There was no reason for them not to accept his resignation. Firstly, there was no particular shortage of people like him. Statisticians were two a penny, or, to put it in their terms, 2.165 a penny . . . He smiled at the joke, relieved that having done such a thing, he was still able to see the humour in anything. Secondly – and this was perhaps the more important consideration – the Supreme Head of Personnel would be delighted to accept the resignation after his performance at the promotion board. He had not minced his words there, and had said things that he – and, he suspected, a lot of other people – had been wanting to say for quite a time. He had long itched to say that he simply did not believe in the utterances that so many organisations made their employees chant: the mission statements, the virtue signalling, the gobbledygook. Why should everybody believe the same thing, sign up to the same ideology? Why should people have to say 'We are here to promote excellence', as they so often had to declare, when what they were doing was a straightforward job of administration? He had dared to say that this was all pious nonsense, and in so doing he had challenged the ideology. They would never accept that and they would be pleased to see the back of him.

He decided to go and treat himself to a long lunch at The Shore, a restaurant on a quay known as The Shore. That, he thought, was honesty: to call yourself The Shore when your address was The Shore. That was the sort of unpretentious, down to earth integrity that was so lacking elsewhere. He wondered whether restaurants had mission statements, and, if they did, what they would be. Feeding people would be a good one, or Serving dinner might also be suitable. There was a mission statement for everybody, if one thought about it. Fixing teeth would do for a dental surgery, and Cleaning clothes might be highly appropriate for a dry-cleaning business. This policy of honesty could be taken even further: a bank might say Looking after your money, but making quite a lot for ourselves in the process. One would applaud a bank that said that, and might even place one's hard-earned money in their hands. An airline might say Flying you from place to place, but charging for your luggage, sandwiches on the plane, and so on. Or they might proclaim, We land and we take off, which had a certain direct charm to it. There were so many possibilities, if only people would get beyond the trite protestations of conformity.

He realised, of course, that he should be giving some thought to things other than mission statements and the confounding of bureaucrats. Usually a resignation was accompanied by the contemplation of all the implications it involved. There were all sorts of schemes whereby the leaving of a secure job may be made more palatable – deals offering six months' salary, or part-time re-engagement, or even early retirement on full pension. Stuart had gone into none of these, and had simply resigned with immediate effect. What would this do to his pension? He had a reasonable number of pensionable years' service: he assumed that whatever benefits had accrued under his pension scheme would sit there until he reached whatever age statisticians retired at. That, of course, was receding into the distant future as the pensionable age continued to be raised. The Greeks had been so fortunate: for years they had allowed many state employees to retire at forty-five on pensions that were close to their final salary. Then the Germans had heard of that, and had disapproved, and spoiled the Greeks' fun. Here, of course, sixty-five had long been the age of retirement, but was rapidly becoming seventy, and beyond. Soon there would be eighty-year-old functionaries and retirement would be limited in many cases to a few years at the most.

Stuart was far too young to worry too much about these matters, but Irene might. She might ask awkward questions about his frozen pension. She might even enquire how he proposed to meet household expenses when there was no salary coming in. That was, admittedly, a pertinent question, but he would find some other source of income. There was so much he could do . . .

But what? As he made his way to The Shore, he thought of the possibilities. He could retrain. He could acquire some sort of trade that was in demand; he did not need to be shackled to a desk for the rest of his working life. He could become a plumber or a joiner. He had always been interested in working with his hands, and now he could do it. He could become a taxi driver, or a commissionaire in the Caledonian Hotel, or a roofer. There were all sorts of honest jobs that he could do once he had fallen out of the white-collar sector into the blue-collar world – if, indeed, it was a fall. It could be seen as a sideways move, or even an ascension.

The restaurant had just started serving lunch, and Stuart was quickly given a table. He looked about him with a satisfied, contented air. He was a free man, sitting down to his lunch at an excellent restaurant. He was a man whose wife was going off to Aberdeen to live with her lover. He was a man who had a flat in a friendly street and had just paid off his mortgage. He was a man who had no job but who would probably be able to find one in a few weeks or a few months. He was a man who had two wonderful small boys who loved him as much as he loved them, and who was twice fortunate because he had a helpful and understanding mother who had expressed her readiness to move in and look after the boys once their mother went off to Aberdeen. There were so many respects in which he was blessed, and he thought of these as he ordered his lunch: hand-dived scallops, a nice piece of grilled haddock, a pint of chilled Guinness, and a piece of strawberry tart.

45. The Slush Pile

At the very time that Stuart was waiting outside that fateful promotion board door, Matthew was crossing Dundas Street to open up his gallery. It was already nine forty-five, the later opening hour being an inevitable concomitant of his having moved out of town to Nine Mile Burn. Matthew had explored the various ways of getting into work and had opted for what he described as the semi-green option. This involved a car journey into Fairmilehead, where he could park well beyond the limits of the controlled parking zone. Then he would wait to catch a bus that would take him all the way into the city centre, dropping him off a mere five minutes from Dundas Street. The entire journey took forty-five minutes, which meant that he had to leave the house at nine if he were to open the gallery before ten.

During the summer, the journey was easy; he had yet to spend a winter in the new house and he was not sure that it would be so pleasant waiting for a bus in the dark, particularly on days when there was rain or sleet. Anticipating this, though, he had reached an agreement with Pat that in the winter months she would come in early on three days a week, while he would do two. Her journey in to work, even in winter, involved not much more than a meander across the Meadows, a stroll down the Mound, and a brief walk thereafter across the ridge of George Street down to Dundas Street.

That morning Pat was due to come in to the gallery, but only later on. She had an appointment with the dental hygienist, she said, and would not be able to be in until half past ten, by which time Matthew would be enjoying his morning cup of coffee at Big Lou's. So it was that when she arrived she found Matthew's usual notice on the door; she let herself in, took down this notice and substituted one saying *Open*. Then she tackled the mail, putting bills to one side, catalogues to another, and dealing with the enquiries from prospective artists seeking representation or an exhibition.

These letters were placed in a folder Matthew described as the slush pile. It was a term used by publishers for unsolicited manuscripts sent in by prospective authors, and Matthew had been told about it by a publisher friend.

'We get the most extraordinary things,' he said. 'The slush pile is never boring.'

'Such as?' asked Matthew.

'Oh, endless memoirs. *Two Years in the French Foreign Legion*, for example. You'd be astonished to discover how many people have spent two years in the Legion – and then written about it.'

Matthew tried to remember whether he had met anybody

who had served in the Foreign Legion. He decided he had not, but then it depended to a great extent, he thought, on the circles one moved in. Presumably there were circles for those who gravitated towards service in the Foreign Legion – people who had something to forget, apparently. Of course, the Legion itself must be aware that many of those who signed up would in due course write their memoirs; perhaps they had a class, as part of basic training, in which memoir-writing was taught to new recruits. Along with instruction in weapons drill, camouflage, and hand-to-hand combat, there would be a weekly lecture on some aspect of biographical writing, or on the merits of obtaining a good literary agent, or on some finer points of copy-editing or grammar.

'And what else?' he asked. 'You presumably don't just get memoirs of the Legion?'

His friend shook his head. 'No, we do get other manuscripts. There's a regular stream of accounts of the life of Bonnie Prince Charlie. They're very common – I get about five a year. They all claim to have new insights, but it's frankly rather difficult to identify what these insights are.' He paused. 'The authors of those particular books all tend to have a certain look in their eye. It's difficult to describe it, but it's there all right.'

Then, he said, there was fiction. 'These manuscripts are usually by people who are quite good at doing other things, but who feel for some reason that they have to write a novel. In fact it's rare these days to find somebody who hasn't written a novel, at least in Edinburgh.' He paused, and smiled at a recollection. 'You know, I went to a dinner party in Great

King Street once where everybody, including the host and hostess, had written an unpublished novel. In fact, it was at that dinner party that I first heard – as an opening gambit – the question: "What novels are your children writing?" This is a variant on the question as to whether children play football or tennis, or are learning how to drive.

'Of course, the vast majority of these novels are unpublishable – some very much so. Then many of them are what used to be called obscene and now are called, simply, adult. We received one of these recently that was all about a man who was kidnapped by a shipload of nuns – and these nuns were – how shall I put it? – very friendly. The author suggested it might be of interest to a Catholic readership, but I think he meant it might appeal to those of catholic tastes. That's a different department, you know.'

'Do you have to read them all?' asked Matthew.

'That depends,' said his friend. 'There are some firms that simply throw them out with the waste paper. I think that's discourteous. Then there are others who ask for them in electronic format, so they can delete them at the push of a button. We take the view that you have to be careful: there are so many cases where publishers have rejected a manuscript only to discover, a short time later, that it has been published to great acclaim – and with great success – by somebody else. A famous Glasgow firm once turned down Enid Blyton. Fredrick Forsyth's *The Day of the Jackal* was rejected, as was *The Spy Who Came in from the Cold*. I could go on.'

Matthew laughed. 'Please do. Hearing about the mistakes of others gives one such a warm feeling.'

'All right,' said his friend. 'Golding's *Lord of the Flies* was rejected twenty-one times and no less a person than T. S. Eliot turned down George Orwell's *Animal Farm* on the grounds that it was not convincing. He'd obviously never met a speaking pig.'

'So, you look at everything in the slush pile?' asked Matthew.

His friend looked embarrassed. 'We don't always actually do what we say we should do,' he said. 'We're only human.'

46. Distressed Oatmeal

Pat handed Matthew the slush pile after he had hung up his lightweight summer scarf. She did not like that scarf, but of course had never expressed her views openly. Clothes were personal in a very special sense: you might compliment another's clothes, but you should never criticise them.

All she could say about his scarf, then, was this: 'That's an interesting colour – what do you call it?' She knew about his distressed-oatmeal sweater, and about his mitigated-beige trousers, but the colour of this scarf, she thought, was something altogether different.

Matthew glanced at his scarf, now hanging on a peg near the office door. 'Understated-brown,' he replied. 'At least that's what they said it was.' He paused. 'Do you like it?'

Pat mustered her thoughts. There were many ways of avoiding questions. 'It suits you,' she said.

Matthew smiled. 'Do you mean I'm understated?'

She made light of this. 'You? No, not at all, Matthew. You're . . . you're just right.'

He thanked her, as he could tell that she meant it. Pat was kind to him; their relationship was an easy one – the relationship of people who may have been more than that to one another in the past, but who were now just old friends.

'You're not so bad yourself,' he said.

She returned his smile. 'What a nice way to start the morning. A compliment or two before work . . . How nice.'

'We don't pay enough compliments,' observed Matthew. 'We should tell people more often that we like them, or that they're doing a good job, or that they look great. It doesn't cost very much, and yet we don't seem to like doing it that often.'

'Some people never do it,' said Pat. 'They can't bring themselves to say something complimentary to anybody else – they just can't. It sticks in their throat.'

Matthew knew what she was talking about. It was something to do with envy, he thought – that most powerful emotion that is there in most of us – to an extent – but that could dominate the entire world view of some.

'Envy,' he said. 'That's what stops us.' He paused to remember his most envious friend, one whose face fell if anybody told him of some piece of good fortune. He found that sad – to go through life resenting what others achieved, or had, because one had not been successful oneself. What a waste of energy it was to sit there and fume, and what a loss. It was so easy to share the joy of another, and thereby experience, at no cost to oneself, some of the pleasure that the other felt. So, if you met a friend who had been invited to a party that you would dearly love to be invited to yourself, then rather than being consumed by envy, you might bask in the pleasure of just knowing that the party in question was taking place and that your friend would be there.

'Two letters,' said Pat, pointing to the file. 'One from a final-year student at the art college offering to interview us – for him to interview us – with a view to our representing him.'

'Oh dear!' said Matthew. But then he thought: what if this young man were the next David Hockney? And so he said, 'I'll look at his work. Are there any photographs?'

'He's attached a set of photos of a series of paintings he's called *The Triumphs of Mother*. He says something about the pictures. They all feature his mother in a number of heroic situations – climbing K2, crossing the finishing line of the New York marathon, meeting the Pope.'

Matthew saw that Pat was grinning. 'Ah!' he said. 'Nothing matters as long as he admires his mother, as the psychiatrist said to Oedipus.'

'And there's a letter from an installation artist from Glasgow.'

'Rubbish bin,' said Matthew.

They moved on to a discussion of the forthcoming visit of a client who was considering the purchase of a work by Edward Atkinson Hornel, *Kirkcudbright Harbour at Low*

Tide. Matthew did not like the painting, but would do his best. 'It would have been so much better if he had put a few Japanese girls in it,' he confessed to Pat. 'Hornel was terrifically good at painting Japanese girls – and flowers. But I suppose neither of those occurs naturally in Kirkcudbright Harbour, even at high tide.'

Pat laughed. 'Don't say that to the client,' she muttered.

Matthew looked towards the door. A customer was about to enter . . . or was it . . . He stood stock still, hardly breathing, chilled within. Mrs Patterson Cowie, his former English teacher, and the victim of that dreadful incident in the bookshop, was poised to enter the front door. She it was whom he had knocked over in his flight from that intolerable and embarrassing situation. And now, just as he was beginning to forget the uncomfortable information that the police were looking for him in connection with that, here she was – the one person in Edinburgh he did not want to see: she would identify him, and he would be arrested.

Pat realised that something was wrong. 'Are you all right?' she asked.

Matthew found himself whispering. 'That woman at the door. I don't want to see her.'

Pat glanced towards the door. 'Why not?'

'I just don't,' said Matthew. 'She was my English teacher.'

Pat looked at him in astonishment. 'And you haven't done your homework? Is that it?'

'Don't joke,' hissed Matthew. 'I'm going to hide.'

And with that, just as Mrs Patterson Cowie opened the door, Matthew ducked under the well of his desk. The space there was large enough – just – to conceal him – although if Mrs Patterson Cowie got too close to the desk, she would be sure to see him.

Pat, struggling with her astonishment, stood up to greet their customer.

'Do you mind if I take a look round?' asked Mrs Patterson Cowie.

'Please do,' said Pat. 'And let me know if I can do anything.'

Mrs Patterson Cowie approached a painting and peered at it closely. 'Venice,' she said.

'Yes,' said Pat, glancing down at what she could see of Matthew. 'Venice. Yes.'

Mrs Patterson Cowie now moved closer to the desk.

'That's a rather interesting painting over there,' said Pat, pointing to a watercolour on the other side of the gallery. 'That's a William Gillies. May I show it to you?'

'Thank you,' said Mrs Patterson Cowie. 'I rather like Gillies. I always have.'

Relieved at being able to steer her away from the desk, Pat led Mrs Patterson Cowie over to the Gillies. 'Lovely, isn't it?'

'Yes,' said Mrs Patterson Cowie. 'It certainly is. That's Temple, isn't it? I love that part of ... what is it, East Lothian or Midlothian? I'm never sure where boundaries lie.'

'Midlothian,' said Pat quickly. 'Or maybe East Lothian. Who knows?'

Mrs Patterson Cowie smiled. 'Well, somebody will know, don't you think?'

From the other side of the room, there came an unexpected sound – a knocking of something against wood. Matthew must have shifted, thought Pat, and bumped a leg against the desk: cramp, perhaps.

Mrs Patterson Cowie heard the noise, too, and turned her head.

47. *Dental Flossing*

Pat had to think quickly, and she did. Looking at her watch, she gave a gasp. 'Oh, my goodness! The time! Would you look at the time!'

Mrs Patterson Cowie glanced at her own watch. 'Well, it's only twenty past ten.' As she spoke, she turned her head to look back in the direction of the desk under which Matthew was hiding. 'Is there something . . . ' she began.

Pat interrupted her. 'Twenty past ten! Oh, heavens, we're going to have to close. Immediately. Right now.'

Mrs Patterson Cowie looked puzzled. 'But you've only just opened. Why on earth do you have to close?'

Pat looked at her reproachfully. 'Operational reasons, of course,' she said, as if this should have been only too apparent.

'And what does that mean?'

'Stocktaking,' said Pat, sounding as firm as possible. 'We have to close for stocktaking.'

Mrs Patterson Cowie looked even more puzzled. 'Stocktaking? Most of your stock, I would have thought, is on the walls. Why do you need to close if . . . '

Again, Pat cut her short. 'Look, I'm terribly sorry,' she said. 'But I'm going to have to ask you to leave. And I can't really discuss management issues with you – it really isn't any of your business.'

It was against Pat's nature to be rude, but she felt that the only way of getting Mrs Patterson Cowie out of the gallery was to give offence; with any luck she would take the hint and storm out.

'No need to be so snippy,' said Mrs Patterson Cowie.

'I'm sorry,' said Pat. 'But you really must go.'

'Well, really,' complained Mrs Patterson Cowie. 'I don't know what I've done to deserve this rudeness. I assure you, I shan't linger.'

'Good,' said Pat, and moved towards the door to let her out.

When Mrs Patterson Cowie had left, Pat made her way over to the desk and peered under it. 'You can come out now, Matthew,' she said. 'Hide and seek finished. Playtime over.'

These comments were delivered with maximum sarcasm, even scorn, but this was lost on Matthew, who only seemed interested in confirming the departure of Mrs Patterson Cowie.

'Yes, she's definitely gone,' said Pat. 'I told her that we were about to close for stocktaking. I was horribly rude to her – and I feel wretched about it.'

'Good,' said Matthew, rubbing at his leg to relieve the cramp that had set in while he was under the desk. 'That was quick thinking, Pat. I owe you.'

'What you owe me is an explanation,' said Pat. 'What a ridiculous performance. The least you can do now is to explain what that was all about.'

Matthew sighed. 'It's very complicated, you know. But I suppose you're right – I suppose I do need to tell you about it.'

'You certainly do,' said Pat. 'She heard you, you know. She heard you bump against the desk. I think she knew there was someone there.'

'You could have told her it was a poltergeist,' said Matthew, grinning. 'You could have said that we're plagued with poltergeists in the New Town and that she had better get out before chairs started whizzing through the air.'

Pat made a dismissive gesture. 'Come on,' she said. 'Tell me.'

Matthew seemed reluctant. 'I tell you what,' he said at last. 'Why don't we go back to Big Lou's? I know I've just come from there, but I only had one cup of coffee and I can have another. We can close up here for half an hour and I'll tell you over a cup of coffee.'

Pat agreed, and as they left the gallery to cross Dundas Street, she asked Matthew again to explain his behaviour.

'I'll tell you in Big Lou's,' he said. 'Just wait.' He paused, and then asked, 'How did you get on at the dental hygienist's?'

'All right,' said Pat. 'She said I had healthy gums.'

'Good,' said Matthew. 'Do you floss after every meal?'

Pat said that she thought that was excessive. 'Once a day is quite enough,' she said. 'I floss in the night before I go to bed. And I use one of those water-pick thingies.'

Matthew shook his head. 'You should floss after every meal. Think of all that stuff in between your teeth being there all day.'

'How do you know I've got stuff between my teeth?'

'You will have,' said Matthew. 'If you eat.'

'There's nothing wrong with my gums,' said Pat stubbornly. 'And what about you? What about your gums?' She sensed her advantage, and pressed home her attack. 'How often do you go to the dental hygienist?' They had reached the other side of the road. Matthew looked away, as if keen to avoid the question.

'Come on,' said Pat. 'Do you even go at all? And I bet you don't floss. Men are useless at flossing.'

Matthew blushed; she could see that, and it gave her the answer.

'You should go to the hygienist, Matthew,' she said, trying to avoid sounding prim, but failing. Nobody, she thought, can tell another person to go to the dental hygienist without sounding prim.

Matthew defended himself. 'Why should I go if I clean my teeth thoroughly?'

'Because nobody,' said Pat, 'can get plaque off by themselves. They need a dental hygienist with a pick. She has to pick it out – you know, to get that white stuff that she wipes off on a tissue on her work tray.'

'White stuff?'

'Yes, little white lumps of plaque – like tiny hard rocks. The hygienist picks them out with her little pick.'

Matthew shivered. 'I don't know if I've got any of that,' he said. 'I'm sure I don't.'

'Then let me look,' said Pat. 'Let me look at your teeth, Matthew. I can tell, you know. I know what to look for between people's teeth.'

Matthew increased the distance between them. 'I have no desire to show you my teeth in the middle of Dundas Street.'

'Because you're in denial, Matthew. You're in denial about dental plaque.' She looked at him pityingly.

'I'm not,' he said.

'Then show me.'

He turned to her suddenly and bared his teeth. 'There,' he said. 'Satisfied?'

'Disgusting,' she said, giving an exaggerated shudder. 'The gaps between your teeth are full of stuff, Matthew. If you went to the dental hygienist she'd need a pneumatic drill. A digger even.'

'You're a dental snob,' snorted Matthew. 'You judge people by their teeth.'

'So?' she challenged. 'Teeth tell you a lot.'

Matthew laughed. 'I can't believe we're having this conversation.'

They had reached the steps down to Big Lou's, and Pat led the way, descending carefully, because these were the steps down which one of Scotland's greatest poets – perhaps her greatest poet since Burns – had stumbled. And they were the steps down which Lard O'Connor, the emerging

Glasgow businessman, had fallen on that fateful visit he had paid to Edinburgh. These steps required caution.

48. You Ran Away

Big Lou welcomed them warmly. 'Return custom,' she said, smiling. 'Matthew had a cappuccino about half an hour ago, Pat. He's addicted, I suppose.'

'Addicted to your company, Lou,' said Matthew quickly.

'Oh, haud your wheesht!' Big Lou retorted. 'I'm not susceptible to flattery, Matthew. You should know that.'

'And as for addiction,' Matthew continued, 'my caffeine intake is very small – compared with some.' He looked at Pat, who loved having a cup of coffee on her desk at all times.

'Most of the time I drink decaf,' said Pat defensively.

Matthew shook his head. 'Except it isn't. A lot of these so-called decaffeinated coffees have quite a bit of caffeine left in them. They have to be treated with the Swiss water process, and then re-treated, if you want all the caffeine removed. With most decaffeinated coffee you end up getting quite a hefty shot of caffeine whether you like it or not.'

'I don't care if I'm addicted,' said Pat. 'I like coffee.'

'And you're entitled to like it,' said Big Lou. 'Dinnae listen to him, hen.'

Big Lou set about preparing their coffees. While she was busying herself with this, Pat and Matthew made their way towards a table at the back of the room; there was nobody else in the café, but if somebody did arrive, they would still be able to avoid being overheard.

'So,' said Pat, as she sat down, 'tell me why I had to go through that ridiculous business with that poor woman. What's her name, by the way?'

'She's called Mrs Patterson Cowie,' said Matthew. 'She used to be a teacher at Watson's – she's retired now, as far as I know.'

'And you didn't like her?'

Matthew shook his head. 'No, quite the opposite. I always rather liked her. She was a great teacher. She made us learn screeds of poetry by heart. I can still remember quite a bit of it. Lars Porsena of Clusium, By the nine gods he swore, that the great house of Tarquin should suffer wrong no more … Do you know that one?' It's all about Horatio and how he defended the bridge over the Tiber. Or Wee sleekit, cow'rin, tim'rous beastie … She liked Burns. And a guy called Cecil Day Lewis who wrote a poem called "Flight to Australia" about two men who flew to Australia in a useless old plane, but somehow got there. I can remember most of that – except the bit where they actually reached Australia.' He paused. 'And then there was D. H. Lawrence and his poem about the snake – you know the one where he throws something at the snake and feels that he's done something petty. And

Iain Crichton Smith and Norman MacCaig and Robert Frost . . . '

'Yes, yes,' said Pat. 'But why did you want to hide from her? What had you done?'

'Not done,' said Matthew forcefully. 'I didn't do it, Pat. Or, if I did, I didn't mean to do it. It was an accident.'

'What was an accident?' asked Pat.

'I was in a shop,' said Matthew. 'And I stumbled – sort of – and knocked Mrs Patterson Cowie down. I didn't mean to, but there was a big fuss and . . . and I ran away.'

Pat's expression showed her astonishment. 'You ran away? Why on earth did you do that?'

Matthew did not answer, but looked down at the floor. Then, after a few moments he looked up and told Pat, 'You heard about the incident.'

'Me? About you knocking over . . . ' She trailed off. Now she realised what he was talking about.

'So you were the perv in that shop,' she muttered. 'It was you.'

'I'm not a perv,' said Matthew, looking down at the floor again.

'But you were trying to steal that *Fifty Shades* book. That's a pretty pervy thing to do, isn't it?'

Matthew began to raise his voice. 'I wasn't trying to steal it,' he protested. 'I had picked it up out of . . . out of curiosity, and then I saw Mrs Patterson Cowie and I didn't want her to see me reading it, so I slipped it into my trousers.'

'Now that's pervy,' said Pat, but corrected herself quickly. 'I'm sorry, Matthew, I know you're not a perv.'

'Thank you.'

'But you're in a serious mess, aren't you? My friend said the police were looking for you because they think you're dangerous. And all it would need would be for Mrs Patterson Cowie to see your face and identify you – which she would.'

'I know,' said Matthew, miserably. 'The police will never believe me.'

Pat agreed. 'Probably not. They'll probably think you're a perv.' She paused. 'Sorry, Matthew, I didn't mean that.'

But Matthew was still miserable. 'I don't know what to do,' he said. 'I really don't.'

'I'll think,' said Pat. 'There must be something – if you're innocent.'

'Which I am,' said Matthew. 'I really am. You know me, Pat – I'd never go around knocking people over.'

'Of course you wouldn't,' said Pat. She now felt sorry for Matthew, and she reached out to pat his hand gently. And at that moment, the door of Big Lou's opened and Mrs Patterson Cowie came in.

Matthew had his back to her, but Pat was in full view. As Mrs Patterson Cowie came in, she saw Pat and immediately recognised her from the gallery. She turned away, to place an order with Big Lou.

'She's just come in,' whispered Pat. 'Mrs Patterson Cow.'

'Cowie,' corrected Matthew. 'You mean, in here?' He did not want to turn round, but had he done so, he would have seen Mrs Patterson Cowie, having ordered coffee, walk purposively across the room towards them.

'Excuse me,' said Mrs Patterson Cowie. 'I really feel

that you were extremely rude to me over the road and I thought. . .'

She stopped. She had seen Matthew, who, feeling her eyes upon him, looked up slowly and with overt dread.

'You!' muttered Mrs Patterson Cowie.

Matthew rose to his feet. 'Mrs Patterson Cowie, please listen to me. I never meant to knock you over – I swear I didn't. It was an accident, and it was all because I felt ashamed. I'd picked up this book, you see, *Fifty Shades of Grey*, and I was so embarrassed . . .'

'Oh that,' said Mrs Patterson Cowie. 'Did you read it all the way through? I did. And do you know, I really didn't enjoy it at all. Not the finest prose in the world, and, frankly, somewhat far-fetched . . . I could have made a far better job of it, you know.'

49. Shafts of Light

Domenica had reached a decision. The previous few weeks had been a strange time for her – she had felt restless. This was unusual for her, as she was normally quite content to allow her life to follow its accustomed patterns, which were quiet and predictable, rather like a river that knows that it is going to reach the sea eventually and is in no particular hurry to get there. Such a river has no need to prove itself by suddenly erupting into rapids or, playing for effect, by becoming a waterfall. Such a river – and such a life – is satisfied with its own course, wants to be nothing else, and is, by and large, happy with its topographical fate.

But then there had come a period in which she began to wonder whether the life she had created for herself – particularly her marriage to Angus – was just too settled, too devoid of excitement. She began to entertain a vague feeling that she should be doing something more; that rather than being content with the company of Angus, she should be seeking new people, encouraging new friendships, and, most unsettlingly of all, finding more passion in her life. It was a seditious, almost frightening thought, and it was one that married people most dreaded. Given oxygen, it could transform happiness and acceptance into misery, despair, and ultimately into disaster.

And that realisation came to Domenica one morning in Scotland Street itself – not in the flat, not inside, but in the street itself. It was a curious moment of enlightenment, and it came to her as was walking back along Royal Crescent, past the old marshalling yards, and found herself standing at the bottom of Scotland Street, looking up the urban brae towards the trees of Drummond Place Gardens.

It was one of those Scottish summer mornings when it was not clear which way the weather would jump. The air was still, and the sky unthreatening, but there had been a slight fall of rain half an hour before and the street's setts were still glistening. Domenica had been out early – it was still only half past seven – to buy a pint of milk and had slowly been walking back to the flat. She had been enjoying the freshness of the morning and the relative quiet: the city, it seemed, had yet to stir. Sometimes, she had noticed, it failed to stir at all – not all cities feel they have to get up every day, and this, she thought, might be one of those days. But then there drifted over from Dundas Street the resigned hum of a 23 bus making its way up the hill and she realised that people were beginning to go to work. This, she decided, would be a Tuesday like any other Tuesday.

And yet, in a sudden moment of insight, she realised it was not – at least it was not for her. The thought came to her with great clarity: what she had was infinitely precious. She did not have to do anything to make her life more exciting; she did not have to change any aspect of how she lived; and, most importantly, she had no reason to be dissatisfied with Angus. This realisation struck her with an almost physical force as she stood at the bottom of the street. I am immensely fortunate. I am alive. In this vast cosmos of swirling planets, so many of them sterile and dead, baking or swathed in clouds of methane or whatever it is they are swathed in, I am alive in a dear green place . . . and there is somebody who actually loves me.

The words *dear green place* came to her unbidden. They were almost an act of cultural, or geographical, appropriation as they have been used most often to describe Glasgow rather than Edinburgh. But they were the right words, exactly the right words, to describe this world: for all its problems, it was dear; for all its wars and hatreds and poisons, it was dear because we loved it and did not want to lose it. Most of us did not want to die; most of us wanted to wake up each morning and find we were still here; most of us did not want to say goodbye to the friends we had and the places we went and the things we did. Most of us wanted the place we lived in to carry on being the place it had always been. Most of us wanted to live under the modest standards of love and acceptance rather than under the strident banners of dislike and rejection.

As she stood there, looking to any who might have seen her like one who was undecided as to whether to walk any further or to turn back the way she had come, she raised her head and saw shafts of light descending on Scotland Street. They were not part of any heavenly manifestation – not the shafts of light depicted in those paintings where the skies open to reveal choirs of angels and cavorting, gravity-defying *putti* – these were ordinary shafts of light of the sort that might fall anywhere and at any time of the day, but that were somehow this morning unusual and unexpected, and, in Domenica's viewpoint, overwhelmingly significant.

She closed her eyes briefly. She felt heady at the moment of mystical insight that she had experienced, but now was sober once more, and needed to get back to the flat. Once there, she opened the milk, pouring a dash into the two blue Spode teacups lined up on the kitchen table, and switched on the kettle. She stared at the two teacups, and smiled. They were just two ordinary blue Spode teacups, but they meant so much. They represented domesticity. They represented companionship, and the compromises of marriage – one teacup was hers and one belonged to

Angus. Angus's teacup had a chip on the rim, hers did not.

Now she had to see him. He was still in bed, and Cyril had not yet stirred from the blanket on which he slept on the kitchen floor. She poured the tea, making sure that his was of just the strength that he preferred. These things were so important. They were everything.

She went through to the bedroom. Angus was awake now and was reading a book.

'I've brought you your tea,' said Domenica. It was what she always said, and he said, in reply, what he always said, which was, 'Thank you, Domenica.'

She placed the cup on his bedside table, and he said, again, 'Thank you.'

'No,' she said. 'I'm the one who must thank you.'

And then she leaned forward and kissed him on the forehead. And Angus, although surprised, understood that this was a kiss of peace.

50. Cyril Thinks

Over breakfast, Domenica said little about the mystical experience she had been vouchsafed at the foot of Scotland Street. Moments of mystical insight are difficult enough for the recipient to understand, let alone explain to others. She had started to speak to Angus about it but had not found the words, and had ended up making a bland remark about the light in Scotland Street at that time of the morning being particularly . . . The right adjective failed to come to mind. Illuminating? No, all light was illuminating. Revealing? Again no: revealing light surely discourages rather than encourages that particular sort of insight.

'Tight?' suggested Angus. 'At this time of year light in Scotland can be tight in the morning and then, in the afternoon, it gets . . . well, a bit more elastic.'

Domenica sighed. She knew that she would be unable to convey the feeling she had experienced. Angus, however, was an artist and was interested in light.

'Have you ever noticed,' he began, 'the difference between the light in the east of Scotland and the light in the west?'

Domenica would have preferred to talk about her mystical experience, but, *faute de mieux*, would settle for light.

'I suppose I have. It's softer over there,' she said. 'Bluer, perhaps.'

Angus reached for a slice of toast. 'Yes, I think of it as gentler. We have this very clear light here in the east. Sharp. But . . . ' He began to butter his toast. 'But it's different again from the sort of clear light you get in Greece – or Australia. It's less powerful.'

Domenica looked out of the window. The sun was on the roofs on the other side of the street, yellow on the grey of the slates; beyond that, the sky; a dash of low cumulus, lonely against the blue.

'Do you know the reason?' asked Angus.

'What reason?'

'Why over in the west – in Argyll and places like that – they have this soft, rather blue light. Or is it white? Sometimes I think it's white. The sort of white you see in a veil of rain. Glowing a bit – in a white sort of way.'

She shook her head.

'It's because of water in the air,' said Angus. 'I never knew that, you know, until I read about the light you see in seventeenth-century Dutch paintings. Think Vermeer.'

She thought Vermeer. 'The woman reading a letter by the window?'

'Yes. That one. Think of the light in that painting. In all of his paintings, in fact. And so many of those Dutch paintings. They're full of light. They're all about light really – light and courtyards and jugs and carpets . . . and everything they had. The Dutch were painting an inventory of their trading success, I suppose.'

'And?'

Angus took a bite of his toast. 'Marmite,' he said, and closed his eyes briefly in appreciation. 'Yes, apparently the reason why Dutch paintings are full of light . . . '

'Rembrandt isn't,' said Domenica.

Angus considered this. 'I see what you mean,' he said.

'They're all gloomy. As if painted in the dark. All those browns. Rembrandt used a lot of brown, didn't he?'

'I wasn't really thinking about Rembrandt,' said Angus. 'Yet there is light in Rembrandt. It's there all right – it finds the faces of his subjects and shines upon them. It's very dim light, though; just enough to create that lovely effect – as if the artist is shining a rather weak torch on the people in his paintings. There isn't enough light for anything but the face and some of the clothing. That's all.' He paused. 'But those other paintings – the landscapes or the illuminated interiors – there's a reason why they seem to have such light.'

'And that reason is?'

'As I said, droplets of water in the air. The Netherlands is very watery. All those canals and the sea all about you has an effect on the air. There were droplets of water, and sunlight was refracted by this water and that's why the light was as it was – and probably still is.'

'And the same applies in the west?'

'Yes. Go to a place like Skye and look at the light. It's that lovely, soft blue. Misty. Watery. And you'll find the same difference between the light in the east of Canada and the light in the west. Vancouver is all blue and soft. Newfoundland and Quebec are all bright and clear. It's to do with geography and the effect of geography on humidity.'

Angus finished his toast. 'I need to get to the studio,' he said. 'My sitter's coming at ten.'

She wanted to say more to him. She wanted to say to him that he could talk to her about light whenever he chose to do so, for as long as he wanted. She wanted to say to him that she loved him not only for what he had to say about light, but for the way he buttered his toast, for the way he liked Marmite, for the way he spoke to Cyril; she loved him for everything. And she loved the flat they lived in; she loved the kitchen and its contents; she loved the marks on the wall that needed painting; she loved the creaking floorboards. And until then, until that moment in Scotland Street, she had not realised how precious all this was and how strangely indifferent she had been to it all. She would never again make that mistake.

Angus left for his studio. She gave him a kiss before he went out of the front door. Cyril watched from his corner, his nose twitching. Angus was his, and he felt a pang of jealousy and resentment when Domenica behaved as if Angus belonged to her. He could not, because he belonged to Cyril. One of these days, he thought, I'll nip her ankles. Not now, not yet; there was a time and place for everything and the time was not yet right for that. And besides, he half-liked Domenica. If one had to have somebody else in the flat, then there were many who would be far worse than this woman. That woman downstairs, for example; the woman with the boy. The boy was nice – he smelled nice – but that woman was another matter altogether. He had bitten her once before, and it had been very satisfying.

But now what is there to do but lie here and think, in so far as I can think, given what I am. A dog. That, as they say, is the bottom line. I'm just a dog, and that is a profoundly sad thing to be.

51. Catching Up

The day ahead promised to be busy. Domenica had correspondence to deal with and, after that, she had arranged to meet her old friend, Dilly Emslie, for coffee at Glass & Thompson, on Dundas Street. That would take her until twelve, when she would return to Scotland Street to prepare a light lunch for Creative Scotland's visiting delegation of pygmies from the forests of Rwanda. Domenica had hoped that Angus would help her to entertain these visitors, but he had asked to be excused on the grounds that his time with his sitter was limited and he needed to make as much progress with the portrait as possible.

Dilly, however, had offered to stand in. 'I'll help you rustle up something,' she said. And then, after a short pause, had enquired what the guests would like to eat.

'I'm not sure,' replied Domenica. 'I took advantage of being at Valvona & Crolla the other day and asked the young man at the counter whether he had any ideas, but he didn't. He thought pasta might be a good option, as long as I didn't serve too piquant a sauce.'

'Do you think they might be vegetarian?' asked Dilly.

'Highly unlikely,' replied Domenica. 'Traditionally they're hunter-gatherers, and as a general rule the hunting bit of that precludes vegetarianism. I've decided to go for mushroom risotto, with a side salad with bits of chicken in it. If they're vegetarian they can leave the chicken – but I don't think they will be.'

She met Dilly at Glass & Thompson just before eleven. They saw one another fairly frequently, but even with regular meetings, there still seemed to be a lot to be caught up on. There were the doings of mutual friends – innocent and unremarkable, for the most part, but with the occasional frisson of excitement. There was news of Scotland Street, and there, of course, Domenica had a substantial report to make.

'Irene Pollock,' Domenica began.

There was a sharp intake of breath from Dilly.

'Yes,' continued Domenica. 'That's what most of us feel.'

'An impossible woman,' said Dilly. 'That poor little boy of hers.'

'Little boys,' corrected Domenica. 'Plural. She has the two. Bertie, who's goodness on wheels, and wee Ulysses who apparently throws up whenever he sees his mother. There are the two of them now.'

Dilly vaguely remembered a story about Ulysses being lost. 'Didn't she . . .'

'Lose him?' interjected Domenica. 'Yes, she left him in his pram outside Valvona & Crolla and he was carted off to the council emergency nursery. She had to go and retrieve him from the social workers – and you can imagine what that was like. Social workers can be very disapproving of anybody . . .'

'As can the government,' observed Dilly.

'Ah yes,' said Domenica. 'The named person legislation. Can you believe it? Can you believe that they're insisting that every child in Scotland should have a sort of official guardian – because that's what it amounts to. Can you conceive of a better way of insulting parents?'

'I suppose they mean well,' said Dilly.

'Well, anyway,' continued Domenica. 'They went to collect little Ulysses from the nursery and she was given a lecture by the social workers. She didn't take that too well, I gather. And when they got back to the flat they found they had the wrong baby. They'd been given a girl instead. Further panic.'

'What a discovery,' said Dilly.

'Yes, indeed. And now Irene has announced that she's going off to Aberdeen to do a PhD under the supervision of Dr Hugo Fairbairn. He was the psychotherapist who was inflicted on poor little Bertie for years and years.'

Dilly thought of something. 'Named psychotherapists,' she mused. 'Do you think the Scottish Government will move on to insisting that we all have named psychotherapists allocated to us – just in case?'

'Don't joke about it,' warned Domenica, semi-seriously.

'Aberdeen,' mused Dilly. 'Is she going to live up there?'

'Apparently so.'

There was a silence. Then Dilly asked, 'And the boys?'

Domenica raised an eyebrow. 'They're staying with the father – with Stuart. His mother, whom I know and like, by the way, is renting a flat round the corner. She's agreed to come and look after the children while Irene is off in Aberdeen with that Fairbairn character ...' Domenica lowered her voice, 'who is, according to Angus, her lover. He says it's the talk of the Cumberland Bar.'

'Well!' exclaimed Dilly.

'And there's more news from Scotland Street,' said Domenica. 'Remember Antonia Collie? My former neighbour?'

'The one whose flat you bought and incorporated into yours?'

'Yes,' said Domenica. 'She came to Italy with us, you may recall, and went down with Stendhal Syndrome in the Uffizi Gallery. Honestly, you should have seen her. Apparently, Stendhal Syndrome occurs when you're exposed to too much great art. She was positively foaming at the mouth and had to be carted off to hospital. She was discharged into the care of a community of nuns and she eventually joined them as a sort of lay sister. Not a fully-blown nun – more a plainclothes version.'

Dilly remembered meeting a nun at a dinner party in Heriot Row. 'Didn't one of them end up coming to Scotland? One of the Italian nuns?'

'Exactly,' said Domenica. 'That was Sister Maria-Fiore dei Fiori di Montagna. She turned up in Scotland Street and decided that she liked Scotland. She stayed. She became quite the social success – all the best parties and so on.'

'She was rather good at aphorisms, wasn't she?' asked Dilly.

'Oh, terrific,' replied Domenica. 'She had an aphorism for every occasion. Shatteringly trite, of course, but people loved them.'

'We hear so few these days,' said Dilly. 'People seem inhibited about coining aphorisms.'

'Not her. Not Sister Maria-Fiore dei Fiori di Montagna. Well, anyway, Antonia's come back,' Domenica continued. 'She's bought a small flat in Dundonald Street, and she's already taken up residence – with Sister Maria-Fiore dei Fiori di Montagna.'

'Is she still working on her lives of the Scottish saints?'

'I believe so, although apparently she's taking an interest in levitation now. She's interested in saints who were reported to levitate. St Joseph of Copertino, for instance, who travelled quite long distances, apparently – horizontally. Rather more interesting than our Scottish saints.'

'Who were more down to earth,' said Dilly.

'Hah!' said Domenica. 'But anyway, that's the news from Scotland Street.' She looked at her watch. 'We must be back there by twelve,' she said. 'The Creative Scotland people are coming at twelve-thirty, and we must be ready.'

'What will we talk about?' asked Dilly.

'Oh, I'm sure there'll be all sorts of things to discuss. I've lived with hunter-gatherers before, you know, and they tend to be utterly charming people, with lots to say.'

After further conversation, they finished their coffee, paid the bill, and then strolled back to Scotland Street for the much-anticipated cultural exchange with their unusual visitors.

52. *A Perfect Boy*

On the day of the resolution of what Matthew came to call, with good-natured self-mockery, *l'affaire Patterson Cowie*, the new au pair boy was due to start at Nine Mile Burn. The business with Mrs Patterson Cowie had been traumatic, but had eventually been settled over a cup of coffee in Big Lou's once Matthew had apologised to the retired teacher. His apology had been graciously accepted and Mrs Patterson Cowie had then telephoned Gayfield Square Police Station, to be put through automatically to a police call centre on the island of Barra. Speaking to a recording device, she had explained that the search for the young man who had knocked her over in the bookshop could now be called off. 'All a misunderstanding,' she said. 'I've had a perfectly good apology from him and have discovered, incidentally, that he is a former pupil of mine and therefore a Watsonian. That's quite enough for me.'

Matthew had been immensely relieved. 'It was awful being wanted by the police,' he confided. 'I felt so furtive in everything I did.'

'It's all over,' said Mrs Patterson Cowie. 'But to get back to that book . . . I really had no time for it, you know. I can't understand what people saw in it.'

'Perhaps they saw that other people were reading it,' suggested Matthew. 'Perhaps that was enough. An immoral panic, perhaps.'

'Possibly,' said Mrs Patterson Cowie. 'But let's not dwell on such things; tell me, Matthew, are you attending Watsonian meetings regularly? You should, you know.'

Matthew promised to do his best. He would have agreed to do anything for Mrs Patterson Cowie now, who by her generosity and forgiveness had taken such a weight off his shoulders.

He returned early to the house at Nine Mile Burn, as he and Elspeth had agreed with the Duke of Johannesburg that he would bring his nephew around at five in the evening, to get settled into his new position as au pair assistant to Elspeth. They had not interviewed this young man, who was called James, and had taken him purely on the Duke's recommendation, so desperate was Elspeth for help.

They waited in the kitchen, nervously sipping at mugs of tea.

'I hope we like him,' Elspeth said, and then immediately reassured herself by adding, 'Of course we shall. The Duke spoke so highly of him, but I suppose one would speak highly of one's nephew . . . ' And reassured herself again with, 'But then it would be terribly embarrassing for him if he recommended a dud, he being a sort of neighbour, and people would talk. No, he'll be fine – I'm sure of it.'

'Just calm down,' said Matthew. 'He'll be fine – he really will.'

They watched as the Duke's unusual-looking car made its way up the drive, disappearing into the cover of the rhododendron bushes before re-emerging a few moments later. Their first sight of James was when he emerged from the back seat. They watched as the Duke straightened the young man's collar, brushed his shoulders in an avuncular fashion, and then led him towards the front door.

Introductions were made in the small entrance hall. Elspeth glanced at James as the Duke introduced him, and then she glanced again. Beautiful, she thought. And then she found herself thinking, Too good to be true.

Matthew smiled at the young man. He thought, Honest. And then he thought, He's not going to stay. Why should he?

'Would you like a cup of tea?' asked Elspeth brightly. 'Then we can bring the boys in. They're in the playroom – go and check on them, Matthew.'

Matthew left Elspeth to lead the guests into the kitchen.

'Young James has just had his exam results,' said the Duke. 'Tell her, James.'

The young man blushed. 'They were all right.'

'Just all right!' exclaimed the Duke. 'They were stellar, James. No false modesty.'

Perhaps it's real modesty, thought Elspeth.

'Go on, James,' urged the Duke. 'All As – every one of them. All starred.'

James blushed a deeper red. 'Lots of people get As,' he said.

'Not in my day,' said the Duke. 'The highest mark I got was C.'

'But Uncle,' said James, 'to get a C in those days counted for something.'

The Duke smiled. 'You're very tactful.'

'And now?' asked Elspeth. 'What are your plans ... I mean, after here?'

Before James could answer, the door opened and Matthew returned, accompanied by the triplets.

'This is Tobermory,' said Matthew, pointing to one of the boys.

'No,' said Elspeth quietly. 'That's Fergus. This one is Tobermory. And this is Rognvald.'

The three toddlers stared at James.

'Hello, boys,' said the young man.

'They can't actually talk yet,' said Matthew. 'They're only fifteen months.'

'They're very well behaved,' said Elspeth quickly. 'You'll have no trouble with them.'

James turned to address the Duke. 'You didn't tell me about them, Uncle,' he said. There was more surprise than reproach in his voice.

The Duke brushed off the comment. 'Oh, I thought I mentioned them.' And then he added, as if by way of explanation – as if one might easily miss three such young infants, 'They're very small, of course.'

'No,' said James. 'You didn't mention them.'

'Well, there we are,' said the Duke breezily. 'You'll get on fine. They're grand wee boys.'

With James delivered and his suitcase being retrieved from the car, the Duke said goodbye to Matthew and Elspeth. He was driving himself on this occasion, Padruig, his driver, being away speaking Gaelic somewhere.

'You'll find this young man no trouble at all,' the Duke said to Matthew. 'Young people these days – well, you know what they're like, but James is quite different.' He paused for a few moments before continuing, 'In fact, I'm prepared to guarantee him, so to speak. If you have the slightest concerns – the slightest – I shall cover the cost of a replacement. You have my word on that.'

'There's no need,' said Matthew.

'But I want you to know how much confidence I have in him,' said the Duke. 'Please – I insist.'

Matthew shrugged. 'If you really want to – but I'm sure he's going to be fine.'

'Of course,' the Duke continued, 'James has his little ways. But then, which one of us doesn't?'

53. James Sets to Work

Once the Duke of Johannesburg had left, Elspeth showed James around the house, explaining to him where everything was kept. She spent some time on the nursery, familiarising him with some of what Matthew called the triplets' *impedimenta* – the changing mats, the wipes, the disinfectants, the endless supplies of shirts and jumpers and socks, the bibs, the plastic drinking mugs, and so on.

'I don't want to pry,' she said, 'but have you ever changed a small child before? You know . . . '

James nodded. 'I learned how to do it for my Duke of Edinburgh's Gold Award programme. I remember how to do it. No problem.'

'Because not everybody likes doing it,' said Elspeth. 'You know how . . . '

'I don't mind,' said James. 'We're all human.'

Elspeth smiled. 'But somehow, small children are more human than the rest of us. Not all the time, of course, but at times they are.'

Then she showed him around the kitchen. 'I love cooking,' he said. 'I've got all the books – well, not all of them, but quite a few. Delia, of course, but also Jamie. And Ottolenghi – you know his books – all that couscous and olives and stuff.'

'Yes, I like them,' said Elspeth.

'And I do Scottish dishes as well,' James continued. 'I've got that book about cooking on Mull and the one about cooking on the puffer – the steamship. I do a lot of their recipes. And that book by that guy who was a medical student but who made fantastic bread.'

'Well!' exclaimed Elspeth.

James looked at her earnestly. 'So I'd like to do most of the cooking, if that's all right with you.'

'Is that all right with me?' echoed Elspeth. 'It most certainly is. When do you want to start?'

'This evening?' said James.

Elspeth hesitated. 'Are you sure? You've only just arrived.'

James indicated that he was perfectly sure. 'I'd like it to be special this evening,' he said. 'I'd like to cook a dinner just for you and Matthew – to have by yourself. With candles. I'll have a snack beforehand. This will just be for the two of you: *à deux*. I'll do the lot – after I've put the boys to bed.'

Elspeth looked at him in astonishment. 'But . . . '

'No buts,' said James. 'You don't need to do a thing. Honestly, you don't.'

She sat down. She felt weak. She had hoped for relief, but had never dared imagine that relief would come on this scale. She looked at him, and he smiled back at her. He was perfection incarnate, she thought. She could gaze at him for hours. She could put him on the mantelpiece and stare at him with wordless appreciation.

She decided to have a rest while James entertained the boys in their nursery. There were shrieks of childish joy; whoops of delight as some game was devised and played with gusto. After that, there was bathtime, accomplished in record time, but with no protest from the triplets; then a story, read by James with a great deal of expression; and thereafter silence as the triplets appeared to go off to sleep without protest.

James appeared in the sitting room off the kitchen, where Elspeth was half-dozing, a barely opened magazine across her lap. He was holding a kitchen towel in one hand, a recipe book in the other.

'May I use anything I find?' he asked. 'In the kitchen, I mean.'

Elspeth made a permissive gesture. 'Of course. Anything at all.' She paused. 'There's not an awful lot, I'm afraid.' In her exhaustion she had let things slip; the trip to the supermarket she had intended to make three days ago had never quite got off the ground, and as a result there were empty spaces on the larder shelves. There were no eggs, she remembered, and the last of the oats she used for making porridge had been used up that morning.

'I've had a look around,' said James. 'And there's quite a lot. I could go to the supermarket for you tomorrow, if you like.'

Elspeth asked him if he drove. 'I've passed my driving test,' he said. 'But I could go by bike; I saw some bikes in the shed.'

'But how would you carry everything?' she asked.

'My rucksack,' he said. 'Honestly, it would be no trouble.'

She smiled. 'You're very kind,' she said. 'I can drive you there. Once we get you on the insurance you'll be able to take the car.'

He nodded. 'And in the meantime, I'm going to start your dinner,' he said. 'I've found some salmon steaks in the freezer and some new potatoes. Do you and Matthew like mustard?'

'We like everything,' said Elspeth.

'I like to use mustard for potatoes,' said James. 'It's a recipe I saw in one of Delia's books.'

A sudden feeling of deep satisfaction came over her. This young man, so eager and so charming, was going to cook. He was going to entertain the triplets. He was going to tidy things up. Now, at last, after over a year of servitude – a year of interrupted sleep and struggling to cook while at the same time watching three toddlers; a year of washing and drying and ironing and scrubbing – she would have time to do the things that she used to do. She could read;

she could see friends; she could go out into the garden and simply smell the roses, if they had any. She had not even had the time to explore their garden, to find out whether there were any roses that were just waiting for somebody with enough time to sniff them.

She went upstairs to run a bath and change. From the window of their bedroom, she saw James in the garden. She watched him idly, wondering what he was doing out there. He glanced up at one point, as if looking over his shoulder towards the house, but he did not seem to see her, as she was well back from the window. She wondered whether he was worried about being observed. What was he going to do?

She watched him wander down the path that led towards the main clump of rhododendrons. Now her curiosity was fully engaged. He said that he was going to start cooking, yet he seemed now to be going off on some sort of errand – into the woods.

On impulse, she decided to follow him. She did not stop to consider whether it was a good idea to follow one's newly employed au pair boy into the woods; for all she knew, he was simply going for a stroll before he started to work in the kitchen; for all she knew he was merely looking for a better place for a signal for his mobile phone; for all she knew, he was merely exploring his new surroundings. But she followed him nonetheless, slipping out through the kitchen door and making her way along the path that led to the dark, secret passages of the clustered rhododendrons and the woods beyond.

Through her mind ran a line from a song she had begun to sing to the triplets. It came complete with a nineteen-thirties big-band backing, and it warned you that if you went down to the woods today you were sure of a big surprise.

54. The End of Bruce

She sat with Matthew in the dining room. It was on the cold side of the house, away from the evening sun that was now, at nine-thirty, just beginning to sink beneath the horizon.

'Our lovely summer evenings,' said Matthew, looking out of the French doors that gave onto a small section of lawn. 'Geographical luck: I feel so sorry for people who have a swift nightfall and no lingering evenings in which . . . well, to linger.'

'Everywhere has its consolations,' said Elspeth. She sighed. 'You know, I still can't quite believe it.' She gestured, with a toss of the head, in the direction of the kitchen. 'Him through there – I just can't believe it. Am I dreaming?'

Matthew shrugged. 'It's early days yet. In fact, it's day one.'

'Yes, but still . . . What did you think of that soup?'

Matthew made a gesture that conveyed his appreciation. 'He made that in what? Half an hour?'

'Yes,' said Elspeth. 'Including picking time. I saw him, you know. I was looking out of our window and I noticed that he was going off on that path – you know, the one that goes to the rhododendrons.'

Matthew looked interested. 'What was he doing?'

'Well, that's exactly what I thought. So I followed him.'

Matthew raised an eyebrow. 'Followed?'

'Yes, I know it sounds a bit melodramatic, but I decided to follow him – keeping a discreet distance, of course.'

'Of course.' Matthew was eager to hear more. 'And then?'

'He went through the rhodies – you know that sort of tunnel that goes right through. He followed that, and then you get to that bit of ground where there's that fireweed and that old shed. And you know what he was doing?'

Matthew shook his head.

'Picking nettles,' said Elspeth. 'There's a patch of nettles there and he was picking them. He had gloves on – I hadn't noticed that before. He was picking nettles for this soup.'

'Did he see you?' asked Matthew.

'No, I turned round and came right back. I felt really rather ashamed of myself. It was as if I were some sort of voyeur.'

Matthew laughed. 'Picking nettles – about as innocent an activity as one can imagine.' He glanced around the dining room. 'And it looks as if he's been gathering flowers too.'

There were several flower arrangements around the room, one on the mantelpiece, another on the sideboard. The flowers were interspersed with random sprigs of greenery – sprigs of honesty, a prickle of gorse, willowy blades of self-seeded wheat.

Matthew shook his head in astonishment. 'Amazing,' he said. 'And how old is he? Eighteen?'

'Yes.'

They lapsed into silence. Two candles, placed in the middle of the table, cast a flicker of light on their wine glasses.

Then Matthew said, 'This morning – after that business with Mrs Patterson Cowie – I had a long talk with Pat. When we got back to the gallery, she really opened up. It all came out. Everything – with tears too.'

'Her love life?' asked Elspeth.

'Bruce.'

Elspeth sighed. 'Him. What's she thinking of? He's the worst possible news for her – or for anyone, for that matter.'

'He has this strange power over her. She's like a rabbit caught in the headlights.'

'Stupid girl.'

Matthew felt that he had to defend her. 'No, she's not stupid – because she knows that he's wrong for her. She understands the situation completely.'

'Well, then, she's due for a lot of heartache. And tears too.'

'Was due,' said Matthew. 'By the end of our conversation, I think things were sorted out. I helped her with a letter to him. I dictated part of it – I feel rather proud of myself.'

'And what did it say?'

'The usual thing. It told him that she thought it would be best for her never to see him again. It asked him not to phone her or e-mail her, or anything. It cut things off.'

Elspeth waited for more.

'She was tremendously relieved. It was as if she had confessed to a bad habit – which, I suppose he was, in a way. It was as if she had suddenly signed a pledge or whatever – as if she had given up smoking or drinking or something like that.' Matthew paused. 'I felt as if I were some sort of Bruce Survivors Support Group. She clung to me – literally.'

Elspeth said nothing, but her eyes narrowed, almost imperceptibly.

'She was weeping,' said Matthew. 'She clung to me. I calmed her down eventually.' He hesitated. 'Mrs Patterson Cowie walked down the street. She saw us through the window.'

Elspeth still did not say anything. And Matthew thought: what more can I say? It was innocent. Pat's just Pat. I was comforting her. And then Mrs Patterson Cowie comes along and she must think that Pat and I . . . What else could she think? And I'd just told her during our conversation in Big Lou's, when she was asking me all about what had happened to me since I left George Watson's, I had told her about Elspeth and having the triplets and now . . . '

He decided to change the subject. 'She told me about Bruce's latest plans. I could hardly believe them.'

'I can believe anything of him,' said Elspeth. 'So, what now?'

'You know the National Monument on top of Calton Hill? That version of the Parthenon – those pillars?'

'Yes.'

'Well, Bruce has got in tow with a group of investors who want to make it into a hotel.'

Elspeth shook her head. 'Did I hear that right? A hotel?'

'Yes,' said Matthew. 'They want to build in between the columns and then out the back. They say it would have a fantastic façade.'

Elspeth did not know what to say. In her mind's eye she saw it, though, those high Grecian pillars with windows between them now and doors and lights, and taxis drawing up outside.

'I thought at first it was utterly absurd,' said Matthew. 'But then I realised that with the way things are going these days there are plenty of people who would probably love the idea. They want hotels everywhere, after all. What use is a half-finished Parthenon? Much rather have the Edinburgh Parthenon Hotel.'

'He's just a Philistine,' said Elspeth.

'Yes,' said Matthew. 'I suppose he is.'

They looked at the flickering candles, at their light, which was so subtle, so gentle, like the faltering light of the spirit that had once infused their city.

55. *The Pygmies Arrive*

They were ready in good time. Dilly had helped Domenica to heat up the risotto she had made the previous night and then to prepare the salad with its optional chicken. Then she had laid the table while Domenica made a jug of iced lemonade that would be served to the officials from Creative Scotland and their two pygmy guests. The pygmies, they had been told, were artists and would be in Scotland for two weeks, during which they would visit not only Edinburgh, but also Glasgow, Mallaig, Inverness and Airdrie.

'It really is a bit odd,' said Domenica as they waited. 'I'm very much out of touch with Rwanda. I was there years ago, doing some fieldwork, and I suppose the Creative Scotland people must have got wind of that somehow. But I would have thought it would have made far more sense for them to take these particular visitors to see somebody involved in the arts.'

'Well, I'm sure they'll enjoy having a varied programme,' said Dilly. 'Is there reciprocation? Are we sending somebody over there?'

'I believe we are,' said Domenica. 'A couple of installation artists from Glasgow are on their way out. Heaven knows what the pygmies will make of them.'

The bell rang. 'Well, here we go,' said Domenica, as she made for the front door.

The Creative Scotland officials were a man and a woman, the man dressed in a blue linen suit, with no tie, and the woman in a pair of elegant jeans, a white blouse, and a green silk scarf.

'Mrs Macdonald?' the man asked.

'Yes. You're Creative Scotland?'

'Well,' said the man, smiling. 'Part of it. My name is Andrew and this is my colleague, Valerie. It was Valerie who wrote to you.'

Domenica looked towards the stair behind them. 'I thought you were bringing your visitors,' she said. 'Have I got the wrong day . . . ?' She broke off. The two officials, who had been standing close together, parted to reveal two small people behind them; Domenica had simply not seen them.

'Oh,' she said, trying to cover her embarrassment. 'I didn't see . . . I mean, there you are. Please come in, everybody.'

The visiting party entered the flat. As they did so, Domenica glanced at the two pygmy visitors. They were not tall – not by any stretch of the imagination – but they had about them a charming conciseness. They were neat – even perjink – one man and one woman, dressed in formal, slightly old-fashioned clothes. The man wore a tie, and the woman a hat.

'I'd like to introduce our visitors from Rwanda,' said Andrew. 'They arrived in Scotland only two days ago.'

Domenica smiled at the two visitors. 'Only two days ago? Well, I do hope that our weather is going to be kind while you're here.'

Andrew smiled. 'I'm sure it will be. And, well, there's something I need to tell you: I'm afraid our visitors don't speak any English.'

Domenica frowned. 'None at all?'

'Not a word,' said Andrew.

'French?'

Andrew shook his head. 'As you know, French is spoken in those parts, but I'm afraid our visitors don't speak it. Nor Swahili.'

Domenica absorbed this information. 'And I take it that neither of you speaks any language known to them?'

Andrew glanced at Valerie. 'I have to admit, we don't. We rather hoped that with your experience with hunter-gatherers in Central Africa you might have a smidgen of local language.' He looked at her hopefully, as if, even at this late stage, an undisclosed linguistic gift might save the situation. 'I gather that it's Efé.'

'It is,' said Domenica. 'But I'm afraid I don't speak it. There was an Efé dictionary compiled some years ago. Jean-Pierre Hallett did it, but I don't have a copy.'

Valerie looked disappointed. 'We were hoping that you'd be able to help us communicate. I suppose we should have arranged an interpreter, but our budget didn't quite stretch to that.'

'And you'd never find one,' said Domenica briskly. 'Theirs is a very isolated culture, you know – and a fragile one too.'

'Perhaps we should give them some lemonade,' suggested Dilly.

The Creative Scotland team seemed pleased with the suggestion. This, at least, was something positive.

Domenica led them into the sitting room, where – by way of gestures – she invited the guests to sit down. Dilly produced glasses of lemonade, which the pygmies accepted graciously, with smiles and small nods of their heads.

'Is this their first visit to Scotland?' asked Domenica.

'It's their first visit anywhere,' said Andrew. 'As far as we know, but . . . '

'But we can't really tell,' added Valerie.

There was a silence. The pygmies were looking at

Domenica and Dilly. The woman turned her head and stared at them with wide, expressive eyes. Then, putting down her glass of lemonade, she rose from her seat to stand next to Dilly. She took Dilly's hand in hers, and held it – gently, as one might hold a bird, a dove. Nothing was said.

After a while, Domenica broke the silence. 'Their world is being destroyed, you know. They are gentle, loving folk, these forest people, but their forests are being cut down and they're being relegated to so-called settlements. The canopies above their heads will be concrete, not the leaves of the forest canopy.'

Andrew shook his head. 'That's very sad.'

'This sort of thing is happening everywhere,' Domenica continued. 'In South America, too. People who have managed to avoid the modern world are being rooted out of their homes in the jungle, hunted down in some cases, all for timber and minerals.'

She looked at the pygmy woman. 'This woman is showing us what we ourselves have lost, and what our grasping world is taking away from them. Their innocence, their gentleness, their friendliness.' She stopped. She had remembered something. 'You know, it's just come back to me. When I was doing my fieldwork out there I had some dealings with the Baka people – they live in the Congo. And they had a word for the spirit of the forest in which they lived: *Jengi*. It's one of the few words that you find in many of the other forest languages in the region. Jengi.'

The effect of Domenica's uttering the word Jengi was electric. The two pygmy guests suddenly sat bolt upright, their eyes shining.

'Jengi,' said the man, and pointed out of the window. 'Jengi.'

'He's telling us something,' said Andrew.

Both of the pygmies now got up from their seats and walked over to the window. They were not quite tall enough to look out of it easily, but standing on their toes, they could just see over the sill.

'Jengi,' said the man once more, pointing now at the tops of the trees in Drummond Place, just visible from the flat.

Then he turned around and gazed at his hosts with an ineffable sadness.

'He's seen God in the Drummond Place trees,' said Domenica quietly. She wanted to cry. She wanted to cry for the loss of so many of the things that had made the world a richly textured place: for community, and local culture, and the forests, and the people who lived in them; because now all that was going, swept away, consumed, cut down, taken away.

56. Stuart Plans his Future

One floor below, unaware of the meeting taking place upstairs in Angus and Domenica's flat, an encounter of a very different sort was about to occur. Since his resignation from his post as a government statistician, Stuart had been busy preparing for his new life, both professional and domestic. The professional side of this preparation had involved a consultation with a financial adviser whom he had met in the Cumberland Bar. This man knew all about redundancy packages and pension entitlements and such things, and was an expert in what he called 'exit strategies'.

'I take it they've offered redundancy terms?' said the adviser, over a pint of McEwan's India Pale Ale. 'The civil service tends to be quite good about those sorts of things. Better than the private sector, on the whole.' He paused, looking momentarily concerned. 'You have been offered something, I take it . . .'

Stuart tried to look nonchalant. 'Actually, I resigned. Handed in my dinner pail – in a manner of speaking. Not permanently, of course – I'm still alive . . .' He smiled weakly. 'But no, I resigned.'

The adviser bit his lip. 'An actual resignation? As in: I quit?'

'As in I quit.'

The adviser took a sip of his McEwan's. 'That's almost unheard of,' he said. 'Nobody resigns from the civil service. They die, yes, and they very, very rarely are nudged out, but they don't go and resign.'

'Well, I did.'

The adviser put down his glass. 'Amicably, I assume.'

Stuart hesitated. But now bravado took over. 'No, I insulted the Supreme Head of Personnel.'

The adviser made a noise somewhere between a whistle and a gasp. 'Well, that's something. Her. I've come across her. Few have survived who've done that. Or not survived in post. You're a brave man, Stuart – a brave, currently unemployed man.'

'Well, it's done,' said Stuart. 'I suppose I'll need to make arrangements.'

The adviser produced a sheet of paper, and listened while Stuart gave him figures. Then he did some quick calculations, checked them, and then shook his head. 'Not good,' he said. 'And your wife? Does she work?'

'She's going back to university to do a PhD,' replied Stuart. 'Up in Aberdeen. She's got hold of some funding for that, but I imagine I'll have to contribute.'

'You need a job pronto,' said the adviser.

'I know,' said Stuart. 'I've registered with a head-hunter and I've been offered a couple of interviews.'

The adviser looked relieved. 'That's fine,' he said. 'I suspect you'll be all right. We'll freeze the pension and start contributions to a private scheme. You can sell your ISAs.' He handed over the sheet of paper. 'There's one thing I want to ask you. What was it like insulting the Supreme Head of Personnel? Was it . . . was it cathartic?'

'Immensely,' said Stuart.

'Then it was worth it,' said the adviser. He leaned forward. 'You know, I think I've met your wife. My own wife is in one of her book groups. She's called Irene, isn't she?'

Stuart nodded.

The adviser took another sip of his beer. 'I don't want to pry,' he said. 'I wouldn't normally ask another chap about this sort of thing, but tell me: are things . . . all right, so to speak?'

Stuart glanced at the other people in the bar, the other Cumberland regulars. How many of them could say that their lives were all right, so to speak? Some, he thought; but only some.

'No, they aren't,' he said. 'She's going off to Aberdeen, and there's somebody there. She hasn't said as much, but I've been able to put two and two together. I should have done that years ago, but I didn't. I was too . . . ' He searched for the word. It was there before him, but he felt loath to make the admission. Then he did. 'I was too weak – far too weak. I allowed her to browbeat me on practically everything. Every so often I'd stand up to her and assert myself, but then, sooner or later, I'd fold, and we'd be back to normal. And normal for us was her calling the shots.'

The adviser was sympathetic. 'Oh, my dear fellow,' he said. 'I'm so sorry. I'd heard a bit of that from others. You know how people speak. Well, they'd said something about all this. They said that you wife was a complete pain . . . ' He stopped himself. 'I'm sorry, I didn't mean to be personal.'

Stuart smiled. 'You don't have to worry.'

'No,' said the adviser. 'I can't possibly.'

'Well,' said Stuart. 'My life is going to change. She's going to be away in Aberdeen and, frankly, I don't think we'll see much of her down here.'

The adviser looked concerned. 'But your boys? You've got two boys, haven't you?'

'Yes, I have. But my mother lives just around the corner and she's going to be moving in. She offered – I didn't have to ask her.'

'Thank heavens for mothers,' said the adviser. 'Well, for some mothers, I suppose – almost all, in fact.' He glanced over his shoulder and leaned forward again. 'It seems to me that you've had a somewhat trying experience.' His voice was now not much louder than a whisper. 'There are lots of men in that position, you know. Oh, and lots of women too – women have had a dreadful time of it at the hands of men in the past – and many still do. There are plenty of bullies out there but . . . ' He lowered his voice further. 'But some of these bullies are women, you know.'

Stuart shrugged. 'Statistically . . . ' he began.

The adviser cut him short. 'Yes, yes, I know about all that. But the point is, Stuart, that you've been a victim. And victims sometimes need to acknowledge their victimhood. That's the first step. Then they need to realise that nobody's going to look after men unless men start looking after themselves.'

Stuart thought for a moment. 'But isn't that what men have been doing for a very long time? Looking after one another? Giving each other jobs and perks and so on? Restricting the freedom of women?'

The adviser raised a finger to his lips. 'Not too loud, old chap. Remember who runs this country now? Women. You never know when they'll be listening in. They've been wiring up our bars for sound.' He paused. 'You're right about that, but that's largely in the past, you know. The boot's on the other foot now. Women are in charge. They're taking over, and you know what? – they're looking after other women. It's men who are threatened now. Look at the intake of universities – men are in the minority in all the student intakes. Look at how our young men are failing. And is anybody saying they should be given a leg up? They aren't.'

'Well, there's been a lot of historical injustice . . .'

'Historical, Stuart! Historical!' hissed the adviser. 'But this is the present.' He reached into his pocket and took out a small card that he handed to Stuart. 'Read that. Commit the telephone number to memory, and then burn it. Then call us when you're ready.'

Stuart read the print on the card. *Men Underground*, it said. And then, under that, *The Male Resistance*. He saw a telephone number.

57. Off to Aberdeen

After that strange meeting in the Cumberland Bar, Stuart had turned his attention to the personal side of his life. He had told his mother, Nicola, of both his resignation and Irene's intention to go to Aberdeen; she had been supportive – and, more than that, she had been positively enthusiastic.

'I'm sorry Irene's going up to Aberdeen,' she said, thinking, I wish it were further. Ulaanbaatar, for instance, or South Georgia.

'Oh well,' said Stuart. 'She's always wanted to do a PhD.'

'Of course,' said Nicola. 'Quite understandable.' She thought: quite understandable if you're an incorrigible intellectual snob with a desire to impress others.

'Her academic career is very important to her,' Stuart went on.

Academic career? thought Nicola. Pontificating at the Carl Gustav Jung Drop-in Centre? Is that meant to be an academic career? 'Of course,' she said. 'Of course it is. She has so much to contribute.' Her unasked-for opinions, for example.

'She knows people up there,' Stuart continued. 'She won't be lonely.'

Nicola smiled. 'Well, that's good to know. And she knows one person particularly well. Her nights certainly won't be lonely.'

Nicola had offered not only to look after Bertie and Ulysses, but also to move in to do so. She had risen to that challenge while Irene had been held in that Persian Gulf desert harem, and she had found that the art of looking after small children, rather like the art of riding a bicycle, never left one. In fact, she was delighted to do it; her life in Edinburgh, although reasonably full, lacked an element of purpose, and day-to-day responsibility for two small grandsons was purpose of the highest nature.

As the meeting was taking place upstairs of Domenica and her pygmy visitors, Nicola was downstairs in the Pollock flat, awaiting with Stuart the return of Irene from a lecture she had been attending at the Scottish National Gallery on the Mound. 'I hope Irene is not going to be awkward about any of this,' she said to Stuart. 'What if she decides to take the boys to Aberdeen?'

'She won't,' said Stuart.

'I must say, darling, I find it a bit strange that she should be so cool about leaving them. That's not very typical behaviour for a mother, if I may say so.'

'Irene is not very typical, Mother,' said Stuart.

'No, dear, she isn't. And I have a feeling – just a tiny, wee feeling – that you might be better off by yourself. And the same goes for Bertie and Ulysses.'

'Possibly,' said Stuart. 'But I don't want any recrimination. I don't want any nastiness.'

Nicola rushed to reassure him. 'Of course not. I'd never say anything.'

They heard the sound of a key in the door, and Stuart went into the hall to greet Irene.

'Well, that was a highly entertaining lecture,' said Irene as she came in. 'It was all about Poussin. A very well-informed lecturer. He concentrated on that painting they have down in London, in the National Gallery. *Man Bitten by a Snake*.'

'Mother's here,' said Stuart. 'She's in the kitchen.'

Irene appeared not to be interested, but wandered through into their bedroom followed by Stuart. 'It's a remarkable painting,' she said. 'I've seen it before, of course, but I'd never really studied it – and it's astonishing how much more you see once you do that. There's that man lying on the ground and the large snake engaged with him. Then there's a figure running off to report the tragedy. It's quite disturbing.'

'Oh well, you were safe in the Scottish National Gallery.'

'Oh, don't be so ridiculous, Stuart.'

'I wasn't being ridiculous. I was simply pointing out that you shouldn't be frightened of a mere painting.'

Irene looked at him disdainfully. 'But that's the whole point of art, Stuart. It engages us, so that the things that the artist portrays become real. And that's exactly what a member of the audience said at the end. He complained.'

'About what?'

'About the failure to warn the audience at the beginning of the lecture. He said the gallery people should have warned us that this particular painting could be distressing. He said we were entitled to safe space.'

Stuart looked at Irene in astonishment. 'This character said that they should have warned you about ... about Poussin?'

Irene nodded. 'And I think he had a perfectly valid point. That's what the safe space movement is all about – ensuring that people aren't made to feel uncomfortable.'

'And only hear the things they want to hear?' said Stuart.

Irene gave him a warning glance. 'You said your mother was here?'

'Yes, she's in the kitchen. I thought we should all talk about the boys.'

Irene looked out of the window. 'I've been thinking, Stuart.'

Stuart held his breath, wondering whether she had changed her mind.

'I've been thinking of going up there next week,' said Irene. 'I can't wait to start work on my PhD.'

Stuart breathed out. 'That's fine,' he said, trying not to sound too eager. 'You must get down to it. You need to commit yourself to it.'

Irene looked at him. 'Has our marriage been a success, Stuart?'

He returned her gaze. There was so much he wanted to say, but he knew that he would never say it.

'I think, by and large, it has. But then . . . '

'Yes, Stuart?'

'But then, I think we've drifted apart. I think we've . . . '

'Been on different vectors? Is that it?'

He had no idea what she meant, but it sounded as if that might be it. Vectors sounded rather like aircraft approach paths, but perhaps there were vectors for people too – vectors that took them through the troubled airspace that was our daily life. The troubled airspace of our daily lives . . . He would have to remember that. That girl – the one he had met in Henderson's Salad Table restaurant, the one studying twentieth-century Scottish poetry; she would appreciate that phrase.

'Irene,' he said. 'May I ask you to do one thing?'

She looked at him. 'In principle, yes.'

'Say thank you to my mother.'

She did not reply immediately. He noticed that her watch strap was frayed. It was strange, he thought, that at moments of great intensity, one sees the details, the things of no consequence in themselves, but things that may say so much about our human frailty.

At last she responded. 'Yes, I'll do that. Because it's very good of her, Stuart.'

He felt relieved. 'I know.'

'And it's good of you, too.'

He was silent.

'It's good of you to give me my freedom, Stuart.'

He leaned forward and kissed her lightly on the cheek. She touched his shoulder. She said, 'Will you forgive me, Stuart?'

He nodded. He could not speak. But he could forgive, and had done so now.

58. How the Truth Emerges

'You can't avoid it, Stuart,' said Nicola. 'Sooner or later you're going to have to talk to Bertie about what's happening.'

Stuart sighed. 'I know, Mother, I know. You're absolutely right. And I shall.'

'When?' asked Nicola.

'Soon.'

'When?' she repeated.

He sighed again. 'This evening. You're collecting him from school, aren't you? When he comes back, I'll talk to him.'

Nicola nodded. 'Fine. And what does he know at the moment? He must suspect that something's up.'

Stuart told her that Bertie had overheard Irene talking to Hugo Fairbairn and had made a few comments about her going to Aberdeen. More than that, he was not sure.

'Has anything been said to him at school? You know how children hear of things.'

Stuart shook his head. 'As far as I know, nobody there will know anything about it.'

In this, he was wrong: the topic of Irene's departure had already been discussed in the Steiner School playground. Olive had broached the subject, having heard her parents talking about it while she was hiding under their bed, which she often did.

'I hear your mummy has a lover, Bertie,' she said. 'Do you know who he is?'

Bertie bit his lip. 'I don't know what you're talking about, Olive.'

'Well, I can tell you, Bertie. It's a person called Hugo Fairbairn. That's right: Hugo Fairbairn. And he lives up in Aberdeen.'

Bertie looked at the ground.

Olive's lieutenant, Pansy, now entered the conversation. 'Don't just look at your shoes, Bertie Pollock,' she said. 'It's rude to look at your shoes when somebody's talking to you.'

'Pansy's right,' said Olive. 'You should look people in the eyes when they talk to you. Everybody knows that.'

Bertie forced himself to meet Olive's gaze. 'How do you know about my mummy?' he asked. 'You just make things up, Olive – you always do that.'

Olive would not let that pass. 'Oh, I make things up, do

I, Bertie? Well, if that's what you say, then you're accusing my mummy and daddy of making things up too – because I heard it from them, so I did!'

Bertie bit his lip once more. He wished that Olive would let him be; he wished that she would no longer taunt him with her knowing remarks; he wished she would drop her claim that he had once promised to marry her when they were both twenty.

'I didn't say that your mummy and daddy were liars, Olive,' he protested. 'I never said that.'

Olive glared at him. 'You can be very insensitive, Bertie Pollock. You don't care what effect what you say has on other people's feelings.'

'That's right,' said Pansy. 'That's typical of boys. They act as if girls had no feelings at all.'

Olive nodded. 'The only reason I'm telling you this, Bertie, is to save you from being hurt. It's far better for you to know that your mummy has gone off with somebody else and that they spend all their time in Aberdeen drinking and kissing and going to dances – it's far better for you to know that.'

'Exactly,' said Pansy.

'My mummy said that she really worries about what will happen to you, Bertie,' Olive continued. 'She said that your father is hopeless.' Olive paused. 'I didn't say that, Bertie – I'm just reporting what I heard. Nor did I say that your father's a well-known wimp. I never said that personally – I'm just reporting.'

Bertie remained silent.

'Poor you, Bertie,' said Olive, putting an arm around

his shoulders. 'It's going to be really tough for you because your dad will be no good at cooking . . . '

'Daddies never are,' said Pansy. 'They're really useless.'

'So you're probably not going to get enough food,' Olive continued. 'But I want you to know that we're here for you, Bertie – aren't we, Pansy?'

'We are,' said Pansy. 'Whenever you need us, Bertie, we'll be here.'

Bertie continued to say nothing.

'Well, I'd have thought that you might just bother to thank us, Bertie,' said Olive, withdrawing her arm. 'There's such a thing as gratitude, you know.'

In a very small voice, Bertie said thank you, and his thanks were acknowledged by a gracious nod from Olive.

So he knew, and, in fact had known for a long time, the way in which children know what nobody imagines they know. He knew that his mother liked Dr Fairbairn; he knew that she seemed impatient and irritated by his father; he knew that his mother was unhappy and that she would be happier elsewhere. And so when Stuart started a long-winded explanation that evening about how it was sometimes the case that mothers and fathers were happier living in different houses, he simply nodded and said that he understood and that he was sure that Irene would be happier living in Aberdeen.

Stuart tried to be as reassuring as possible. 'She'll come to see you quite a lot, Bertie. She'll be down for weekends.'

Bertie looked at his father. 'Oh, Mummy shouldn't bother, Daddy. I really wouldn't want her to have to come all the way from Aberdeen. Couldn't she just write a letter from time to time – not every month, say every other month?'

Nicola, who was present in the background when this conversation was being had, caught Stuart's eye. 'I'll be here all the time, Bertie,' she said. 'I'm going to live in the spare room and look after you and Ulysses.'

Bertie smiled. 'I'm really happy about that, Granny,' he said. 'And I hope Ulysses will stop throwing up so much.'

'I'm sure he will,' said Nicola.

'You're being a very brave boy, Bertie,' said Stuart. He swallowed hard. He could not cry in front of his son, much as he wanted to, because this little boy was indeed the bravest, noblest, kindest little boy he could ever have wished to know – and I, he thought, I am his father.

Bertie turned to Nicola. 'Do you think you'll be able to get me another kilt, Granny?' he asked.

'But don't you have one already, Bertie?' replied Nicola.

'Mummy made my kilt into a cushion cover,' said Bertie. 'She doesn't like tartan and kilts and all those things.' Nor cub scouts, nor Swiss Army knives, nor pizza with five different toppings.

Nicola gasped, but quickly regained her composure. 'Tomorrow, Bertie,' she said. 'We'll go tomorrow when you get back from school. We'll get you a new kilt.'

Stuart rubbed his hands together. 'Just in time,' he said. 'Because the day after that is Saturday, isn't it, and Scotland will be playing rugby against New Zealand at Murrayfield. And we're going to go – you, me, and, if you'd like to invite him, your pal, Ranald Braveheart Macpherson.'

Bertie replied that he would like that very much.

'Will Scotland win, Daddy?' he asked.

Stuart hesitated, but only for a split second. Then he replied, 'Bound to, Bertie.'

59. The Existential Happiness of 13–0.

Ranald Braveheart Macpherson was delivered to the Pollock flat in Scotland Street wearing his Macpherson tartan kilt with a blue sweater into which the word SCITLAND had been carefully stitched.

Bertie noticed the error immediately and raised it with Ranald. 'I don't think you spell Scotland like that,' he said. 'I think there's an O after the C rather than an I.'

Ranald seemed unconcerned. 'It was knitted in China,' he said. 'My mummy says that sometimes they spell things wrong in China.'

Bertie nodded. 'My dad says Chinese goods are rubbish,' he said, but then added quickly, 'Except for sweaters. He says that Chinese sweaters are really good.'

Ranald seemed pleased. 'I like your kilt, Bertie.'

Bertie acknowledged the compliment. His new kilt, purchased for him the day before by his grandmother, was having its inaugural outing – and what better occasion for that than the end-of-season rugby match between New Zealand and Scotland, to be played on the hallowed turf of Murrayfield Stadium? It would be a very important match, Stuart explained, as Scotland had never beaten the all-powerful New Zealanders. There came a time, though, when David overcame Goliath, and so all hope of a victory should not be abandoned.

It was a short bus ride to Murrayfield. Walking the rest of the way, they mingled with a growing stream of people heading for the stadium. Here and there along the road, the bagpipes of some optimistic busker skirled through the bright afternoon air. The crowd was good-natured, as rugby crowds invariably are, and numerous saltires reminded those present of the fact that this was a national occasion – a time for pride and courage in the face of almost certain defeat.

Stuart had prepared the boys for disappointment. 'I think we're going to win,' he said as they made their way towards the ground's entrance, 'but we must remember that these New Zealanders are mighty men. They're a very strong opposition.'

'But we're strong too, aren't we, Daddy?' asked Bertie.

'Sort of,' said Stuart. He did not go into it, but he knew it was a question of selective breeding. In the past, all Scottish rugby players of any note came from the Borders and were the sons of farmers and grain merchants selected by both nature and nurture to push and shove against one another on muddy fields and to hurl themselves against similarly built opponents – all in pursuit of a curiously shaped leather ball. The eugenics that had produced such sturdy young men now seemed no longer to be practised, and Borders farmers were not paying the same attention to build and strength in their selection of a wife. The results were now felt on the rugby pitch.

Once inside the stadium and seated in their allotted places, Bertie and Ranald Braveheart Macpherson could scarcely contain their excitement. When a pipe band marched onto the pitch, they watched in awe, and when at last the Scottish team came out, running courageously through the tunnel from the dressing rooms, both Ranald and Bertie cheered at the top of their lungs. Now came the solemn moment of the singing of 'Flower of Scotland', that stirring evocation of national spirit in the face of devious English machinations. That the song referred to the fourteenth century was neither here nor there: for many the fourteenth century was but yesterday, and the New Zealanders should bear that in mind.

New Zealand responded, as they always do, with their *haka*, the Maori challenge with all its curious gestures – the rolling of eyes, the sticking out of tongues, and the general presentation of a less than welcoming demeanour.

'The *haka*'s jolly rude, isn't it, Daddy?' observed Bertie.

Stuart smiled. 'I think it's just superficial, Bertie,' he said. 'I'm sure the New Zealanders are quite sensitive underneath.'

The whistle blew and the game began. Scotland, having won the toss, kicked off and thundered after the ball, which was caught by a tree-sized New Zealander. He was immediately jumped upon by a knot of large Scotsmen.

When the hapless New Zealander failed to give up the ball, the referee's whistle went and a penalty was awarded to Scotland. This was an opportunity for the Scottish scrum-half to kick the ball neatly over the posts. 3–0 to Scotland. A further penalty, awarded against New Zealand for general attitude, took the score to 6–0 to Scotland by half-time.

There were no tries in the first half, but in the second half there was a scrum five metres from the Scottish line. With a huge effort the Scots forwards kept the scrum firm and the ball emerged in the hands of the scrum-half. He kicked the ball soundly, hoping to put it out of play, but ended up kicking it up the field. The left winger chased after it and it bounced into his hands. He then kicked it across to the right winger, a kick that was beautifully timed and placed. With the ball in his possession, the winger raced towards the line, neatly sidestepping past his opposite number. As the stadium erupted in a roar of applause, the Scottish player surged across the line and touched down. Bertie and Ranald leapt to their feet, waving their arms in sheer delight. And they did that again when the try was effortlessly converted by the same player who had kicked that first penalty. 13–0 to Scotland; and that was where the score was when the final whistle brought the game to a close.

The defeated New Zealanders, a dispirited, diminished band of men, stood despondent on the pitch. The noble Scotsmen, generous in victory, shook hands with them and offered them such condolences as good sportsmen accord to those they have vanquished.

Bertie turned to Ranald and said, 'We did it, Ranald! We did it!'

Ranald nodded. Behind the SCITLAND on his sweater, his heart, like Bertie's, was full. In the following few minutes, while they waited their turn to leave the stadium, another small boy who had been sitting nearby offered to show Bertie and Ranald how to paint a saltire on their faces. This offer was gratefully received, and soon the two friends had the familiar blue flag displayed in greasepaint from brow to chin.

It was a time of great pride for Bertie. He was at a rugby match, with his father and his greatest friend, the loyal Ranald Braveheart Macpherson. Scotland had won – and won convincingly; the New Zealand *haka*, with all its threats and hollow gestures, had met its match in clear-eyed, firm rugby played with Presbyterian rectitude and according to the principles of the Scottish Enlightenment.

They walked all the way back, spurning buses to savour the bonhomie of the dispersing victorious crowd. As they passed Haymarket Station, Bertie muttered something that his father did not quite hear.

'Did you say something, Bertie?' Stuart enquired.

Bertie looked up at his father, and slipped his hand into his. 'I'm very happy,' he replied. 'That's what I said.'

60. For What is Not, and Cannot Be

By the time that Stuart arrived back in Scotland Street along with his two saltire-faced charges, a celebration of Scotland's victory had already begun in Angus Lordie's flat. The sounds of this party – a hubbub of conversation drifting down the common stair – could be heard the moment Stuart opened the front door.

This was remarked upon by Bertie. 'Mr Lordie has friends in, Daddy,' he said. 'He's probably celebrating the result.'

'My dad will also be having a party tonight,' said Ranald Braveheart Macpherson. 'He always gets drunk when Scotland wins.'

'That's all right, Ranald,' said Bertie. 'You can stay with us tonight if your dad's too drunk to collect you.'

'Thanks, Bertie,' said Ranald. 'He will be, I think.'

Drawn by the sounds of merriment above, they climbed the final flight to Angus and Domenica's landing, and saw that the front door of the flat was open. Angus, standing in the hall, glimpsed them and came to the doorway. 'Just in time,' he said, reaching out to shake Stuart's hand. Then, looking down at Bertie and Ranald, he said, 'And who do we have behind these splendid saltires? Young Bertie and young Ranald, I believe. How patriotic you boys look – and how appropriate for such a day as this.'

'We were there, Mr Lordie,' said Bertie. 'We saw Scotland beat New Zealand.'

'Well, you'll remember that for the rest of your lives, boys – largely because the possibility of its recurrence is slight.' He turned to Stuart. 'You're the statistician, Stuart, how would you work out the probability of that?'

Stuart laughed. 'I'm taking a rest from statistics, you know.'

'Of course,' said Angus. 'You told me. But look, the party's just beginning – please come in. I can probably find some Irn Bru for the boys and a dram for yourself.'

Stuart looked at his watch. It was an automatic response – one motivated by anxiety – but then, in a moment of sudden realisation, he remembered that he was free. He could go to parties if he wished; he could take Bertie and Ranald with him; he had no need to report to anyone. Nicola would already have put Ulysses to bed and had said that she was not proposing to go anywhere. He really was free.

He looked down at Bertie. 'Would you boys like that?' he asked.

Bertie nodded vigorously. 'Yes, please.'

They followed Angus into the kitchen, where most people seemed to have drifted. There, grouped around the table, perched on the window seat, astride kitchen stools, were the friends and neighbours who made up this charmed circle. Matthew and Elspeth were there, released from the triplets by the offer of James, their new au pair, to babysit while they went off to the match. They had brought the Duke of Johannesburg, as Matthew had met him at Murrayfield and had suggested that Angus and Domenica would not mind if he came along with them to Scotland Street. There was James Holloway, whom Bertie and Ranald had last seen at Abbotsford when they had discovered the long-lost spurtle of Mary Queen of Scots. There was Big Lou, by herself, and Pat with a young man she had met in the Elephant House (not Bruce).

And there, to Stuart's surprise, was Antonia Collie, Domenica's former neighbour, who had been rescued from Stendhal Syndrome in Italy and then looked after by a convent of nuns in Tuscany. And she was with that remarkable nun who had come back to Scotland with her, Sister Maria-Fiore dei Fiori di Montagna, whose social success in Edinburgh, Glasgow and Perth had been reported almost monthly in *Scottish Field* and *Edinburgh Life*.

There was much to talk about. Stuart engaged Antonia in a brief conversation about the new flat she had bought in Dundonald Street before Sister Maria-Fiore dei Fiori di Montagna interrupted with a long description of her recent outing to the Skye Ball. After this, Big Lou took him aside and told him that she had heard about Irene and Aberdeen and while she was sorry, she thought that he would be just fine. 'If you're ever lonely, just give me a ring,' she said, with what Stuart thought might be a wink, but he was not sure. And suddenly he thought: Big Lou ... Sometimes the people for whom we are really destined escape our attention: they may be there in full view, but unnoticed because we take them for granted. But then he thought: no. Big Lou was more of a sister, and he was not sure that he was ready for anybody else. Then he noticed a set of eyes upon him, and these were those of Sister Maria-Fiore dei Fiori di Montagna. No. Definitely no.

On the other side of the room, Domenica came to where Angus was standing and whispered, 'You must read one of your poems, Angus. You always do.'

James Holloway overheard. 'Yes,' he urged. 'We would be disappointed if you didn't.'

Angus hesitated. 'Very well,' he said at last. Then people, sensing the moment, fell silent; sentences left hanging in the air; heads turning in anticipation towards their host.

'This is a poem that I wrote a few months ago,' Angus announced. 'I wrote it when Domenica and I went to Mull. If you'll allow me, Domenica . . . '

Domenica looked at him and smiled. She remembered the poem; it was personal, but they were among friends. She inclined her head in acceptance.

Angus glanced at those around him and then, from memory, so that he might look at the woman he loved so much while he recited, he started his poem.

'"On Clouds over Mull",' he began. '"A Love Song".'

White the shifting veils of rain
That fall like tears, like tears, so white,
And soft upon your cheek, my dear,
So soft and wet upon your cheek;
And Mull stands guard against
The green sea, stands guard
Against the green sea.

And if our hearts will have to weep,
As all hearts will, and ours must do,
Then we shall shed on this soft isle,
These human tears, like tears of rain
That fall so soft upon the land
So gentle in their quiet regret
For what is not, and cannot be,
For what is not, and cannot be.

He stopped. Nobody spoke. Bertie looked at Ranald Braveheart Macpherson, who was eating a piece of shortbread. Stuart looked out of the window; Cyril looked at his master, thinking thoughts that in their canine profundity none would be able to fathom. Domenica looked at Angus, and he looked back at her.